MUSCLE CUB

A BEAR CAMP NOVEL

SLADE JAMES

Copyright © 2023 by Slade James

Cover Design: Slade James

Editing: Susie Selva

Proofreading: Lori Parks

Beta Reading: M.K. Varrich and A.M. Johnson

ISBN (ebook) - 978-0-9916523-8-9

ISBN (print) - 978-0-9916523-9-6

SYNOPSIS

He's a little too young and way too hot for me.

Austin Fox is a twentysomething beefcake living his best life working at a clothing-optional campground. He's the reigning Best Cub of Bear Mountain Lodge. With a twinkle in his eye and a mischievous smile, he radiates body positivity and self-esteem.

He could have anyone he wants.

I'm a forty-two-year-old, once-celebrated author with a bad case of writer's block, a dad bod, and "performance anxiety" in bed.

He picks me.

On paper, he's offering me exactly what I came here for —a weekend of no-strings fun to reboot, "get my groove back," and find my muse before summer ends.

But there's more to Austin's story than his title and appearance. He's empathetic, wise beyond his years, and he challenges me to see myself in a new light. Despite our age difference, we're in the same place, hoping to find a renewed sense of purpose.

If we choose to let go of the stories that no longer serve us, we can write our next chapter together.

Muscle Cub is an age gap, surly/sunshine gay romance that starts with a one-night stand and turns into a deeper reflection on identity and self-image. It's the second full-length book in the Bear Camp series, featuring cringe-inducing karaoke, a makeover, and a man-pageant. It can be read as a standalone.

This one's for Sam

AUTHOR'S NOTE

Muscle Cub takes place in the mountains of North Georgia at Bear Mountain Lodge Men's Resort & Campground.

This clothing-optional campground is a fictional amalgamation of the men's campgrounds I've frequented for the past twenty-five years.

1

OVER THE YEARS, WHENEVER MY FRIENDS TALKED ABOUT THE local men's campground, I'd always assumed the term *clothing-optional* referred to a simple binary choice—keep your clothes on or take them off.

Now that they'd finally convinced me to come meet them at Bear Mountain Lodge for the long Memorial Day weekend, I quickly discovered just how many *clothing options* there were.

It was intimidating in every way I'd dreaded and a few I could never have imagined.

A surprisingly high proportion of the men pitching their tents alongside mine this afternoon opted to do so while wearing nothing more than ball caps, flip-flops, and jockstraps.

With ball caps being the obvious exception, these choices seemed... impractical for manual labor.

Possibly dangerous.

I'd opted for a T-shirt, trail-running sneakers, and a pair of cargo shorts, which were an eternally useful and functional item of clothing that transcended all trends in perpetuity. Like many men of my generation, I was prepared to die on a hill of cargo shorts.

What else would you wear when camping out in warm weather?

For at least a few people, the answer to that question was a cock ring and motorcycle boots.

I kept my head down, eyes forward, and continued hauling my equipment back and forth from my truck to the perfectly idyllic campsite I'd chosen by the creek. It was about a three-hundred-yard trip in one direction, a path which led right through the pool area and a gauntlet of several dozen minimally attired or buck-ass-naked men who lounged in deck chairs, sipping from large drink tumblers and treating the pedestrian walkway as something of an undergarments and fetish-wear fashion show.

This seemed an awful lot like the kind of thing I might have had a bad dream about, but it was happening, right here, right now, at a campground swimming pool in the Blue Ridge Mountains.

Who knew?

One thing I did know for sure, I was definitely not a model, and yet I found myself on a catwalk of concrete pavers and red Georgia clay, sweating like hell in the late May sunshine and dying to take my shirt off.

I stopped and dropped armloads of gear at my feet.

Stripping to the waist didn't seem like that big a deal—the most justifiable of options really, given the environment and circumstances—as long as I ignored the fact that nothing accentuated a gut quite like the straps of a heavy backpack.

I doubted they were paying much attention to me anyway. Why would they? There was *so* much more to look at.

But apparently, the audience of leering, gawking sunbathers greatly approved of my modest offering of middle-aged torso, and they treated it as a kind of performance.

The catcalls elicited a complicated mixture of flattery and mortification I hadn't experienced many times before, and the wolf-whistle was definitely a first for me.

Eric and Ben swore this would be the perfect place to hook up with age-appropriate men who'd appreciate me as I was—a forty-two-year-old man with a great upper body if you overlooked the yard-work tan and the little bit of a belly. I was definitely better than average looking. My gray eyes passed for blue sometimes, and I had a nice beard, even if there was a bit too much red in it. If I saw myself through another man's eyes, and I didn't know what I'd looked like before my hair had started thinning and I'd put on extra weight, I would've thought, *he's attractive.*

But the *applause*...

Well.

Nothing could have prepared me for fucking *applause*.

I wished I'd worn mirrored sunglasses so I wouldn't have had to make eye contact with anyone. I plastered on a grin and held up my hands in a gesture of acknowledgment and surrender.

Just some dad bod here, guys. Nothing much to see. Carry on.

I still had three or four more trips to make, and calls for me to *take it all off* weren't dying away as quickly as I'd hoped. I wrestled a stack of folded tarps under one arm and reached for the bag with the inflatable air mattress with the other.

"We have wheelbarrows over there."

The voice startled me.

I'd bowed my head to avoid the attention and scrutiny, so I hadn't seen him standing so close.

Now *this* guy was handsome. He was over six feet tall, muscled and furry, with buzzed hair, beard scruff, and warm brown eyes gleaming above an easy smile. An avatar of masculine beauty, probably somewhere in his mid to late twenties.

Definitely way too young for me.

How was it even fucking possible there were men this good-looking just walking around in everyday life? Not online, where they seemed to be everywhere and yet always somewhere else—Provincetown, Miami, São Paulo, Ibiza— but right here in fucking Edgewood, Georgia.

Every now and then, they stepped out of their charmed realm and crossed briefly through mine—on a sidewalk between buildings on campus, in the window of a passing car, around the turn of a grocery store aisle—before they vanished like apparitions.

The guy who'd spoken to me was one of those men, and I hadn't heard a thing he'd said.

He was stunning, and I was just... *stunned*. "Sorry?"

He raised a tanned, veined forearm and pointed in the direction of a large ice cooler. "We have some wheelbarrows over there." He was wearing a gray staff T-shirt. The fact that someone with a body like his was the one person still fully dressed was the most obscene thing about this place so far.

I'd heard him this time, yet still I gaped.

"You know, for carting your stuff back and forth." He patiently mimed pushing a buggy. "There're only a few, but I saw one free. If you hurry, you can snag it, or..." His brown eyes softened. "I don't mind grabbing it for you if you want me to."

Oh dear God, he was probably starting to get concerned

I was either not in full control of my mental faculties—I kinda wasn't—or that I didn't speak English.

Feeling foolish but grateful, I stammered like a new kid on his first day at school. "Ah, no. That's cool. I totally appreciate it. I can get it. Thanks, man."

He looked me up and down, a slow glance I felt on every pasty inch of my bare chest. "Sure, bro. No problem." He smiled.

He's just being nice. Doing his job.

I fled to the plastic wheelbarrow and stacked my things inside. I'd only ever used a metal one with a rubber tire. When I started up the path, the plastic wheels made a hideous racket on the concrete pavers, and the waking nightmare of being the center of everyone's attention returned.

As I trundled past at an excruciatingly slow pace, Wheelbarrow Boy watched from the shade of the cabana bar, his lips twisted in a half smile of commiseration.

Adorable.

I felt his eyes on me all the way up the trail.

Don't look back.

Of course, I couldn't help myself.

He was still watching me.

No way.

Probably one of those chance synchronicities where he'd happened to glance up at the same moment.

Just in time to catch me checking him out and stumbling over a tree root.

2

I SPENT THE NEXT HOUR SETTING UP MY TENT AND SUSPENDING a tarp between the trees above it, but there was no sign of Eric and Ben. Hoping to find them at dinner, I hiked up to the lodge. I'd been warned about the lack of cell coverage, but I brought my phone, thinking I might be able to use the Wi-Fi to message or even email them where they could find my campsite.

The nominal building at Bear Mountain Lodge was exactly what I'd pictured when I heard the name—a rustic log chalet with chunky wood beams, dry-stacked river stones, leather furniture, and windows overlooking spectacular views of the woods. To be honest, it was nicer than I'd anticipated. The structural materials were rich and authentic, and the decor had whimsical touches like oil portraits of black bears on the walls and cushions that appeared at first glance to be black-and-white toile but were actually tiny Tom of Finland characters doing tiny leather daddy things.

There was a library nook stuffed with books and knickknacks. Introvert that I was, I imagined what it must be like when it was quiet during the off-season. I fantasized about going for long walks with the trees as my muses and writing for hours in a big cozy chair by a fire with Wheelbarrow Boy on a bearskin rug...

Writing for hours. Please. Talk about a real fantasy. My muses hadn't spoken to me in years.

Eric said I was blocked because I needed to get laid.

He wasn't wrong—I needed a *reboot* to get back to writing—which was one of the reasons I agreed to join them for their shared thirty-ninth birthday party.

I joined the line of guys waiting to enter the dining hall. Everyone was fully dressed in Hawaiian shirts, snarky graphic tees, shorts, and jeans, looking like a big gay family reunion at the state park. A sign proclaimed you must be wearing clothes and shoes to be served at meals. I hadn't considered that one of the more potentially awkward aspects of being in a clothing-optional environment might be knowing when to put your clothes back *on*, but having never eaten in public and indoors without wearing a shirt, it had been a no-brainer for me.

The dining hall was a large space with more windows and rows of long wooden tables that could seat dozens of men. With all their unmentionables tucked away, the crowd looked like the kind you might find at a sports bar. Eric and Ben hadn't prepared me for the pool complex, but this scene certainly fit with what I'd imagined when they'd sold me on joining them.

I relaxed a little.

After filling my plate at the buffet, I tried to slip onto the end of a table without drawing too much attention to myself. The handful of men sitting closest introduced themselves with a friendly, although mostly useless, blur of first names.

"Paul," I said, summoning my best smile.

"Where're you from, Paul?" asked the guy to my right—Grant, I believed he'd said.

"Edgewood."

"Lucky you," said the man sitting on his other side. "So close. You can come all the time."

I didn't volunteer that this was my first time here. Over the years, plenty of local men had made too big a deal about my being a *Bear Camp virgin*. I was here now, so there was no point in defending my reasons for not coming sooner or broadcasting my relatively nonexistent social life.

The conversation remained superficial and cheery—when everyone had arrived, where on the property they were staying. Some of them seemed to know each other, others not at all, but it didn't seem to matter.

I listened while enjoying the food in pleasant quasi-anonymity.

Until Wheelbarrow Boy appeared with iced tea and water pitchers. As he worked his way down the table offering refills, several of the guests made suggestive comments to him and found excuses to touch him.

Nothing vulgar, really, just small squeezes on the arm or pats on the back. He responded with an unflappable smirk and flirty comebacks like an old-school waitress in a diner full of hard-up truckers. He was probably used to it.

He arrived at my side, seeming to loom over me with the bulge of his crotch right at my eye level. When he reached over my shoulder to fill my glass, I caught a whiff of his citrus body wash.

I glanced up and murmured, "Thanks."

His eyes flashed. "My pleasure, sir."

He retreated, but the heat of his body lingered on my flushed cheeks.

"Oh my," Grant purred. "I think you've caught the attention of the most popular boy in school."

God, if he only knew what an awful metaphor that was to use with me. I tossed my napkin onto my empty plate. "I'm sure he's just doing his job."

As if on cue, Wheelbarrow Boy appeared at my side again, one hand on the back of my chair for the briefest moment before he whisked away my plate. He looked back over his shoulder and grinned.

Grant made a skeptical noise, but it was teasing, not unkind. "The guys who work here don't even attempt to offer full service at meals. A tea refill here or there, sure. But just so you know, I've never *not* carried my own dirty dishes to the bus tub." He quirked an eyebrow. "And I've been coming here for twenty years."

AFTER I'D FAILED to find a stable Wi-Fi connection, I went looking for Eric and Ben.

I finally located Ben's truck up a distant hill parked at a dark and silent cabin next door to what I presumed to be the campground bar. The sign above the door proclaimed it the *Cubby Hole*, which was unfortunate since *cubbyhole* was one word. If I'd thought to bring pen and paper, I could have left a note on Ben's windshield, but the plan had always been to meet up later this evening.

I went for a shower at the bathhouse near the pool—an eye-opening voyeuristic experience—and puttered around my tent organizing my clothes and snacks until it was time to head back to the bar.

The geodesic building reminded me of a wooden igloo elevated on a pedestal with a steep staircase and wraparound decking. It must have been adapted from some kind of eighties prefab round cabin kit.

I pressed through the crowd of men in religious-themed costumes and stepped through the door.

What gay hell is this?

Inside was a circular dance floor beneath a domed ceiling with various alcoves and additions built off its perimeter—a DJ station, a bathroom, a bar, and a billiards room.

Dressed in head-to-toe latex, the DJ operated a laptop keyboard with one hand while holding a tall plastic pitchfork in the other. With puffs from a smoke machine and lighting changes, the dance floor alternated between the third ring of the seventh circle of Dante's inferno and disco Xanadu. Baby doll cherubs with glitter wings pasted on their backs hovered in a ring around a mirror ball suspended over the heads of the dancers.

I skirted the dance floor and headed toward the bar, which would've made a damned good theater set for a pearly gates scene. The bar area was bathed in blue light, flanked by false classical columns and draped in silk with white puffy clouds hung from fishing line.

I definitely needed a drink for this.

The beer selection was pretty fucking atrocious, so I purchased a can of something cheap from an angry-looking guy about my age, muscular, bearded, handsome, and still wearing a staff T-shirt. He was one of the only men other than me not wearing a costume. He looked like he was only just managing to suffer the foolishness around us by sheer will. A pretty blond surfer type leaned across the bar and said something to him, and he lost his surliness in a smile.

Maybe this wasn't gay hell after all but some kind of gay heaven.

I found a wall where I could blend in and observe this whole new level of *clothing options*. There were bearded nuns in comically oversized wimples, monks in rope-belted tunics, and more than a few Jesuses in bad wigs. Among the variety of scantily clad angels, one seraphim wore a set of wings with a pulley apparatus that allowed for a full human-scale wing extension. Although the engineering was impressive, he kept clearing the dance floor around him. Someone was going to lose an eye before the party was over. The extremely realistic-looking arrows piercing Saint Sebastian were similarly unlikely to survive long in a crowd this tight without actually goring someone.

My personal favorite concept was the shirtless foursome in priest collars, black jockstraps, and combat boots. They looked like a sacrilegious male exotic dance troupe.

Kudos on the coordination, boys.

Clueless and unprepared, I'd shown up in the most damning drag of all—the unimaginative uniform of the average middle-aged gay man venturing out to the bar on a Friday night for the first time in forever: khaki shorts, white sneakers, and a white knit polo shirt that I'd ironed before leaving home. I'd hung it in my truck so I'd have something unwrinkled to wear to my friends' birthday party. As if wrinkles would have been the part of my outfit to call attention to me. My shirt and sneakers were now glowing faintly purple from a nearby black light.

I was calculating how long I should stay and look for the birthday boys before slipping out and going back to my tent to read when I heard my name being shouted over the din.

Finally, there were Eric and Ben. They wore matching devil horn headbands, and Eric's arm was draped across Ben's shoulders.

What the fuck?

"Paul! You're here!" Eric pulled me into a hug. He was obviously wasted.

Okay. This was unexpected, but considering what I knew of their long history together, it wasn't a complete shock. They'd dated when they were younger and had remained friends for years. I'd certainly never seen them being physical with each other, but they'd always felt like an old married couple who might have outgrown some of their affection.

"What the fuck is this?" I smiled and gestured at them hanging all over each other, but Eric must have thought I meant the party.

"It's Saints and Sinners!" he said, raising his cup in a toast.

Ben grinned at me through slitted eyelids, either drunk, stoned, blissed out on Eric, or all of the above.

"Come to Bear Camp, you said." I had to shout so they could hear me over the music. "Lots of regular guys like us just hanging out by the pool and sitting around a campfire."

Eric waved it away like a minor scheduling conflict. "That's tomorrow. Tonight it's a dance party."

"You never said anything about costumes."

Eric rolled his eyes. "It's not that big a deal."

At that moment, a pope with a bedazzled miter on his head and a hand-beaded robe squeezed between us. I had no idea which pope he was supposed to be, but I could feel the weight of the costume. In terms of time, materials, labor, and concept, everything about it screamed *kind of a big deal*.

Eric's eyes crossed a little, then refocused on me. He looked chastened. "Okay. Yeah. Some of these queens go all out. But it doesn't have to be that deep. Ben and I usually just throw some shit together, or we borrow a few accessories from those who overprepare." He carefully touched his horns. "You just need the tiniest makeover."

I held up my hands in a universal warding off gesture. "No thanks."

Eric leaned in to whisper sloppily against my ear. "Dude, you kinda look like somebody's dad." He pulled back suddenly, opening his eyes wide. "Or was that what you were going for?"

I crossed my arms and glared at him. "I'm good."

"No, wait. I got you covered. This is a very sharing environment. Give me two seconds."

Eric, at that level of drunk and enthusiastic that couldn't be argued with, had already disappeared into the crowd and was conferring with a guy as he rummaged in a backpack. He returned bearing a headband with a silver tinsel halo, and, despite my protests, mounted it on my skull.

"Oh my God. It totally suits you!" He grabbed my shoulders and turned me toward a mirror on the wall.

Through the beer logo frosted across its surface and with the smoke and lights behind me, I resembled a character who had died and gone to heaven in a bad sitcom dream sequence. "I look fucking ridiculous."

"You look *hot*. You're totally gonna get your groove back this weekend."

Get my groove back. The expression made me cringe, but I couldn't fault Eric for not knowing the full story. I'd never confided to him that it was less about an opportunity to hunt and more about my ability to follow through. "We'll see."

"You haven't spotted any of your students yet, have you?" Eric waggled his eyebrows.

I huffed. For years, I'd resisted coming to the campground for the same reason I wouldn't be found on any dating apps. I didn't want to run into one of my students. "Thankfully, no."

"See? You were being paranoid."

"I honestly haven't seen anyone that young here." The youngest person I'd encountered so far had to have been Wheelbarrow Boy. "I thought you guys started coming when you were barely old enough to drink?"

"Ah, yes." Eric nodded with the graveness of the inebriated. "We were adventurous. Early adopters. The guy who owned the place back then didn't give a shit either. He liked twinks." Eric turned suddenly and grabbed both Ben and me by the shoulder, shaking us. "You guys! Take this moment in." He looked back and forth between us, and then he leaned back and yelled at the top of his lungs. "Paul's at fucking Bear Camp!"

Ben spoke for the first time. "Finally."

"Ta-da!" I attempted a single jazz-hand while raising my cheap beer with the other.

I toasted their birthday, we all drank, and they made out right in front of me, which was... new. I'd always envied their connection. It wasn't that I necessarily wanted a serious relationship again, but if I could have one, I'd want it to be like theirs.

I looked away, my eyes straying to the door at the exact moment Wheelbarrow Boy arrived.

Maybe it was another one of those synchronicities.

3

I almost didn't recognize him, but even dressed in an elaborate devil costume with a solid stripe of black makeup across his eyes, an irrepressible twinkle shone through.

He wore a black horned headdress, a pair of black shorts small enough to qualify as underwear in the outside world, and black leather thigh-high platform boots. He towered over everyone in the room. From horn to toe he was easily over seven feet tall.

Holy Son of Maleficent.

Beside me, Eric cupped his hands around his mouth and yelled, "Austin!" Wheelbarrow Boy turned, and Eric waved him over, unnecessarily hissing the name close to my ear. "This is Austin."

Austin's linebacker build had been intimidating in his work uniform, but now, in a costume that exaggerated his size and with his glorious hairy chest on full display, he was a beast on another level.

I bet he knew it too.

Austin's eyes never left mine even as Eric went up on

tiptoe to share what I presumed was the other side of our introduction. I couldn't read Eric's lips, but I could definitely tell he was using a lot more words than *This is our friend Paul.* There was no telling what he might be saying about me. Eric had been notoriously heavy-handed and misguided with his matchmaking attempts a few times in the recent past.

Of course, I recognized Austin from earlier, and he surely recognized me. When he offered his hand—I didn't know what possessed me—I blurted out my snarky nickname for him. "Wheelbarrow Boy."

For a moment, I was lost in the feel of the smooth hard calluses on his palm. A weightlifter; no surprise there.

Austin squeezed my hand and smirked. "Cursed Campsite Dad. Nice to officially meet you."

Record scratch. "Wait. What?"

Austin chuckled at my confounded expression. "Nothing."

"What does that even mean? Why is my campsite cursed?"

He looked away and shrugged off my question. "Nothing. I'm just fucking with you." He moved closer to stand shoulder to shoulder with me against the wall. "So you're the professor?" His voice was loud enough for me to hear him over the music but intimate in the proximity it required. "I had the hugest crush on one of my professors sophomore year." Eric, Ben, and some of the crew who had arrived with Austin were watching us, but I couldn't tell if they could make out what was being said. "Care if I call you *Prof*?"

Surprised by Austin's forwardness, my protest came out sounding like a question. "Um, I'd rather you didn't?"

Austin laughed at my glare, crinkles forming at the corners of his eyes. One day, those lines would make him even more gorgeous. "Yeah, my professor hated it every time I called him that."

Oh God. He was probably one of *those* students—the bros who treated a lecture hall like an open mic night at a comedy club.

Eric obviously heard our conversation because he leaned past me to interrupt. "Paul is also a famous author."

I could have killed him. For a number of reasons.

"Really?" Austin turned toward me, only one shoulder against the wall now. The bulge in his shorts was perilously close to my elbow. The latex material made the hairs on my forearm rise. "What do you write?" He looked as seriously interested as a devil in a disco could look.

I knew he thought he was being polite by asking, but there was nothing more specifically awkward than having to convince someone who clearly isn't your audience that they didn't have to act interested in your book. And nothing made that more difficult than having to yell about it in a crowded bar over loud dance music. "Literary fiction. It's really just one book that anyone would know me for."

"Two books!" Eric corrected, shoving his fingers in our faces.

Technically, it was three books if you counted my research, which was academically published due to the success of the first novel. But we were at a naked campground, where I still held some small hope of getting laid, and it probably wouldn't be because of my fiction or my thoughts on twentieth century British literature.

"We don't speak of the second book," I shouted at Eric for the hundredth time. To Austin, I said, "It was all a while ago." I meant the hoopla—the "fame"—as much as the publication dates. At the rate things were going, there might never be a third novel.

"That's really interesting."

"Is it?" I arched an eyebrow, daring him to show me how easily he might lose interest. "Why? Do you read?"

"I mean, I *can*." Austin's expression was so believably innocent and earnest like he was pleading with me to find him worthy of the conversation. It was disarmingly sweet, and if the humor had been intentional, it was a pretty fucking clever comeback to my bitchiness.

I didn't want to smile, but I couldn't help myself.

Austin grinned too. Smugly. He knew he'd won something. A little battle of wits.

Cross conversations between Austin's friends and mine demanded our attention for a while, but Austin remained standing close to me. I studied him as he interacted with others. As I'd witnessed at dinner, there was a stream of men who came up to him for a small verbal exchange or a touch, adoration on their faces like they were meeting a celebrity. They seemed happy to have any attention from him, and he was generous with it. He made eye contact with them and smiled and nodded along to whatever they were saying.

I was impressed. At my signings, I'd often taken sedatives and hid in bookstore bathrooms until the very last possible minute. This guy knew how to be a star. It was about sharing your light, making other people feel seen.

"Isn't he precious?" Eric shouted close to my ear. He elbowed me, pointedly cutting his eyes to Austin. "He likes you."

I rolled my eyes.

"He chatted you up pretty hard, and he hasn't moved from your side. He's usually bouncing all over the bar."

As if on cue, the music changed to something thumping and sinister. Austin and his friends clearly recognized it, and they started dragging him toward the dance floor.

Austin grabbed my hand. "Come dance with us."

"Oh, no, no, no." I shook my head. "Thanks, but I'm good."

"*Please.*" He obviously thought pouting was effective, and it nearly was. For a second, I thought I might do anything to keep him holding my hand like this.

"I really don't dance."

Austin pinned me with a side-eye. "Can't or won't?"

I'd just said *don't*. It was like he was purposefully mishearing me as a *tactic*. I grasped at a more convincing argument. "I'm terrible at it. Truly. Really awful."

"You don't have to be good at it." Austin pulled a face. "You just have to do it."

"Trust me." My self-consciousness and four decades of awkwardness was hardwired at this point. "It's not a pretty sight. I would only embarrass you."

"Prof." Austin tilted his head like he pitied me, which was a disturbing way to be looked at by a creature with large black horns. "You're supposed to dance like nobody's watching."

"Oh Jesus Christ." I rolled my eyes.

He was shameless with his cheesiness. He grinned, but he dropped my hand. He pointed at me. "All right. But just know, before this is over, I'm gonna get you to dance with me."

Before what was over? The night? The weekend? Whatever he was implying, it definitely sounded like it went beyond this moment.

"But until then," Austin continued, "I'm gonna dance *for* you."

What the fuck did he mean by that?

Austin threw out his arms, the set of his jaw determined, his body language clearly transitioning into performance mode.

Oh shit. What had I done?

By refusing to dance with him, I'd only succeeded in drawing even more attention to myself. Everyone was watching Austin, and by holding eye contact with me as he backed onto the dance floor, he trapped me in the spotlight with him.

I kept trying to look away, but he was relentlessly dancing *at* me. Sexually suggestive yet clearly playing the clown, and with a body like his and the way he moved—he was an incredibly good fucking dancer—it was impossible not to watch him.

Other men attempted to join him, to grind on him. Austin didn't exactly push them away, but he didn't draw anyone to him either.

A couple of guys in matching Catholic schoolgirl skirts approached, one of them cupping his hands over Austin's ear and shouting something. A grin split Austin's face, and he nodded. They warned everyone to back up and give them space, and the dancing crowd morphed into a half circle of audience.

Small metallic pompoms materialized out of nowhere—because... *of course they did*—and the three of them launched into a synchronized *routine*.

Sweet muscled Christ, this husky, seven-foot-tall devil bear-boy was doing a motherfucking *cheerleading* routine with a pair of backup dancers.

I'd never seen a grown man perform anything like that in my life. How was he not on tour with someone?

Austin stuck his tongue out at me and laughed.

This was what he'd meant by dancing for me.

The trio threw their arms up and leapt. The backup dancers hit the ground in unison in near perfect splits, and the crowd roared, but Austin had aborted at the last minute.

Shaking his head, he reached down to each of his teammates and hauled them up from the floor. I could read Austin's lips: *Not in these shoes.*

He had turned a moment's hesitation or a lack of ability —maybe a moment of clarity and common sense—into a fake out, a gag, a comedy bit.

Who the fuck is this guy, and what dimension did he come from?

He trotted over to me smiling, panting, and seemingly oblivious to the applause.

"Holy shit." I couldn't think of what else to say.

"Didya like that?" He batted his eyelashes.

"It was"—I nodded like a bobblehead—"something else."

He stood there, beaming at me, catching his breath. The heat of his exertion came off his body in waves, his citrusy fragrance mingling with fresh sweat. His eye makeup ran down his cheeks, and his horns were starting to droop a little bit.

And fuck me if I didn't still find him incredibly appealing.

Someone passed a tray crammed with colorful Jell-O shots to us. "You want one?" Austin asked.

I lifted the slightly warm, half-full can I'd been holding and avoiding this entire time. "I'm good with beer."

Austin pulled a disgusted face. "Nobody's good with *that* piss water. Come with me. We're getting you a real beer."

He laced my fingers with his and pulled me toward the door. The crowd parted for us, and a gauntlet of faces rushed past. I was painfully aware of all the eyes on us. Eyes on *Austin*, I assumed. I couldn't blame anyone for ogling him, and all I could really think about was my hand in his.

Outside on the deck, Austin dragged me through cigarette smoke that seemed like a theatrical effect as unseen men called out to him from the dark.

"Oh, handsome devil!"

"I tell you what, that's a big sinner right there!"

Invitations came from left and right, but Austin moved past, bantering and flirting with ease, suggesting all kinds of things and promising nothing. "I'll catch you in there," he said.

"I'll catch you anywhere you want!"

"I bet you would." Austin laughed, managing to sound fond and genuine and never saying no outright.

Austin led me to a covered veranda at the corner of the deck with fairy lights, bench seats, and a view of the moon over the nearest blue ridge of mountains. The walls of the bar muffled the music from inside, leaving the spot feeling quiet and intimate, not exactly romantic because there were so many others out here with us, but it felt familial and special. Like I was backstage or beyond the velvet rope.

"Give me that." Austin snatched the can out of my hand and threw it into a recycling bin tucked beneath a built-in counter. "I'd like to claim they serve some of these beer brands ironically, but I wouldn't stake my reputation on it. Between you and me, I see no evidence to suggest there's any good reason for it other than just being cheap. Lemme get you taken care of. Ryan!" His sudden shout made me jump. "I'm raiding your cooler, bro. The Prof needs a decent beer."

A young guy who looked like a slightly smaller, heavily tattooed version of Austin nodded. Ryan seemed unconcerned with whoever the hell *the Prof* might be, even though I felt a need to justify why I deserved access to his special stash. "Y'all can have whatever."

Austin strode over to a corner, where the deck and the building converged against the mountainside, a rhododendron spilling over the railing almost to the boards, creating a natural screen. He motioned me to his side to peer into the rollaway cooler where bottle necks peeked from a bed of crushed ice. "We've got some Blue Moon, Corona, and looks like a sampling of local IPAs."

"Blue Moon would be great. I wouldn't have minded paying for one at the bar."

"Oh, they don't sell these. Something about the beer license. You can brown bag liquor but not your own beer because they sell it. I don't know. I've never understood it. It's one of the great mysteries of this place. It's probably all a bunch of cobbled together, grandfathered licenses from back in the day when the original owner was still alive."

"Shit. I didn't know you couldn't bring your own beer." I lowered my voice. "I have a full cooler down at my campsite."

"Are you inviting me to your campsite already?"

"What? No, I-I was just hoping they're not going to throw me out."

"Nobody's going to throw you out."

A voice boomed close behind us. "Well, what the hell do y'all think you're drinking?"

I startled.

It was the big guy from the front office who'd checked

me in earlier. I guessed he was about my age, maybe a little older, midforties. Hard to tell through his makeup. He was dressed in something that resembled both a nun and a mime. "This is entirely against the rules, boys. I'm afraid I'm gonna have to report you to Sawyer."

"Go ahead!" Austin sassed. To me, he explained, "Sawyer's the owner. Big, handsome, mean-looking motherfucker behind the bar with no costume because he has no sense of humor." I cringed, wondering how I was getting by on my flimsy halo. "And for the record, this one here's just fucking with you. This is Jim Savage, the general manager," Austin continued, "and apparently one of the Sisters of Perpetual Indulgence."

I had no idea what that meant, although I felt like I should. It was surely a gay cultural reference that went over my head as so many of them did. I made a mental note to ask someone later at a more appropriate moment.

"I am not technically a member of the Order. But I probably should be." Jim looked me up and down. "Jim Savage." He placed a big paw on my forearm. "Honey, I know it's your first time here, so I haven't learned your name yet."

"This is the Prof," Austin said unhelpfully but with great enthusiasm.

I offered my hand to Jim. "I'd prefer to be called Paul." I shot Austin a pointed glare, aware that it might backfire and only goad him into doubling down on the nickname. After seeing what happened as a result of declining to dance with him, I had good reason to be wary.

"You having a good time so far, Paul?" Jim asked.

I found it noteworthy that he didn't immediately want to know what subject I taught or to tell me what he'd majored in as so many other people did at parties when they heard what I did for a living. I was grateful for the simple acknowledgment that I was on vacation.

I assured him I was indeed enjoying myself, surprised to find that was truer than I would have predicted when I'd left home this afternoon in a state of dread.

"So what you boys getting into?" Jim asked.

"We just came out here to talk," Austin said.

"Talk?" Jim's raised eyebrows put air quotes around the word. "You? Okay, honey, we'll go with that."

Austin groaned and jutted out his chin, making a shooing motion at Jim.

Jim acted offended, but he shot me a wink before fading into the crowd farther along the deck.

"Jim likes to bust my ass, but he's cool. He's kinda family to me. Like an adopted gay uncle."

"He seems nice," I said. "He has good energy."

Austin considered me for a moment, then nodded slowly. "He does."

We stared at each other, his grin mirroring the one I felt overtaking my face. Neither of us seemed to know what to do next.

I glanced away to take in the view of the moon and the streaks of blue clouds over the dark woods, trying to buy myself some time to think of an appropriate topic of conversation. It was a gorgeous night with a pleasant spring chill. Perfect camping weather.

Beside me, Austin took a deep breath as if to say something, but then he paused. Before he could speak, he was interrupted by someone yelling his name.

"Dude. There you are." It was a cute, preppy-looking blond, one of the guys he'd arrived with. "You coming back in to dance or what? I just requested the 'Jolene' remix."

"Right on," Austin said in his noncommittal way.

Here it was, the perfect moment, the perfect excuse to release me. The party was in full swing, he was all dolled up, and there were hundreds of men vying for his attention.

I expected Austin to make his excuses to me, but instead, he told his friend he'd *catch up*, and then he leaned in close.

"Hey." His low, breathy voice against my ear raised the hairs on the back of my neck. "You wanna go take a walk?"

4

I WASN'T ENTIRELY SURE IF *LET'S GO TAKE A WALK* WAS A euphemism for *let's go fuck* or not, so it took me a few seconds to realize my answer was the same either way. "Um. Yeah." I hoped I sounded casual. "Let's do it."

"Need to tell your friends you're leaving?"

I waved away his concern. "They're probably too wasted to notice." The truth was, given Eric's cartoonish thumbs-up and extreme eyebrow waggling when Austin and I had left the bar together, I wasn't sure what kind of a scene he might make over this development.

I followed Austin through the crowd to the top of the stairs, where he hesitated. "I may need you to go down in front of me. The soles of these boots are basically bricks, and my feet feel like they weigh about twenty pounds each."

"That's fine. Just... Why don't you give me the damn beer so you can hold on to the railings with both hands?"

"How are you gonna hold on?"

I rolled my eyes. "I've only had two drinks. I'll be fine. And I'll sacrifice the beers if I need to."

As we reached the bottom, someone above us shouted

Austin's name. It was his buddy with the ginger mohawk. "Where the hell are you going?"

"On a little walkabout."

"Don't fuck up my girls!"

"I won't!" Austin stumbled on the uneven gravel as he turned, and I reached out a hand to steady him. He draped his arm over my shoulders and pulled me close. "Sorry. I'm not that drunk, I swear. It's the boots." He dropped his voice to a whisper. "Gunner names all his shoes. Individually. I'm wearing Hedwig and Hagatha, but I have no idea which one is which."

I managed a convincing chuckle, although ninety percent of my cognitive function was engaged in processing his scent and how much more of his body now touched mine.

Austin proceeded to stroll down the hill with his arm around me like it was the most normal thing in the world, pointing out the various buildings in this part of the campground. They called it the Village. In addition to the bar, there was a chapel, a barber shop, and a café. Farther down the path was a bathhouse with a gym attached to it.

"How long have you been working here?" I asked.

"Just a few weeks so far this season. I worked here last summer too."

"You're not a student are you?" I braced for the answer.

"No. I graduated from UGA. Go Dawgs!"

"Oh, okay." *Thank God.* "So what do you do during the rest of the year?"

"I'll show you." He released me. The absence of his touch made me regret my attempt at small talk. He angled off the path to our left, and I followed him. On the door of the gym was a colored flyer with a picture of Austin, smiling, his impressive arm flexed in a classic Rosie the Riveter pose.

A bold typeface read *The Morning-After Drill with Austin*. "My class," he said unnecessarily.

"Ah. So you don't just look like this for fun. You're a professional." It was the closest I'd come to flirting or overtly commenting on his looks, but he didn't take the bait.

"A professional meathead."

"Not a cheerleader, then?"

His eyes lit up. "God, I'd love to be a professional cheerleader. Like, if only the Dallas Cowboys Cheerleaders had men on their team, that would be my dream job. The DCC style with the tailgating tunes they love..." He made a sound like he'd tasted something delicious. "I was made for that shit. Almost."

"After what I witnessed at the bar, I'd say it's their loss."

"I was actually a cheerleader in high school. I always thought it'd be fun to be a cheerleading coach, but I don't have any dance training. I'm just a gym rat."

"You know, you could call yourself a *fitness instructor*. I wouldn't be offended."

He chuckled. "Why, yes. That's a much classier term."

"Is that what you'll do when the summer's over?"

We resumed our walk back down the hill, but without me to augment his balance, Austin moved at a snail's pace.

"Um. That's a good question." It was the first time I'd glimpsed anything resembling a frown on Austin's face. "I'm kinda hoping if my class is popular, they'll hire me on as full-time resident staff. I could live here year-round. I'd stay here forever if they'd have me."

I smiled. I didn't want to interrupt him.

"But just in case, I'm working on some additional fitness certifications too. At this point, I kinda think it's the only thing of value I really have to offer."

I made a wordless sound of protest. I didn't like hearing him talk about himself that way.

Austin held up a hand. "It's not like that. I'm not putting myself down. I like to work out, and gyms are expensive. Teaching's a win-win. I always wanted to be a teacher or a coach. I like kids."

Hearing the passion in his voice I felt guilty. I didn't love teaching. At first, I'd been satisfied to work at the same institution as my partner, but after the second book had been such a failure, I couldn't get the expression *Those who can't do, teach* out of my mind. I associated my job with fear. I tended to forget there were people like him who considered it a calling. "Why didn't you pursue that?"

"Oh, I did." This time, Austin's chuckle was bitter. "Kinda fucked it up. Burned a bridge. It's a long story. Probably not what you think."

I didn't know what he thought I might have presumed, but from the shift in his energy, I could tell it was something he didn't want to talk about. I didn't press him.

He changed the subject, turning the focus on me. "How long have you been in Edgewood?"

"Well, I grew up here and stayed for my undergrad." I didn't say *and fell in love with my English professor.* "Moved away to complete my graduate work and came back to teach seven years ago."

"And you've never been here before?"

"For a long time, I was in a relationship. After that, I was afraid of running into one of my students."

"Oh. Okay. I thought maybe it was because you're famous."

"Pfft. I was never *that* kind of famous. Few authors are."

"I've met two other authors here," Austin said.

"Really? Anybody I might have heard of?"

"Jody Summers."

"The romance author?" The one with a bajillion titles I'd never read who was nevertheless a household name.

"Yep."

"Jody Summers is a *man*?"

"Was." Austin smiled softly. "Joseph passed away in October."

"Oh." It took me a moment to process both revelations. "I'm sorry to hear that." A few follow-up questions formed, but before I could get them out, Austin moved the conversation along.

"So what are your books?"

I doubted my writing would interest him much—maybe the fact that I was a writer but not the work itself—so I responded with the short answer like I did whenever anyone only asked as a way of being polite. "*The Boy Who Didn't Come Back* and *Divining Virginia.* They're magical realism."

He seemed excited by the sound of that. "Like paranormal?"

I hated to disappoint him. "No."

"I'm gonna buy them," Austin said.

"That's sweet of you. If I had copies with me, I'd gladly give them to you."

"Do they have your picture on the back?"

"Uh... yeah." Was that why he wanted them? "Not that you'd recognize me."

"No?"

"Oh no. That headshot was taken years ago. About thirty pounds ago"—a lie; it was at least forty—"before my metabolism ground to a halt and my hairline receded." Was I daring him to like me anyway? "My barber's been trying to convince me I should just shave it all off."

"Well, we like bigger guys around here." His voice grew husky. "And bald men are totally hot. Receding hairlines are hot too if you ask me. I think there's something... virile about them."

"*Virile*, huh?" *Well, fuck me.* He'd left a party full of sexy, willing men—after having gone to a shitload of trouble to get into a costume for it—to walk a quarter of a mile in platforms, downhill, in the dark, while acting interested in my career.

He was probably out of my league, but maybe there was a god up in gay heaven after all.

5

AUSTIN TEETERED A BIT ON THE LAST STEEP STRETCH OF HILL before the pool complex. He softly cursed the boots and muttered something about the *things we do for fashion*. I offered him my arm, hoping he might hang all over me again, but he placed a hand on my shoulder to steady himself.

"Now's when we could've used a wheelbarrow," I said.

He chuckled. "Who couldn't use a good wheelbarrow every now and then?"

Him on his back, feet in the air, me grabbing him by the ankles...

I swallowed and turned my head to look at him. His face was so close. "For the record, I prefer to drive the wheelbarrow."

"I'm good with that." He flashed a feral grin. "Lemme get out of this costume."

He led me into the main bathhouse, where I'd showered earlier. A fan roared somewhere, stirring the humid air, and there was a loud hiss from the steam room, but with everyone up at the Cubby Hole, it seemed too quiet.

"I hope I'm not pulling you away from the party," I lied.

"Nah. We can always go back if we want to." Austin stood on one foot and braced his hand against the sink counter. "Besides, this whole place is a party. Everybody's gonna migrate down here soon anyway. Especially when the bar closes." He struggled to pull off one of the boots. He hadn't unzipped it far enough.

"Let me." I set down our beers, squatted in front of him, then carefully moved the zipper all the way down his inseam. I did the other boot, looking up to find him watching me. I had assumed the intimate position for practical reasons, and I wouldn't have minded being on my knees for him in another context, but I didn't have the confidence to claim it as boldly as his expression said I could.

I circled his bare ankle with one hand, tugged off the boot, removed the other, and hurriedly stood, my knees popping.

Austin sighed loudly. "Thank God those are off!" He flexed and wiggled his toes. He had nicely shaped feet with cute stubby toes. They did look a bit blue like the circulation might have been cut off. "My foot's a little wider than Gunner's, so I fully expected to be cussing this decision before the night was over, but *fuck*." He turned to the mirror, looked at me in the reflection, and chuckled.

"What?" I asked, shoving my hands into my pockets. I never knew what to do with my hands.

"You must be what my guardian angel looks like, standing around in the bathhouse looking slightly uncomfortable."

I'd forgotten I was wearing a fucking halo headband. I rolled my eyes and yanked it off, setting it on the counter beside him.

"Aww," he pouted. "I'm sad to see it go. It suited you."

"You think? Do I come across as particularly angelic?"

"Not really." He looked me up and down. "More like a surly professor teddy bear."

"Are professor teddy bears a thing?"

"Oh, absolutely." Austin nodded, his tone serious. "They come wearing little vests and bowties. And no pants."

I blushed. *Sweet Jesus.*

With a loud ripping sound, Austin tore the horns from his forehead.

I winced. "Shit. Are those made out of duct tape?"

"Yeah, and that hurt like a motherfucker." He grabbed a paper towel and ran it under cold water before pressing it against the angry skin at his hairline.

I gestured toward the remains of the headdress on the counter next to my crooked little halo. "Pretty ingenious, though."

"Gunner's super creative."

I looked around at the bins of condoms and lube packets on the wall and the sign prohibiting photography and sex in the public areas.

Austin followed my line of sight. "Few people want to be photographed, so that one's easy enough to follow. The sex in public areas, though... not so much. Virtually ignored. People behave fairly well during the day, especially in the mornings when it's crowded with hungover guys legitimately looking to shower and shave and make it to the lodge while they're still serving breakfast. But nighttime in here is a whole different world. A few hours from now... You might not want to be in here. Or maybe you would." He scrubbed at the eyeshadow on his face.

"I hate that you're having to take everything off early."

He arched a brow. "Do you really?"

"Well, it obviously took a lot of time and effort. It was quite a look."

"Legend has it this is what Gunner was wearing the night he met Hank. They convinced me it's charmed."

And now you're wearing it the night you met me. I blamed his attention for thoughts like that. He pulled them from me with his bold eye contact, his unselfconscious smirks, and his cheeky, eat-me-alive looks. He probably enjoyed making regular guys like me squirm and eat our hearts out.

"You staying through the holiday on Monday?" he asked.

"Um, I was probably gonna head out before then." *Tomorrow.*

Austin's eyes went wide. "You can't do that!"

I balked at his disappointment. "Maybe Sunday. Depending on how it goes."

"Prof." He spread his hands and shook his head like he couldn't believe the *insanity* he was hearing. "You'll miss the fireworks."

The steam room door slammed open, and two flushed men emerged in a cloud of heat and moisture. I shifted to allow them to pass into the shower area, looking away from their semierect, swinging cocks.

Austin gave them an up-nod in the mirror. "How's it going?"

One answered with a husky, "Hey," and the other shyly smiled.

We heard the spray of water start, and I met Austin's eyes in the mirror. "I feel like we're interrupting," I murmured out of the side of my mouth.

"Nah." He mopped the back of his neck with the wet paper towel. He leaned close, his voice so low it was little more than lip reading. Voices carried in here, bouncing around off all the tiled surfaces. "They're probably taking a break from the heat. Or they could've just finished. Trust me, if they want privacy, they'll take it back to their cabins. I keep it quick when I'm only in here for official business. I don't like to send any mixed signals."

It was hardly a shock that Austin would come to the bathhouse for reasons other than bathing, and I didn't want him to feel any shame about it, but his confessing it confused me. I could've taken it as evidence of how easily he could be had without consequence, or it could've been the kind of locker-room banter reserved for the friend zone.

It did cross my mind that if I'd first encountered him here instead of at the bar, I might never have properly met him at all. He could've just been a hunk stumbling out of the steam room while I was brushing my teeth before bed. I might have only gotten an eyeful and a "Sup, bro."

Austin picked up the boots and flopped them over his shoulder like a towel. "I keep a locker down here. Let's see if I can get these bitches in there."

I grabbed our beers, hesitating for a second before choosing to abandon my halo, and followed him out the side entrance to a covered walkway that led to the pool. The underwater lights threw shimmering waves on the dark cabana and the undersides of the trees. The industrial-sized dryers in the adjacent laundry facility blew a steady hum that almost drowned out the screaming of the cicadas, and the chilly night was kept at bay by the oasis of warmth and light.

There was a row of metal lockers like the kind found in a school hallway I hadn't noticed before. Austin worked open a combination lock and peered into the locker while wondering aloud about the sweatshirt he liked to keep for golf-cart rides and long walks back to the employee bunkhouse. "Nope. No sign of it. Not even a T-shirt."

Something brightly colored fell out onto the concrete. "Whoops!" Chuckling, he snatched up the red jockstrap and stuffed it deep into the locker. "These boots are never gonna fit in here. I'll just have to keep them with me. Don't let me lose them or Gunner'll kill me. No telling what they cost. I try to keep some flip-flops in here too, but I keep wearing them places."

A bottle of spray sunscreen fell out with a clatter. He picked it up and held it under my nose. "Smell that? Lemony. That's the expensive shit." He dropped his voice to a whisper. "I snagged it from the lost and found." He grinned in a way I suspected he knew was irresistibly charming. "Let's go hang by the pool."

6

————

AUSTIN PADDED BAREFOOT TO THE CLOSEST COVERED PATIO table, deposited the boots in a chair, and plopped down in another with an exaggerated sigh.

I took the seat closest to his and handed him his beer. Mine was a little warmer than I would've liked, but Austin made me nervous, and sipping it gave me something to do.

Steam rose from the pool's surface, and silence stretched between us, long enough to make me uncomfortable. I didn't know whether or not I should attempt more small talk about our lives or if he might fill it with more of his willfully unselfconscious chatter.

"Your buddies told me about you last night," Austin said. Bluntness was definitely a key part of his communication style.

"Oh, really?"

"Well, Eric did. I don't think Ben said much of anything."

"That sounds accurate. At least I know you're telling the truth. What was he saying?"

"Nothing bad. Just that they had a friend meeting up

with them who was..." He paused, choosing his words carefully. "Looking to have a good time."

I pretended to gag. "*Looking to have a good time?* Seriously? Please tell me you're paraphrasing."

"Maybe it was *looking to get your groove on*. Something like that. He kinda pimped you out." He held my gaze, waiting for a reaction, his smile turning wicked. "Nothing wrong with it. You've definitely come to the right place." I doubted Eric had offered much detail. Austin wouldn't have enjoyed putting me on the spot this much if he thought it was a big deal to me. He was a shit-talking flirt, but he wasn't a bully. He laughed. "I asked if you were hot."

I opened my mouth to fish for a more direct compliment, but we were interrupted by loud laughter and footsteps on the gravel path.

Three men came around the corner of the bathhouse. One was a thin Black guy dressed in a gold metallic jockstrap and matching winged harness. If Austin's costume devil persona had had minions, this guy would have been one of them. The other two wore matching red briefs, red muscle tees, red high-top sneakers, and the ubiquitous red plastic horned headbands. One had waxed his mustache into curled tips and his goatee into a point. They didn't seem to have noticed us yet. They opened lockers and began peeling off their clothes.

The first golden devil walked right past us to grab towels that were draped over nearby lounge chairs, but he spotted us on his return and startled with a gasp. "Shit! I didn't see y'all sitting there." He covered his eyes and squinted at Austin. "Oh. It's you!" He ducked beneath the canopy, and Austin rose to greet him with a hug. "We saw you leaving the Hole earlier, and we were like, 'bitch ain't even been on the dance floor for fifteen minutes and she's already hooked up for the night.' And you're already out of costume, so this must be about to get serious." He looked between us. "Or did it already?"

He studied me openly in that forward, hungry manner a lot of the men here displayed. Maybe it was alcohol that made them bold or knowing they were somewhere they didn't have to hide who they were or what they wanted. Their barriers were down.

Austin gave me a wincing, apologetic smile over the guy's shoulder. "We're just hanging out."

"Oooh, hanging out," he purred like that was the most risqué and suggestive thing he'd ever heard. He quickly shifted to a friendly tone typically used when meeting someone for the first time. "I'm Jay, by the way." He reached out to shake my hand.

"Paul," I said, relieved by the normality of the gesture. For a moment there, I thought he might demand a hug from me too.

"And those two hookers over there are the Chrises." The pair of red devils, now naked, waved in unison. Jay turned back to us and whispered, "Chris and Chris." He rolled his eyes.

Austin chuckled. "One of *those* couples."

"Don't you know it." Jay glanced over at his companions and said under his breath, "Also, hung and hung, in case you haven't noticed."

I had, but I willed myself not to look a second time.

Austin played along, giving them a slow once-over and clucking his tongue admiringly. He shot Jay a sly look. "You love to do a couple, don't you?"

"Girl, *couple* my ass. I'm about to throuple up with them full-time."

Austin's eyebrows shot up. "For real?"

"Hell yes. This is our last test run before I move to Charlotte."

"To live with them?"

"Mmmhmm."

"Well, alrighty then!" Austin held out his fist for a bump, but Jay gave it a sassy little pat instead.

Jay looked between the two of us. "Are we gonna see you guys in the sauna?"

I prayed Austin wouldn't volunteer us for some kind of... *quintuple* situation. Or whatever it was called when it involved five people. Oh, wait. There were two other men in the bathhouse.

This could quickly slide into orgy territory.

"Um." Austin made eye contact with me as if it were something we'd been discussing before Jay showed up. "I think we might take a little skinny dip in the pool while we have it to ourselves."

"How romantic." Jay waved his finger at us in a circular motion. "This is giving me a daddy-and-his-boy fantasy."

My cheeks flushed, but fortunately, nobody could see it in the dark. The objectification and the labeling mortified me, but I was also desperate to know if that was how Austin saw us too.

Us. One witness and we'd become an *us.*

Austin didn't seem to mind. "Shut the fuck up." He playfully shoved Jay toward the Chrises. "We might see you in there later. If you're real lucky."

With a smirk, Jay left us. The screen door screeched and banged closed behind the three men, leaving Austin and me relatively alone again in the dark.

"You kinda say yes to everyone, don't you?" I asked.

Austin shrugged. "It's just easier. Given my reputation."

"What kind of reputation is that?" Of course, I could

have guessed, but I wanted to know how he would present it to me. I was also a little proud of myself for turning the tables on him, putting him on the spot.

Austin shot me a look that said, *Seriously. You're gonna make me spell it out?* He sighed. "If I blow somebody off, it's gonna make him feel like he's the one and only guy I won't flirt with."

Interesting. Austin wasn't concerned about the labels anyone might impose on him; he was concerned about how he might make them feel. "You have the right to say no."

Austin hummed skeptically. "I'm not good at saying no, and I hate hurting people's feelings. I just don't want to make anybody feel undesirable, or ugly, or too old, or not good enough. I have ways of putting people off gently. Usually without them even noticing."

"A little glamour spell?"

Austin's mouth dropped open. "That's what Jim calls it!"

It crossed my mind that I might see his careful, compassionate magic in action before the night was over. He might've promised Eric and Ben he'd keep me company and stroke my ego a bit. Nothing like a little attention from the youngest, hottest guy at camp to rekindle a spark of hope in their pitiful friend. "Good to know you wield your power benevolently."

Austin batted his lashes, convincingly bashful. "I'm not all that."

"Oh, please, *bro*. I don't believe for one second you don't know what people see when they look at you."

"Well, yeah, what they *see*." He uncrossed and recrossed his legs. "But, you know, deep down, once a chubby kid, always a chubby kid."

I squinted. The confession did change how I saw him. The kind of physical transformation he must have undergone had the power to either make a monster or armor a tender heart, depending on the soul inhabiting the body. I'd been small-minded. I should have suspected there was complexity behind his considerable charm and quick wit.

Austin leaned back in his chair and folded his arms across his chest, his massive pecs bunching together. "I'm gonna ask you something point blank. I'm just gonna blurt it out, okay?"

"Okay." I dragged out the word warily.

"Would you ever consider being with a guy like me?"

I almost choked on my tongue.

A guy like *him*? Was this a move? Something vulnerable intended to disarm me and make me feel like *I* was the special one? I would have liked some clarity on what he meant by *being* with him—a hookup? Dating?—but I didn't have the guts to confront him on that directly. Besides, another honest question popped out of my mouth, "Does anyone ever say no to you?"

Austin rolled his eyes. "Uh, yeah. You. Like, what, an hour ago?"

"I said I wouldn't *dance* with you."

"I know. It gutted me." Austin pressed a hand to his chest. "Please don't make me relive it."

I laughed. "Now I'm back to wondering how sincere you're being."

Austin was one of those people who smiled when he talked—everything he said was accompanied by a twinkle—but now, with a slack fierceness in his expression, he said, "I'm always sincere."

He was so earnest I found it difficult to maintain eye contact with him. I swallowed, and my throat clicked.

"Let's get in the pool," Austin said.

This time the suggestion wasn't framed as a question. I could say yes to him with pure action, by simply following his lead.

He stripped out of his booty shorts in seconds.

He had the kind of body even straight men would have ogled. From sheer envy if nothing else. At my peak physical condition, when I'd worked out in my late teens and early twenties, I'd never had a body like his. I never would, and, unfortunately, being conscious of negative thoughts did little to silence them.

Eric had insisted being in this environment would shift my perspective. It was different from other queer spaces. There was a higher proportion of men who would actually prefer me at this stage of my life. When I'd taken off my shirt this afternoon—in this same spot—they had applauded. Maybe they'd cheered me on for vanquishing modesty.

It wasn't impossible to believe Austin found me attractive. At least for tonight. I had my doubts about how quickly the thrill of the hunt might dissipate once he felt like he'd *caught* me, but in this moment, right here, right now, an incredibly hot guy was already naked and waiting for me in the swimming pool.

I couldn't *not* get in. It was a little late for that.

So here it was at last, the opportunity to fully exercise my clothing options. I wished I could simply choose to feel sexy.

Fuck it.

I undressed quickly, grateful for the relative darkness and the lack of a large audience this time. I carefully folded and placed my clothes where they'd cover Gunner's boots, walked to the deep end, and stepped off the edge.

7

AUSTIN MOVED TOWARD ME, TREADING WATER. "YOU HAVE NO idea how hot you are, do you?"

"Jesus." He'd been watching me undress. A compliment like that—from him—was almost unbearable. "You're killing me." I wrapped my arm around his neck and pulled him against me. After slipping closer and closer all evening long, I was relieved to finally touch him like this.

His furry knees knocked against mine, and our feet flopped together as we treaded water. He held on to the edge of the pool to anchor us.

His mouth was only inches from mine.

He wet his bottom lip with his tongue and—

A shadow passed over our heads, and we both ducked reflexively.

There was a catcall, a battle cry, and a cannonball splash.

Someone yelled Austin's name, then suddenly there were a dozen men in the pool with us. Twenty more invaded the patio tables. Dance music blared from a small speaker, tinny, manic, and aggravating.

Austin kissed me quickly. It was something more than a peck—a *smoosh*. The kind of kiss your boyfriend might've given you in public after he'd already kissed you thousands of other ways in private.

He'd skipped to a... kiss from the future.

It felt like a *maybe* or a *later*.

It was entirely unsatisfying but enough to keep me hanging on to him as other men moved in close to us in the water.

I felt like we were being abducted by a gang of mermen.

Austin shifted me onto his back, clutching my wrists at his chest, wearing me like a backpack, so I was making eye contact with his friends as they all joked and chatted.

Gunner and Hank—I believed that was Hank—and the other guys whose names I didn't know all started talking to Austin as if I belonged there, but they also ignored me like I was an accessory. My presence wasn't unwelcome, but I suspected they didn't find a random stranger on Austin's arm—or on his *back*—all that unusual.

Austin pulled my knees against his waist, and he toyed with my fingers. I rubbed my facial hair against his neck—because I couldn't resist the opportunity—and pressed my swelling cock against his spine.

It was intimate—the kind of intimacy exhibited by couples—but not being able to see his face made me feel self-conscious.

Someone called for another toast to the Summer of Lust —apparently there had been one before the Saints and Sinners party—and all the men around us whooped and cackled, but Austin went still.

While a few of the guys exited the pool to grab everyone fresh drinks, Ryan, Keeper of the Cooler of Good Shit, flashed a wicked grin. "How's your Summer of Lust going, by the way?"

I slipped from Austin's back as he lunged for Ryan. He dunked him, grabbed him in a headlock, and dragged him across the pool. The wrestling match went on and on, cheered by an audience of shit-talkers, but I wasn't enjoying it.

Their grappling was more brotherly than sexual, and they were acting like fourteen-year-olds, but they looked like they belonged together in a way Austin and I never would.

The realization was a gut punch.

If it hadn't been me at this point in the evening, it would surely have been someone else clinging to Austin, wet and ready.

What the fuck am I doing? I must look ridiculous.

I swam to the ladder near the corner of the deep end and climbed out of the pool.

It was freezing once I left the water. I grabbed a towel from a stack on a nearby lounger, vaguely hoping I wasn't stealing it from someone.

"Hey!" Austin called out.

I hugged the towel around me and pressed it into my eyes, irrationally thinking I could ignore him if I didn't look at him.

"Prof!"

I ground my teeth, refusing to answer to that fucking nickname.

"Paul!" His voice was pitched higher than normal. "Are you getting out?"

Considering I was already standing on the concrete, it was a stupid question, but hearing him use my name, I couldn't help but turn.

Austin's hands were on the edge of the pool, and he was preparing to haul himself out.

I squatted down close to him. "Stay. It's warmer if you just stay in. I think I'm gonna crash."

"What?" He looked stricken, bewildered. "No."

Seeing the genuine disappointment in his eyes, I almost changed my mind. Almost. I'd enjoyed spending some time alone with him. I'd even started to feel comfortable. I could've happily convinced myself kissing him in the pool made sense as a fantasy come true, but this party was just getting started, and these guys—his friends—weren't going anywhere anytime soon. I couldn't see myself hanging out with a bunch of twentysomethings drinking five times more than I already had and winding up in some obscene puppy pile in the sauna sometime close to dawn. "Yeah. It's been a long day. I'm pretty wiped."

"Are you mad?" Even his frown was adorable.

"Why would I be mad?" I was irritated by the circumstances of our being interrupted. I was annoyed with myself for either looking like a fool or giving up this chance like an idiot, but I couldn't be mad at him for being who and what he was.

Young. Handsome. Sexy. Funny.

Out of your league.

Austin stuck out his bottom lip in a pout. "We didn't even get to make out."

"Is that what you thought was gonna happen?" Teasing him provided an opportunity to prove I wasn't angry.

"Well, yeah. Duh."

I chuckled. "I had fun with you tonight. Thank you."

"Why does it have to be over? I can walk you to your tent." He wasn't making any more moves to get out of the pool.

"It's not necessary. Stay and have fun with your boys." Taking a line from his playbook, I said, "I'll catch you later." I stood and turned to leave, but then I remembered a promise I'd made to him. "Oh!"

"Yeah?" He looked expectant, hopeful.

"Don't forget"—I mouthed the names silently—"Hedwig and Hagatha. They're presently unchaperoned."

Austin's eyes shifted toward Gunner, careful not to turn his head. He grimaced and gave me a thumbs-up.

I didn't even put my clothes back on, just bundled them against my chest, and stepped into my shoes.

"I'll be here for a little while," Austin said, "if you change your mind."

"Cool." Holding the towel at my throat like a cape, I walked away quickly and fled up the trail into the woods.

The campsites around me were all silent. It was way too early for bed by most people's vacation standards. I didn't feel remotely sleepy. I put my clothes back on while listening to the rumble of music, conversation, and laughter coming from the pool.

If I were being honest with myself, no longer being the center of Austin's attention and feeling like I couldn't compete with all those younger guys had triggered me. It reminded me a little too much of the jealousy and humiliation I'd experienced with my ex.

The sickening part was that I'd told Austin to stay, even though on some level I really wanted him to come after me.

Jesus.

I should have said, *Fuck what anybody else thinks I look like.* Was it too late to march back down there, jump in the water next to Austin, and tell him I'd changed my mind?

I went back.

I figured I could at least return the towel.

The crowd at the pool had grown, but I didn't see Austin in the water or among the people hanging out at the tables.

I ducked into the bathhouse, but there was no sign of him. Unless he'd gone into the sauna or the steam room. I couldn't be sure unless I went in to investigate, and I certainly didn't want to find him there. Besides, if he or any of his friends saw me skulking around, they'd think I was cruising for someone else.

Fuck. I needed to stop embarrassing myself and go to bed.

Before I headed up the trail, I stopped beside the dark, empty cabana bar to survey the crowd one last time.

At that moment, Ryan and Austin came around the side of the bathhouse from the path that led to the Village. They were naked and carrying six-packs of beer and stacks of cups.

As they deposited their haul on the table where we'd been sitting earlier, Austin glanced across the pool in my direction.

He looked right at me.

And for absolutely no good reason other than a knee-jerk response at being caught watching him, I jumped back into the shadows.

Relieved but also embarrassed, I hurried back to my tent, turned off my lantern, and lay on the air mattress in the dark.

I heard footsteps coming up the trail, then leaves crunching a few feet away.

A shadow grew up the wall of my tent.

"Prof?" Austin's voice was quiet, uncertain, not a whisper but the low, normal speaking voice you use when you think you might possibly be talking to yourself. "You up?"

He had followed me after all.

I was so busted, lying there on the bed fully clothed with my shoes still on. "Yeah." I cleared my throat. "I'm still up."

His silhouette on the tent wall grew as he stepped closer. "Want some company?"

8

———

I TURNED ON THE LANTERN, STOOD AS MUCH AS THE TENT allowed, and unzipped the door flap.

Austin stood clutching his shorts with a single platform boot slung over each shoulder. He glanced down. "Oh, look at your tidy little mat."

"I, uh... wasn't going to allow shoes in the tent," I mumbled, toeing them off.

"Will you make an exception for Hedwig and Hagatha?" He brushed pine straw off the soles of his bare feet with his fingertips. "I'm not technically wearing them in. I just don't want to risk them getting damp with dew or something."

"That's fine." I didn't mention that the dew wouldn't fall until morning. Hours from now. I stepped back to let him tiptoe inside and zipped the flap up behind him.

There was really nowhere for him to go but onto the bed. I stole a quick eyeful of his bubble butt as he crawled onto the far side of the mattress.

"I've never seen an airbed with a head bolster." He rolled onto his back, laced his fingers behind his head, and crossed his ankles. "Nice." His cock and balls were drawn up tight from the slight chill in the air, but he seemed completely unselfconscious about it.

"Yeah, it was marketed on the box as a *headboard*." I remained standing, my head awkwardly bowed under the curve of the tent's dome, eyes on his, trying not to ogle his body. "I don't know that I'd call it that, but at least I can still prop up in bed and read."

"Read?" He scoffed. "Is that what you came here to do?" He sighed and shook his head at me like he found me incorrigible.

I couldn't go on stooping and looming over him, so I joined him. I lay back with my legs straight and my hands stacked on my belly like it wasn't a big deal at all that we were lying on my bed together alone in my tent.

My heart pounded so hard he could probably feel the mattress moving.

Austin turned toward me and resettled on his side, bouncing and jostling against me more than was probably necessary. His greater weight created a gravity well, and I rolled helplessly against him, ending up with my shoulder pressed into his chest and my ankle resting over his calf. I tensed, instinctively trying to hold the weight of my leg off his, which was stupid and unnecessary; it wasn't like I was going to hurt him.

I willed myself to relax, to try not to overthink every detail of being with him.

"I should've offered you some water," I said.

"Maybe later. Don't get up now."

"I don't usually drink much alcohol."

"You're on vacation," he said softly. "Nobody's judging you."

Out of the corner of my eye, I saw Austin studying my

face as I stared at the tent ceiling and counted my breaths. "What do you want to happen here?" he asked bluntly.

I didn't look at him. "What do you mean?"

"What do you like to do?"

"Is this like a detailed negotiation or…"

"Sorry." He chuckled. "I'm used to sluts like me who rattle off their preferences in shorthand."

I turned my head and caught his eye. "You're not a slut." I wasn't sure he wasn't or how convinced I sounded, but the self-deprecating humor had landed wrong with me.

Austin twisted his lips. "Well…"

"Why would you call yourself that?"

"I'm just playfully reclaiming the term. I think it's only right you should know what you're getting with me. Which, for the record, is versatile/bottom, negative for STIs, on PrEP, and happy to play at whatever level of safety you feel comfortable with."

"I gathered that you're… *popular*."

"Aww. What a sweet way to put it." He sounded genuinely flattered. He waited a few heartbeats to see if I would say anything more, and then he sighed. "So… why don't we go back to the kiss that almost happened in the pool and see how it goes from there. Is that cool?"

I swallowed and nodded.

Austin reached over and gently cupped my jaw. His eyelids fluttered closed.

The initial touch of our lips was soft and dry.

The kiss was patient and tender, nothing like the fast, hot, open-mouthed tongue-wrestling I'd seen happening in the showers earlier. It wasn't a confirmation of pheromones or a gratuitous prelude to fucking. This kiss was a *thing* in its own right, like the most private and intimate conversation we could have.

I was grateful to him for initiating it, but I couldn't maintain the simple, passive sweetness. My nostrils filled with the warmth of Austin's breath and the smell of chlorine. Need took over, and I rolled on top of him, deepening the kiss with greedy, urgent thrusts of my tongue.

I could have made out with him for hours.

I'd come to the campground hoping something like this might happen, and my expectations may have been way too low. At least in terms of a partner. But I could still fuck up the act itself. For several years since becoming single, whenever I'd tried to hook up with another person, I had an issue getting hard enough or staying hard long enough. I woke up with morning wood, and I didn't have any problem jerking off alone.

It was some kind of performance anxiety. Another mental block like the one I was experiencing with writing. My therapist suggested I overanalyzed perceived judgment by strangers, so casual partners didn't provide me with enough *emotional safety*.

Ask your doctor if you're healthy enough for sex.

I had.

He'd assured me my testosterone levels were normal, and there was nothing physically wrong. It wasn't unheard of for any man, especially one over forty... ED medication wouldn't hurt if I wanted to try it.

I definitely wanted to try it with Austin.

If it went badly, at worst, it'd be a temporary blow to my ego, a few minutes of awkwardness while I either got rid of him or he made his own excuses to leave. Since it was a one-night stand, I'd never have to know what he thought of me. Whether or not I was *any good*.

God. I was so in my head. This wasn't an *audition*.

There'd be no *review*. But I already wanted Austin to go on liking me after tonight.

I trembled with the effort of hovering over him in a plank.

He tapped the backs of my arms, urging me to let go, to lie fully on top of him. He'd never know the leap of faith I took in that moment. My hope bordered on recklessness.

I allowed myself to melt onto him.

We both groaned at the revelation of our bodies pressed together with only the fabric of my clothes separating us.

I ground against him, wishing I could crawl into him.

Crushed between our bellies, his cock felt huge. I was suddenly overcome with a need to see it. I wanted to see all of him. Not a glimpse from the corner of my eye before he slipped into the pool or the casual nudity he displayed for anyone. I wanted to see him here laid bare for me, excited to give himself to me.

I pulled out of the kiss, sat back, and looked down at him. I'd seen a lot of naked men in the last eight hours—as many in a single day as I'd seen in a lifetime—but in the glow of the lantern light, edged in shadow, Austin's body was a miracle. His cock was nicely shaped, shorter and thicker than mine, with a shaft that tapered into the head. It was like the rest of his body—a little too thick for its length and too pretty to be believed.

He rose up on his elbows, probably wondering why I'd stopped, and grinned. "What are you doing?"

"Just looking at you." My voice came out thin and rusty. I'd never touched anyone with a physique like his. Maybe I was a dorky angel after all, coming to earth for the first time and seeing a new creature lying naked in the Garden. It was a strange epiphany to find such beauty willingly laid out before me. "I don't mean to be creepy, but I'd probably be happy just to look at you all night."

His eyes gleamed in the dark. "Well, throw in some touch, Prof. At least for my sake. And you can do anything you want."

Anything.

He was better than perfect. He was real.

I explored him with my fingertips. I stroked the scruff of his beard, the hair on his chest, the fur on his belly. I traced the thick veins down his biceps and forearms to his heavy, callused palms. I massaged his feet and squeezed his thighs. I gently lifted his nuts, weighing his sac.

God, I'm petting him.

It might have gone on for five minutes; it might've been a half hour.

Austin watched me, his expression shifting from amusement to wonder to torture. I grazed the sides of his stomach, and he sucked in a breath and contracted his abs. When I finally rubbed the slit at the head of his cock, his eyebrows drew together, and his mouth opened in a silent cry. I dipped my thumb into the precum pooling in his navel, painted the underside of his cock with it, and he hissed.

He looked like a Renaissance painting of a beautiful saint in agony.

I caught his eye, and his expression broke into a bright, encouraging smile. He seemed to delight in my objectification of him, not because he needed the attention but because he was giving me an experience.

He was letting me play with him.

Anything.

He arched an eyebrow like we shared some devious, delicious secret.

I grabbed his cock around the base, opened my mouth wide, and took as much of him as I could all at once.

I held him there, tasting his brine on my tongue, letting the heat of him fill my mouth. He writhed on the bed, cursing, talking out of his head like he might have been dreaming.

I hadn't even moved my tongue yet, but taking his reaction as encouragement, I began to suck in earnest.

After a few minutes of wordless cries, he tugged the neck of my shirt. I'd remained fully clothed the entire time, but it wasn't because of modesty or even insecurity. I'd simply forgotten myself in him.

"Take everything off," he whispered. "I want to see you too."

I allowed him to strip my shirt over my head, only releasing his cock with an audible pop at the last possible second. I stood clumsily, unbuttoned my shorts, shoved them with my boxer briefs down my legs, and stepped out of them.

Still wearing my socks.

This was the clothing option I couldn't fail to catalog. Nothing felt more naked than being *almost* naked in socks. If it turned Austin off, he was kind enough not to show it.

My dick swung heavily, filling faster now that it was freed.

Austin's grin turned wolfish. He sat up on the mattress and pulled at the backs of my thighs, gently nuzzling my balls and pressing his cheek against my cock.

It felt amazing, but I couldn't remain standing in a stooped position, so I squatted at the foot of the bed.

"Come back up here," Austin said.

I surreptitiously stripped off my socks, crawled between his legs, and pushed him flat on his back again. *That* was when I finally experienced the sensation of my fully naked body against his.

I didn't want to change anything, but there was no universe where I could have also stayed still. I moved on top of him, humping, frotting, trying to find every possible nuance of contact.

We were too tightly intertwined to kiss. I groaned, and he murmured "Fuuuck" into the side of my neck like he couldn't believe this was happening any more than I could.

I felt like I was seconds away from shooting all over his belly—which was a miracle in its own right, one I didn't want to squander—but I didn't want any of this to end, so I let the sensation pass and kept driving along that edge.

"D'you wanna fuck me?" he whispered.

I'd lost my faculty for words, but I managed an affirmative grunt.

Austin raised his head and strained to peer at my backpack in the corner. "You got some kind of little trick kit around here somewhere?"

Indeed I had. With a flourish, I produced a clear zipper pouch with a brand-new box of condoms, a pristinely new bottle of lube, and the full, unopened bottle of ED medication I'd acquired in time for this weekend. It was still in the paper bag from the pharmacy with the prescription information stapled to the front. The pills rattled like maracas.

Austin chuckled. "Blue ones or yellow ones?"

"Uh..." Were they yellow? I hadn't seen them yet. My doctor had said most people found the side effects more tolerable. "Not the blue ones."

"Okay." Austin grimaced. "Well, the yellow ones work more slowly. They're usually more effective if you take them some time *before* you're gonna get lucky." A frustrated sound escaped my mouth, and he rushed on. "But it's cool. It'll be fine."

I didn't care so much that Austin knew I needed the pills, but I was mortified I hadn't known to take them in time.

Unless I'd been scheduling date night with a partner, an adventurous weekend at a naked campground should have been the ideal circumstance for predicting when I might *get lucky*.

The last thing I needed at that moment was to contemplate my luck, and now there was also *packaging* to contend with.

I managed to shake out a tablet and place it under my tongue. It was probably way too late, but I prayed it might somehow get into my bloodstream faster.

Just *thinking* about needing the pills was enough to make me spin out. The fear I *might* lose my erection was one of the most likely ways to ensure that I did.

Talk about a feedback loop.

I was hard now, but I'd fallen for that fleeting certainty before.

The what-if thoughts went straight to my dick, and here I was at *that* shitty spiral.

No, no, no, no, no.

I was losing it.

Austin thought I was only struggling with the seal on the new lube bottle. "Hand that over." He clawed off the plastic wrapping, squirted a few drops on his fingertips, and reached between his legs to prep himself. Within seconds, he was lying back, ready for me.

I would've enjoyed doing that to him. It also would've helped to drag it out a bit longer. Rushing things definitely did not.

I tore the condom package open with my teeth, hoping I still looked like I knew what I was doing.

Austin watched me with heat and anticipation, playing with his cock. He scooted down closer to where I knelt on the bed and lifted his legs.

Goddamn, that was my kryptonite—a man with his feet in the air for me. *Wheelbarrow Boy.*

At least I'd have the image in my head to jack off to for the rest of my days.

I fumbled with the condom, bumping into his nuts as I tried to roll it on in the right direction. He pulled his sac out of the way to give me easier access, and then I tried to sort of *stuff* the condom full of *not quite hard enough* dick into him.

Which, as anyone who has ever tried this last-ditch, desperate move knows, doesn't work.

I pulled back and futilely slapped my sheathed, softening dick against his perfect, willing hole.

"Everything okay down there?" he asked.

"Yeah." I groaned in frustration. "The condom just…"

"I'm on PrEP…" he said, putting an option out there.

"Yeah, me too, but…" I'd been taking it for months like a tiny seed of dormant hope that someday I'd need it, but even if Austin and I had discussed barebacking earlier—and no matter how much the thought appealed to me—I likely couldn't now. I was unprepared for this much *luck*. I was the proverbial dog who'd caught the fucking car. I sighed and reached for words that would let him off the hook. "I'm sorry. You're gorgeous. It's just been a while for me, and…"

Austin dropped his feet, sat up, and leaned toward me. "It happens to everybody. It's okay."

"It's not." Without meeting his eyes, I shook my head and removed the condom. "It sucks being a top who can't get hard enough to fuck." I chuckled bitterly.

He took my hand. "Then let me take care of you." He pulled me back onto the mattress with him, rolled me onto my back, and kissed me until I finally surrendered and relaxed. He slid down my body, propped on his elbows, between my legs, and took my half-hard dick into his mouth.

Thank God for options. It was heaven.

I watched him as if it were happening to someone else, but there was no way he was only doing this to make me feel better. He was enjoying himself too. He was hungry for me. At one point, he lay with his head against my hip, his eyes were open, looking up at my body. He spread his hand across my belly and moaned.

My orgasm pulled from every extremity and coiled in my core. It paused for one, two, three heartbeats, and finally released.

With a roar, I came down Austin's throat. They surely heard me all up and down the holler.

I could've sworn I heard someone somewhere applaud.

9

IT WAS THE FIRST TIME I'D COME WITH SOMEONE ELSE IN longer than I could remember. While I was still panting and seeing stars, Austin crawled up beside me, threw a massive arm over my chest, and nuzzled his face between my neck and shoulder. He wriggled a few times, settled his limbs into the empty spaces between mine, and, with a big sigh, promptly fell asleep.

Under most circumstances, I couldn't have slept without reading first, but I couldn't reach my Kindle without moving, and I was in no hurry to disturb him. His weight, his warmth, his scent... Beyond seduction and sex, this was a comfort we all dreamed of.

My ex had usually fallen asleep right after we'd finished. I'd always wanted him to stay, but he'd rouse after dozing for fifteen or twenty minutes, dress in a hurry, and flee my dorm room before anyone caught him there. Years later, when we'd been living together, he'd steal down the hall to sleep in the guest room.

Once we'd stopped having sex at all, it had shifted seamlessly into separate bedrooms.

Austin hadn't even gotten off, though.

I shifted a few times, testing to see if he'd jump up and make excuses to stumble off into the night, but he turned me on my side as if I were a body pillow and pulled my back against his chest.

I lay awake tracing his fingers as he held my hand under my chin.

He ran hot. I was thirsty, almost feverish, with a headache forming behind my eyes. I was going to be hungover as shit in the morning, but tonight wouldn't last forever. I could suffer tomorrow.

For now, I'd absorb the details of what it felt like to share a bed with someone who never stopped touching you. I might need to write about it sometime. And until this moment, it hadn't happened to me.

I BLINKED in the gray morning light. Somewhere nearby, a bird made a god-awful racket. The only thing more disturbing would have been the literal crowing of a cock. By comparison, a bugle playing "Reveille" would've been a lullaby.

Austin lay on the small strip of empty floor beside the mattress, trying to work his tiny shorts up his thighs as quietly as possible. I remained still, one eye cracked, watching him. For a few moments, his cock and balls were nicely presented, squeezed from below by the tight fabric, but then, with a small curse, he manfully stuffed everything out of sight.

I grimaced in sympathy, sucking in a loud, sharp breath.

He heard me.

I'd blown any chance I might have had of pretending to

be asleep and letting him slip away without any awkward morning-after conversation.

Austin crawled partially onto the mattress, placed one hand near my head and the other between my legs, and kissed me.

I hadn't anticipated it. My mouth tasted like sour beer and ass—not in a good way—so I'd hesitated. Thankfully, it was a quick, chaste smack of the lips.

"Morning," I murmured.

"Good morning," Austin said. His brown eyes were puffy. "I didn't want to leave without saying goodbye, but I'm super late for work—oh, wait. What do we have here?" He squeezed my morning erection through the thin fabric of the sleeping bag. "It looks like your package has arrived, sir."

I instinctively pushed into his grip. God, it felt good, but my sinuses were congested and my head throbbed. I groaned. "Damn. I don't think I've ever had a hangover like this. I didn't drink *that* much, did I?"

Austin grimaced. "Yeah, the stuffy nose is a pretty shitty side effect. Have you never taken dick meds before?"

I avoided his question. "Have *you* taken them before?"

"Yeah."

"Why?"

"Um..." I could see him thinking. "Athletic performance," he said with a questioning lilt. "I've also been with other guys who take them." To change the subject, he tore back the covers and grabbed my dick again. "But check out this fucking tool, Prof."

God, I'd forgotten what it was like to be *this* hard. Unable to help myself, I fucked his warm fist. "Sorry," I said through gritted teeth.

Austin laughed. "What have you got to be sorry for?"

66

"Badly timing my medication." I grimaced. "And leaving you blue-balled."

He shrugged. "Not everybody has to get off every time."

I propped myself up on one elbow. "Well, that's awfully mature of you."

"I'm very mature for my age."

"Are you?" I teased. I wanted to ask him how old he was exactly, but our age difference wasn't something I wanted to call attention to.

"I am. It makes me feel good to make you feel good. And the other stuff—the making out, the body contact, the spooning—is what I love most. It's so much harder to find."

I would have never guessed that physical affection was the thing he was after, but considering the kind of attention others presumed to give him, it made sense. I also would never have predicted he would stay the night, but I couldn't say any of that without sounding like an asshole.

"Then I'm also sorry"—I had to clear my throat—"you can't stay."

"I guess I could quit my job, but being a no-show's not my style."

"Don't do that."

He tapped my phone and the time flashed on the screen. "I was supposed to be at the lodge about ten minutes ago. I still need to run by the bunkhouse and grab some work clothes."

"Wait. You're gonna walk up the trail to the lodge shirtless and barefoot?"

He looked at Gunner's boots and twisted his lips. "Trust me, going barefoot will hurt less."

"What size are you?"

"Twelve-and-a-half."

I arched a brow. "Well, this is your lucky day."

He smiled. "For so many reasons."

I reached into the corner where I'd organized my clothes and pulled out the largest item I'd brought, a threadbare University of Georgia sweatshirt.

"Your alma mater." I tossed it to him. "I don't know where or when I got that, and"—I held up a finger—"before you even think about it, it's way too fucking early for a Go Dawgs cheer. 'K?"

He pouted. "You're grouchy in the morning." He pulled the faded red sweatshirt over his head, and holding the collar to his nose, inhaled deeply. "Mm. It smells like you."

His doing that, his saying it—and the thought of him wearing my scent—made my pulse race more than when he'd grabbed my cock.

"Oh, look." I shoved a pair of red Nikes at him. "Shoes to match."

"Aww, Prof. I can't take your shoes."

"They're my shitty work in the yard shoes. I brought them as an extra pair in case it gets muddy."

Austin slipped them on. "Nice. They're all broken in and comfortable. I can feel the shape of your foot." He was killing me with all this clothing *intimacy*. "It's kinda like wearing your boyfriend's jacket in high school."

"Did you ever do that?" I asked, genuinely curious.

"Nah. I wish. Never had the chance." He tied the laces. "Red shoes, huh? How very Dorothy of you."

"I got them on clearance. I can't tell you how many times I've found red sneakers on clearance. I guess it's the least desirable color."

"I used to wear red shoes on purpose all the time. On days when I needed to feel a little more magical. Brave. Special. Whatever."

"Did you click them together?"

"Maybe. I wish I could click them together right now and be at the lodge and not getting fired."

"Go." I looked away, releasing him.

"Come find me," he said.

If you'd asked me this time yesterday, I would've said I'd probably stay the night and leave in the morning. My sabbatical from teaching was ending soon, and I needed to get home and get some writing done. Last night, lying in his arms, I would've given myself till this afternoon—enough time to have breakfast with the guys, hang out at the pool for a bit, maybe talk to Austin again, at least to say goodbye.

Now I dreaded leaving.

He leaned in for another sweet, simple kiss.

I sent him off with one of his own lines, "I'll catch you later." Only I sincerely meant it.

10

MORNING TEMPERATURES WERE STILL CHILLY AT THE END OF May in the North Georgia mountains, so I pulled on an old hoodie, and, after casting a regretful look at the formerly white Vans I'd worn last night, I sighed and stomped into them.

As soon as I popped my head out of the tent, someone called my name.

Ben and Eric were coming up the trail, both of them sporting bedhead and matching blood-red lips. The expression *good and fucked* came to mind.

"Perfect timing!" Eric was happier than I'd ever seen him. It creeped me out a little.

"Coming to see if you want to grab breakfast with us," Ben said.

"Sure. I was just heading up to the lodge in search of coffee."

"I meant," Eric said, "it was perfect timing to see who just left your tent. You're looking a little mauled and red-faced this morning."

"Um, don't even start on me when you've yet to

explain"—I gestured between them—"whatever the fuck has happened here in the last thirty-six hours."

Eric sighed. "The long, slow hands of fate." Ben only grinned down at the trail and said nothing. Behind his back, Eric mouthed, "I'll fill you in later."

We hiked for a bit, marveling at the dozens of campsites that seemed to have materialized overnight.

"So," Eric said. "Everybody saw you guys leave the bar together last night. And it has been confirmed that neither of you came back."

"Confirmed?" I scoffed. "By whom?"

"Sources," Eric said. "Now stop stalling. We need details."

"*He* needs details," Ben muttered. Ben was the one I saw the most often, and if I hadn't witnessed them together, it might have been weeks or even months before he brought it up. Ben traded in zero gossip; Eric, blow-by-blow accounts.

I teased Eric with a brief, intentionally maddening summary. "We hung out down here at the pool for a bit. Then we came back to my tent."

"And?" Eric's voice cracked.

I shrugged. "He spent the night." And before Eric could grill me further, I turned the inquisition on him. "How do you know him again?"

"Everybody here knows Austin Fox." He must have realized his tone carried a ton of innuendo because he quickly added, "He's the reigning Best Cub of the annual Bear Mountain Lodge Bear Run."

I carefully picked my way up a steep section of the trail where tree roots and rocks formed natural steps, waiting for the string of words to make sense to my uncaffeinated brain. "What the fuck is that?"

Eric hummed, searching for an explanation. "Think

high school superlatives crossed with like International Mr. Leather. But *way* local."

"So it's a fucking beauty pageant?"

Eric nodded once. "It's a fucking beauty pageant." He held up a finger. "But butch."

Ben snorted.

I rolled my eyes. "Of course."

"Very, very butch."

"I wouldn't dare think otherwise."

We reached the end of the trail and took our places on the lodge steps behind all the other men waiting to get in. There was a self-service coffee station set up out on the deck to appease us while we waited for breakfast to be served.

Eric took Ben's hand, gazed lovingly at him, and something unspoken passed between them. When Eric saw me staring, he said, "We agreed it's finally time for us to be together again. As more than friends."

I hadn't known them back when they'd dated in college —I was a few years older—but I knew they'd been close for twenty years. I toasted them with my coffee cup. "It's about damn time."

BREAKFAST WAS a muted event compared to dinner. Most of the men looked a bit bleary-eyed, shuffling forward like zombies in the buffet line, drawn by the smells of bacon and biscuits. Other than mumbled good mornings, conversation was limited to ubiquitous complaints about hangovers and jokes about sausages that the staff surely had suffered before.

One exception was a chatterbox in a *Golden Girls* T-shirt who sat at our table and bragged about how early he'd gone to bed, how *fabulously* he'd slept, and all the remote work tasks he'd managed to accomplish on his smart phone by hiking out to the front gate. He went into great detail about the precise location of the strongest cellular signal—an electrical pole about a quarter mile up the drive toward the main road.

As if we were in the presence of a wild animal, we instinctively and collectively avoided making eye contact until his chipper monologue transitioned into chewing noises.

To distract myself from visions of his grizzly murder, I looked for Austin.

Austin carried a heavy urn, headed for the coffee table outside. "Hot stuff coming through!" he warned everyone in his path. His muscles strained under the weight of the canister, making everyone's morning a little brighter for so many reasons.

Since I'd last seen him, he'd changed into a staff T-shirt a few sizes too small for his upper body and khaki shorts, but he still wore my shoes. He hadn't spoken to me yet, but the shoes felt like a secret communication. Every time his duties brought him near our table, I had to raise my cup to cover the smile I couldn't suppress.

Catching me grinning like a fool, Eric smirked through the entire meal.

I didn't know what kind of attention I'd expected from Austin this morning. Maybe more of the glances I'd received last night at dinner, the overzealous drink refills, the cleared plates, maybe an extra smile or even a wink.

Austin struck me as the type who'd wink under the right circumstances, and serving breakfast to the man he blew last night sure seemed like it would have been in the ballpark.

I'd expected more than *no* attention.

Maybe I was a sad, middle-aged fool who'd gotten lucky at a naked campground bar with a guy who'd swindled me out of my favorite yard-work clothes.

But then, he *was* working, and he'd been running late this morning. Hell, maybe he'd been chewed out by his boss. Sawyer, the campground owner, was definitely glowering at *someone*.

Austin also had more at stake today than an early morning shift with a hangover. It was the launch of his fitness class, and considering his association with red shoes, he was probably really in his head worrying about how that was going to go. His lips moved as if he were muttering to himself, probably rehearsing what he was going to say when he got up in front of everyone.

That's what I'd always done on the first day of a new class.

I should have wished him luck.

Austin stopped between Eric's and Ben's chairs, facing me. For a second, I thought he was finally going to say something to me, but then, in a loud voice, he asked for everyone's attention. "Hey, guys! Listen up!" I realized we happened to be sitting in the middle of the room.

The murmuring voices ceased and silverware clattered to a halt. Every face in the room turned in Austin's direction with either a smile or an expression of curiosity.

"If you wanna get rid of your hangover, I've got the cure." Austin paused, looking around and making eye contact with a variety of men. "It's a little routine I call the Morning-After Drill. It's high intensity interval training with all bodyweight exercises that can be modified for any level of fitness including beginners." The diners collectively groaned, but Austin ignored it and pressed on. "We're gonna do some stretching, some light cardio, and just enough strength training to give you that little pump you're gonna want when you're strutting around the pool later."

There was some heckling, negative enough that a cold tendril of dread crawled up from my stomach. Someone yelled, "The last thing I wanna do on vacation is work out, son!"

But Austin treated it as if it were good-natured trash talk. "You know you wanna look cute." He didn't seem bothered by his reception at all. Maybe he'd expected it. "This is gonna be a lot of fun, and"—someone said something to him that I couldn't make out—"No, fuck you very much, my playlist is *not* all country music, and it definitely does not suck."

The room erupted in crosstalk. Austin had completely lost the floor, but he cupped his hand around his mouth and attempted to finish up his pitch. "I promise you, hair of the dog is not the answer. Bring your water bottle and meet me in the gym next to Bathhouse Three at ten."

I doubted anyone else had noticed the flash of disappointment that passed through Austin's eyes. He projected a convincing smile. If he felt embarrassed or harassed, he didn't show it. He was comfortable being in the spotlight.

Or at least used to being there.

"It actually *is* a pretty good way to get rid of a hangover," I said to Eric and Ben. I hadn't intended to speak so loudly, but it was one of those weird moments in a crowd where there was a sudden, random lull in conversation, and by contrast my voice had carried.

Austin held his hand out to me like he was presenting me to the room. "Thank you!" He nodded and beamed at me for a solid five seconds, vindicated, and then, before he turned to flee through the kitchen doors, he winked.

I *knew* he was a winker.

"You gonna go get you some of Austin's *drill*?" Eric teased.

I placed a hand over my full, distended belly. "As much as I probably need to, I'm not about to make a fool of myself in front of him." *Not after what happened last night*, I thought. "I can't remember the last time I went to a fitness class."

I'd tried to work out all through my twenties. When my ex, Charles, and I had been together, he'd had an eye for the young jock types. He always seemed to be tutoring some guy who was in danger of losing his athletic scholarship. Toward the end of our relationship, I'd avoided dropping by during his office hours, afraid I might interrupt him receiving some extra credit from one of his students.

Eric sighed. "Well, if I were more motivated, I'd at least go to watch, but—"

"Excuse me?" Ben huffed, affronted.

Eric grabbed Ben's thigh under the table and nuzzled his ear. "You didn't let me finish. I was gonna say, I can't imagine a better workout than a post-breakfast nap."

The way he popped the *P* at the end of *nap* implied there would be other *P*s involved.

The chemistry between them—and the affection more than anything—was palpable. They turned heads. All the flirting, the cruising, the hooking up here... Even if they wouldn't admit it, a lot of these men ultimately wanted to end up in something that looked like whatever Eric and Ben had.

"Well, hey. We hiked up here, and we're hiking back. That's gotta count for something, right?" I stood and gathered my dirty dishes. "I think I'm gonna shower and go read by the pool."

Eric and Ben followed me to the bus tubs near the kitchen.

"Beware the Bloody Marys down by the pool," Eric said. "Sometimes it's mimosas. Sometimes it's both. They're poured heavy-handed, and if you're not careful, your lightweight ass'll end up trashed before noon and sleeping it off the rest of the day."

11

I'D SERIOUSLY CONSIDERED WALKING OVER TO BATHHOUSE Three to take a shower and shave this time. Maybe sneak a peek at Austin teaching. But if he were to see me, it'd be obvious what I was doing.

Possibly a little pathetic.

My legitimately attending was out of the question. He didn't need some random older dude he'd hooked up with stalking him, then passing out in his class.

I believed the chemistry between us was genuine and mutual, but I had no delusions about how I might fare in a side-by-side comparison with a bunch of gym-going types.

Bathhouse Two, the one at the pool complex where we'd gone last night, was only a hundred yards from my tent and the obvious and sensible choice. The communal showers were packed with naked guys, but after my night with Austin, I didn't enjoy the view nearly as much today. I was afraid I might become unintentionally aroused due to my chemically assisted dick, but I was relieved to discover the medicine didn't automatically override my lack of interest.

Austin had probably ruined me for anyone else for a

long time.

When I saw my reflection in the mirror, I was mortified by how red-faced I still was from the medication. It was a glaring spotlight on my situation. I peered at the other men going about their morning routines, wondering who else might share my affliction, but so many of them seemed to have unusually flushed complexions. It was probably only the heat from the sauna and the showers, and I hoped once I got out of this sweatbox, my own persistent blush would subside.

I returned to my tent to change into a pair of board shorts. I downed an extra bottle of water and took a few over-the-counter fever reducers. I grabbed my e-reader, sunglasses, sunscreen, and a towel, and went to claim a spot near the pool.

It was still early. A handful of leather-skinned sunbathers who'd clearly been working on their tans since the eighties were quietly dozing, and a raucous group at a nearby table poured drinks and handed them out.

One of the men waved to me and raised his voice. "Mimosa or Mary, Mary?"

At first, I wasn't sure he was talking to me, but a quick glance confirmed there was nobody seated behind me. I raised my eyebrows.

He squinted, playfully biting the end of his finger, and then he pointed it at me. "You look like a Bloody Mary to me." He held up a cup with a celery stalk and a toothpick stacked with olives sticking out of the top. "Want one?"

My hangover plus these hellacious side effects weren't likely to cure themselves. Fuck whatever Austin had to say about hair of the dog; at the moment, it was definitely more appealing than exercise. "Um, yeah. That'd be great." I jumped up and met him halfway so he wouldn't have to serve me. The first sip was heavenly, the salty, sour taste of the juice and the scent of black pepper filling my nose. I groaned with pleasure. "Oh my God. That's delicious. Thank you."

"Sure thing, baby," he said.

I was oddly touched by this random person—a guest, clearly, not a staff member—making and serving drinks to strangers *just because*. There was a camaraderie here I'd never encountered in the outside world. Few queer-friendly environments I'd been in could claim this level of instant inclusiveness. I often felt a little judged and overlooked.

The sudden wave of fond feelings might have been due to my being sleep-deprived, hungover, and having gotten laid for the first time in forever, but it could also have been evidence of the welcoming camp society Eric had evangelized for years.

I sipped my drink and pretended to read while people-watching behind my sunglasses. The Bloody Marys kept offering me a refill, but I heeded Eric's warning. Eric and Ben arrived, carrying a cooler between them, with Eric's musician friends/clients Alex, Noah, and Lance trailing close behind. They descended on my quiet, shady spot, dragging a few extra chairs over so we could all squeeze in around the same table.

Alex grumbled about having slept through breakfast, and Noah wondered aloud if there might be coffee at the cabana bar. Lance said he was fine with skipping the caffeine and going right into day drinking.

Ben poured and passed around cups of something that smelled like pineapple and rum. The proportion of alcohol was enough to make my eyes water, not to mention it would've been a terrible flavor progression from tomato juice and Worcestershire, so I declined.

Lance took the cup from me and declared it *breakfasty enough*.

Austin walked by carrying a bag of ice on each shoulder. He'd changed again, this time into a staff T-shirt with the sleeves cut out, a pair of retro, white athletic shorts, and tall striped tube socks.

He was still wearing my red sneakers.

I was shocked at how fast that made my dick hard. Not the sight of a naked body, not a grope, not even a kiss—the thought of Austin choosing to put my shoes on again.

A lot of heads turned in unison to check out Austin's ass before he disappeared behind the bar. Someone at the Bloody Marys' table made a loud comment about a *muscle cub*, and they all laughed.

Eric caught my eye and smirked.

"Okay." I would've preferred to talk to Eric and Ben without these other guys overhearing, but fuck it. I nodded toward the Marys and dropped my voice. "So explain that to me."

Eric cocked his head. "Explain..."

"A *muscle cub*. What the hell is that exactly?"

Eric was kind enough to answer seriously. "In bear speak, a *cub* is generally a younger or younger-looking guy who will probably grow into a full-blown bear. Usually, he's a bear chaser or often the boyfriend of an older bear. Austin's one of the youngest guys here. What is he, like, twenty-five?"

God, I hoped he was at least that old.

"So he qualifies as a *muscle* cub because, well... look at him."

We all did. Everyone at our table turned to stare at Austin, who was lining up beer cans on the bar and popping them open for customers.

Eric chewed the inside of his lip, considering. "He's actually pretty tall for a cub. You usually think of them as being on the shorter side. His face has that sweet, boyish quality, though, so even if he was seven feet tall and forty, he'd still have a cubbyness about him, you know?"

"So what does that make me?" I cleared my throat. "In bear slang or whatever."

All five of them studied me. It was like being surrounded by a circle of people miming *thinking hard*.

Alex spoke up first. "You're a little young to be a daddy, I guess, but—"

"No, he's not," Eric said. "He's right at the beginning of prime daddy years."

Alex snorted and said to Eric, "I don't think of *you* as a daddy."

Ben shook his head slowly, repressing a smile as Eric's mouth dropped open in mock horror.

"Of course not, dude." Eric pointed at me. "Paul is three years older than I am."

Alex raised his hands in a gesture of surrender.

"You do have a killer dad bod, though," Lance said.

My head whipped around. Lance was indeed talking to me. I gave him a stern frown.

"You look great," Lance said earnestly, his eyebrows raised. He didn't *look me up and down* exactly, but he held my gaze in a way that felt the same.

"This!" Eric slapped the table, then presented Lance to me with an open hand. "This is why I wanted you to come here. So you can finally realize once and for all how hot you are."

"Um..." My face felt like it was on fire. At least maybe the flush from the medication and the Bloody Mary hid my actual embarrassment. I managed to shoot Lance a tight smile. "Thanks."

"You bet." Lance leaned toward me. Under his breath, he said, "I'm in Cabin Six, by the way. If the muscle cub doesn't work out for you."

"Okay, back off, buddy," Eric said a little too loudly, shaking his head at Lance. "You've looked, you've complimented. Thank you for your service to Paul's ego, but he and Austin have established a connection. They're close to having their own hashtag if I have anything to say about it."

Austin glanced at our table, his brows knitting together in a questioning frown.

"He's looking right over here," I spat through clenched teeth.

Eric made a dismissive gesture. "He can't hear us."

To confirm for themselves whether or not that was possible, Ben, Lance, Alex, and Noah all turned to peer at Austin.

Austin smiled and waved.

And everyone—*everyone* at the fucking table, except me—waved back.

Great. "He definitely knows we're talking about him now."

Eric huffed. "I'm sure he's used to it. Half the men here are probably talking about him."

And he could have his pick of any of them.

Eric must have read my mind because he reached past Ben and laid his hand on my arm. "He spent the night with you."

I rolled my eyes. Eric was now one of *those* people, so in love he wanted everyone else to feel what he was feeling. "It was a hookup."

"Was he too drunk to make it back to the bunkhouse?"

"No."

"Was there spooning?" Eric held up a hand to stop my protest. "I'm not asking for sex details. I want to know if cuddling occurred."

I half shrugged, half nodded. His cross-examination deserved a petulant gesture.

"Ah-ha!" Eric slapped the tabletop a second time. "See? Nobody crashes in a fucking tent when they've got a real bed within walking distance unless they can't physically get to it or there's something way better in the tent. Some of these dudes won't even fuck a guy in a tent unless he's really hot." Alex and Noah snickered. "No, seriously. It's true. It's a thing. Ask around." He turned back to me. "I think Austin's genuinely into you. When you guys were talking out on the side deck at the bar last night, we went and peeked."

"*You* went and peeked," Ben corrected him.

Eric ignored him. "I saw how he was looking at you, Paul. And he told us the other night that he was into older guys."

"So I'm like... a fetish or something."

"Dude. He was *dancing* for you. He was dancing *at* you."

Ben hummed, a wordless sound of agreement. "He's also been wearing your shoes all day."

I stared at him. Ben wasn't quick to share his opinion about anything trivial, and when he did choose to speak, it was worth paying attention to.

"Paulstin." Eric snapped his fingers, the name having just occurred to him. "Hashtag fucking Paulstin."

While the boys were high-fiving Eric's wordplay, Ben raised his eyebrows at me. "It's not nothing." He was still referring to the shoes.

Austin had already changed clothes twice that I knew of

before noon. He'd had to have taken the shoes off both times—once to get those tiny shorts off; another to put those socks on. He'd definitely chosen to keep wearing my shoes.

And I didn't know for sure how much he'd had to drink or what kind of tolerance he had, but at any point in the night, he could've crept out and gone back to his own bed.

I motioned for the guys to settle the fuck down. Not only were other people looking over now, wondering what the joke was, but Austin and his coworker were watching us while speaking intently with their heads together.

"It was hot," I said to Ben as if he was the only one listening. "It was nice. But I'm pretty sure it was probably like, you know, a... one-night stand."

"The weekend's not over," Eric said. "Hashtag Paulstin."

I hadn't told them my intentions to leave either this morning or maybe this afternoon, and the Bloody Mary buzz had already made it unlikely I'd get out of there before tomorrow morning. Eric had been right to warn me; that may have been the strongest drink I'd ever consumed in my life.

With the sun shining, the pool deck filling up with men, and the DJ setting up beside the bar, the thought of packing all my shit and carrying it to the truck seemed like some kind of punishment.

Missing out on whatever today might have to offer, what tonight might bring, the opportunity to talk to Austin more...

That would be self-imposed exile.

As long as there might be any chance I'd get to hang out with Austin again, I couldn't leave.

But even if I harbored the tiniest secret hope, I couldn't help voicing my doubts. "Why would someone like him, who's clearly living his best life in his best body in a twenty-four seven playground, want a forty-two-year-old doctor of English literature whose idea of the perfect weekend is getting up early enough on Saturday to beat the crowds at the home improvement stores?" I laughed as if I were being self-deprecating. I was trying to spar with Eric, to challenge his idea of Austin and me as a match, to see if he could convince me it wasn't a ridiculous notion.

Ben shrugged. "Sounds pretty fucking nice. A lot of men want a home and somebody they can trust to build one with. The party can't last forever."

I watched Austin opening a beer for a shirtless, muscular guy with a mullet that was probably meant to be *ironic* but nevertheless made me question how hot that hairstyle could actually be on the right person. Austin grinned at him, his teeth brilliant white against his tan, scruffy face.

Maybe he would want to settle down at some point, but surely it would be with someone his own age and with someone who looked like him.

I could see it.

They'd go to the gym together six days a week and spend Sundays prepping high-protein meals of bland chicken cutlets and recovery shakes. They'd adopt a pair of pit bull rescues and drive them to the park in their Jeep. They'd invite their buddies over to watch sportsball on a TV the size of a wall. They'd get married in matching tuxes they could barely move in because no suit could be tailored to the bulk of their shoulders and thighs.

Austin came out from behind the bar and headed straight for our table.

"Shit," I said. "He's coming over."

12

"Can I get you gentlemen anything from the bar?" Austin asked.

Everyone declined except Noah, who asked if it would be possible to get a coffee.

"Sure. I can put a pot on." Austin glanced over at me. "Hey."

"Hey." I pointedly looked down at his shoes. My shoes.

"Sorry." He grimaced. "They're so fucking comfortable."

I shook my head. "Don't be. I'm sorry they're so fucking old."

"I like wearing them." I remembered his commenting on how he could feel the shape of my foot.

I almost said, *Wear them every day and think of me*, but I managed to bite my tongue at the last second. I was definitely tipsy.

"Are you blushing, Prof?"

I lowered my chin and glared at him through my eyelashes. Surely he wasn't going to make me remind him about the medication.

"Oh, right!" He glanced at my lap, and his dark eyes flashed. "Is that still working for ya?"

If it hadn't been for the table, he might've seen the fabric of my shorts visibly throb.

Before I could think of a coherent answer, Eric interrupted to invite Austin to their cabin for drinks this evening before the bonfire.

Austin nodded. "I'll try to swing by." He told Noah to give him a couple minutes on the coffee, and after making an excuse about not wanting to leave the bar unattended for too long, he left.

Eric turned to me with a smug expression. "You're welcome."

I shook my head. "'I'll swing by' is what he says so he doesn't have to say no. He told me so himself."

"He'll be there."

"We'll see."

THE POPULATION of the campground might have doubled during the day. The pool area was jammed with bodies. Austin was slammed at the cabana bar for hours. We didn't get a chance to speak again, but I never stopped watching him. The few times I caught his eye, he smiled.

Dinner was madness. We had to wait outside for tables to empty before we could rotate into the line for food. The staff all had harried, focused expressions, and their usual banter was terse.

Austin was serving desserts, and with the size of the crowd, I didn't expect him to have time for any meaningful interaction with me. I also didn't want to appear desperate, so I opted to stand in line for a much needed after-dinner coffee instead of dessert.

After I returned to our table, Austin materialized bearing two plates, one with cobbler, one with cake. "We're supposed to only let you have one kind, but..." He waggled his eyebrows at me before dashing away.

Eric gushed, Lance asked if he could eat my cake, and I eye-fucked Austin across the dining hall until we had to leave to make room for others.

I hoped he would come to the guys' cabin later.

I ATTEMPTED a disco nap to sleep off my buzz, but I failed again. All I did was lie in my tent replaying every interaction with Austin and kicking myself for not taking this prescription sooner. I wasn't really masturbating so much as marveling at my miraculous erection. I toyed with it, edging myself, but I worried an orgasm might diminish my newfound libido. I didn't want to get off alone if I had another chance with Austin later.

To sober up a bit and refresh my energy, I went for a shower, then headed to Eric and Ben's cabin. Alex and Noah and a few random campers I didn't know were there. We sat on their hot tub deck drinking, admiring the crescent moon and Venus above golden clouds in a purple sky.

I hadn't expected Austin to be there yet, if ever—certainly not before me—but I was surprised not to see Lance. I casually asked where he was, and Alex said, "Off whoring."

For a horrible moment, I imagined Austin and Lance somewhere together. There was absolutely no reason to think that was actually happening. The thought was more like a lingering echo of the shitty things my ex had been notorious for. Charles had particularly enjoyed fucking guys he perceived as having been interested in me, flirting with me, or checking me out. Whenever he'd cheated, he was never satisfied to hook up with a stranger. He had to make it messy—my high school boyfriend, a friend of my parents, my teaching assistant.

If anything, it was evidence of how much I secretly liked Austin. Even though most of Ben and Eric's friends wouldn't even have known to expect him, and Alex and Noah probably couldn't have cared less, it felt like everybody was waiting for Austin. Ben would never have paid attention to something of personal concern to me unless I'd asked him to, but Eric was definitely as hyperaware of Austin's absence as I was. He kept offering me drink refills I wasn't ready for, and as the night wore on, he seemed unable to look me in the eye.

Which made me feel like an asshole, even though Eric was the one trying to turn my one-night stand into some instant love story.

By this point, I'd overheard the claims that it wasn't uncommon to experience weeks and months' worth of a love affair in a single day at camp, then be on to someone new the next day. You could potentially fall in love a handful of times in a long weekend.

I wasn't quick to believe that could happen to me, and as for Austin... Well, it seemed unlikely someone who worked here would fall under that spell, especially so early in the season.

It was his *Summer of Lust* after all. Surely, he would know to pace himself.

I reset my expectations accordingly.

When it was time to leave for the bonfire and Austin still hadn't *swung by*, I decided to let Eric off the hook by being the one to drain my beer, stand, and suggest we head out.

· · ·

THE LONG-HAIRED BLOND guy on staff, Luke, was singing and playing guitar beside an unlit pyre in a grassy field in the center of the campground. He was the one I'd seen chatting with the owner at the Cubby Hole and talking to Austin at the bar this afternoon. "Sunshine Kurt Cobain," Eric called him.

The music was a little on the country side for my tastes, but Luke had a nice voice, and he played recognizable covers, crowd pleasers that could be ironic or earnest—or, intelligently, both. I overheard Eric telling Alex he thought Luke was *the real deal.*

After the set, people milled around and chatted as a tentative drum circle took over and the bonfire was officially lit.

Austin finally appeared with Luke and eagerly introduced him to Eric, Alex, and Noah. Austin was hoarse from cheering; he was clearly Luke's biggest fan.

While the guys chatted about gigs and rigs and a flurry of other band-dude terms that went over my head, Austin came to stand near me. He tossed out an apology for not finding us earlier, and when I didn't respond he hip-checked me.

He was probably attempting to bro-zone me with casual playfulness that I was expected to go along with. No doubt this was how he usually moved on from his hookups so he could remain friends with everyone.

His grin fell when I shot him a nasty scowl.

But instead of backing off, he proceeded to lean against me like a Great Dane. Like he intended to wear me down with puppy energy.

He was still wearing my shoes.

"So what'd'ya think of Luke?"

"He's definitely talented."

"I found him busking on the street in Edgewood a few weeks ago and brought him here."

"Did you now?"

"Sure did." Austin obviously took pride in discovering Luke, but I was reluctant to give him much attention after he'd finally officially blown me off with one of his trademark no's that sounded like a maybe. He either didn't pick up on my coolness, or he chose to ignore it. "What kind of music are you into?"

He wasn't going anywhere—I didn't entirely want him to —so with a defeated sigh, I chose to engage. "Alternative. Nineties Grunge. Smashing Pumpkins, Nirvana. That kinda shit."

Austin chuckled. "For real?"

I shrugged. "Alice in Chains. Tool. Nine Inch Nails."

He shook his head. "I totally imagined you listening to Tori Amos and writing angsty poetry about boys in your diary."

"My journals are filled with mostly angsty prose. But I do like Tori."

"I knew it," he said smugly.

"I like a lot of women artists. Alanis. Fiona Apple—" The smirk on his face grew. "Hey. Don't make me school you about how edgy Tori Amos can be."

"That's what my mom says!" Austin's eyes sparkled. "She's a big Tori fan too."

I gave him some hard side-eye. "If that was intended to be an insult, it only made your mom sound cool." I wandered away from the crowd toward the dark creek, and he followed.

"My mama is cool. But I know you're not *that* old, so where'd all the grunge come from?"

I resisted asking his mom's age. "An older neighbor kid growing up. He was in college when I was, like, twelve."

Austin poked my shoulder. "Ah-ha! That explains a lot."

"I actually do prefer harder music, though. I probably have a lot of unexpressed rage or something."

"I can get down with some harder stuff if it's a little funky too."

"Red Hot Chili Peppers?"

Austin bounced on his toes. "I fucking love them."

"Do you?"

"Yeah, I used to listen to them all the time." He paused for a beat before adding, "With my dad."

"Okay." I turned to walk away as if I were well and truly offended. "You can fuck off now."

Austin laughed and grabbed my arm to stop me. "No, seriously. My dad and I used to rock out in the car together. Chili Peppers. No Doubt. Green Day. But then I went through my teen rebellion phase and started listening to country."

"You rebelled by listening to country music?"

"Yeah. I blasted that shit. My parents didn't know what the fuck was happening. I put up a poster of Keith Urban and my dad was like, 'I don't even know who you are.'" Austin giggled. "But I didn't do it just to piss them off. It speaks to me. I'm an emotional person. I'm rarely angry, though. I'm either ready for some tailgating, or I'm wallowing in heartache. So country's perfect for me." He fixed me with a serious look. "I'd think as a writer you'd at least appreciate the storytelling aspect."

I made a loud, juvenile gagging noise.

"Okay. Because of that outburst, I'm gonna have to make you a country playlist." Austin shrugged like it was out of his hands. "That's all there is to it."

"That really won't be necessary."

"I must."

"Please don't."

"Let me, Prof. I can open you up to parts of yourself you've never accessed before. Let me in."

He was being intentionally cheesy, but language like that with a smile like his... It was a dangerous combination. Not to mention the last time a guy had made me a playlist, it had been a mix tape, and it was the most romantic thing that had ever happened to me.

I wasn't about to share that with Austin. I shook my head at him and pretended I was going back to the bonfire.

Austin jumped in front of me and crossed his arms. "What's your current go-to karaoke number?"

"Um, zero, as in never going to happen."

"Prof!" He put his hands on his hips. "Everybody needs at least one karaoke classic they can whip out when the situation calls for it."

"Like, for what? A karaoke emergency?"

Austin nodded. "Absolutely. You need to be prepared."

"Okay." I pinched the bridge of my nose as if this conversation was giving me a headache. "I know you're dying to tell me what your *number* is, so just get it over with."

He rubbed his hands together. "I've been rehearsing 'Strawberry Wine' by the incomparable Deanna Carter."

I knew the song, one of those ubiquitous hits you didn't have to listen to country music *by choice* to recognize. I'd heard it in the background of television shows or while pumping gas at the convenience store. I prayed it wouldn't get stuck in my head now.

Austin must have thought I didn't know the song by only its title—or maybe he didn't care—and instead of mumble-singing it or shyly humming a few bars like most people would, he launched into a full-throated, tone-deaf wail of the chorus.

It wasn't *country music* terrible or *can't carry a tune in a bucket* bad, this was *hounds baying at a passing siren* horrible.

God-awful.

I couldn't breathe because I was laughing too hard. When I was finally able to compose myself, I gasped. "That was truly one of the worst things I've ever heard in my life."

Austin's mouth dropped open, and he clutched his chest as if he'd been stabbed in the heart. "How can you say that? My voice brings joy to others. Look how happy it's making you right now." He sounded so sincere. If he was acting, his talents were truly being wasted.

Against my will, I burst into another fit of laughter. I sounded like a hyena, but I couldn't control it. Once I'd wiped the tears from my eyes, I saw that he was struggling to suppress a grin.

And I forgave him for not *swinging by* earlier.

"Another insult." Austin shook his head at me. "Damn, Prof. You're really coming for me today."

"What? When did I insult you?"

"You totally bailed on my class." The look on his face was serious. I didn't know him well enough to be sure his feelings weren't truly hurt, but based on my experience, he had to be teasing me.

I held my hand up between us. "You don't want to get into it with me about being a no-show, *sir*. And I didn't come to your class because I didn't want to make a fool of myself in front of you again."

Austin pulled a face. "Again? When did you make a fool of yourself in front of me ever?"

"Uh, last night."

"Oh, okay. Gotcha." Austin nodded thoughtfully. "I guess my class was kinda like last night"—he paused—"not everybody came."

My jaw dropped. He did not just call me out after feeding me that line about how *everybody doesn't have to get off every time.*

"I'm fucking with you, Prof. I meant what I said last night. But I do love that pissed-off look on your face." He toed at a rock in the grass and shifted tone. "Class turnout could have been better." And just like that, it was as if we'd been having a straightforward conversation all along.

"Oh?"

"Five people."

"Oh." *Only five? Shit.* I grimaced.

Austin gestured toward the camp at large. "Yeah, there's like five *hundred* people here this weekend. One percent's not gonna cut it."

"Do you have a quota for your job, or..."

"No. I'm not officially the campground trainer or anything like that. Yet. I'm a glorified pool boy for the summer. I know that. But I was kinda hoping the workout would be really popular so I could show Sawyer and Jim they do need to have a trainer on staff, and it might, you know, lead to something permanent."

"I see." I didn't know much about the fitness industry, and I didn't want to discount his ambition. I wanted to say something encouraging. "But it was the first one, right? Maybe you need to give it a little more time to catch on."

Austin scratched the back of his neck. "I don't really have a lot of time, but... You're probably right. Now that I think about it, I could've gone bigger with my flyer. Where did you see it?"

"On the door of the gym, where you showed it to me." I

scrambled to think of where else I might have seen the damn thing. "I think I spotted one on a bulletin board at check-in, although I didn't know what it was at the time."

He raised a finger. "Exactly! Because that bulletin board is ten feet from the counter. I told Jim nobody was gonna see it unless they specifically walked over there. It needs to be bigger. Like, life-size. I'm gonna put one on the motherfucking bathhouse wall right when you come out of the steam room as you're walking into the showers. How expensive do you think it'd be to have one of those foam-core cut-outs made?"

"Um..." I didn't know if I was meant to endorse this or fully enable it. Hopefully it had been a rhetorical question.

Austin pointed at my facial expression and grinned. "I'm fucking with you again. Listen, I know these guys are on vacation. They came here to drink and fuck. I get it. As for the staff, I mean, some of them would work out with me during the week or between holidays, but they're the ones who're already into it anyway. It's not like that's going to turn into a *career*."

I imagined if he taught in the right location, he'd have people lined up around the block just to *watch* him teach. "I'm sure you've already considered this, but what about being a trainer at one of the gyms in town?"

"Yeah. That's definitely a possibility. I've already been putting myself out there as a substitute. You kinda have to sub for a while to get your foot in the door."

"Of course."

Austin shoved his hands deep into his pockets. "Next time I pick up a class in town"—his voice was soft, almost shy for him—"you promise you'll come?"

I gaped. After all the banter and teasing with bits of confession tossed out like breadcrumbs, the direct question surprised me. I was also taken off guard by how quickly I wanted to say yes to him without processing what he'd asked.

Nobody had said the sparring was over, though, and I hadn't entirely surrendered to his charms. Yet. I wanted him to know that. "I might swing by," I said.

Austin drew in a sharp breath, and his mouth opened in an *O* of surprise. "Burn."

I grinned, pleased with myself.

"Speaking of which." Austin inclined his head. "Savage magic. Incoming."

I didn't know what he was talking about.

He pointed with his chin at an approaching figure, a silhouette against the fire. "Jim Savage's bonfire spell. Get into it."

"Hey, boys," Jim called out. "Y'all enjoying yourselves?" We murmured that we were, and he put his hand on my shoulder. "Paul, honey, let me ask you something."

"Sure."

"Do you consider yourself a spiritual person?" Jim didn't wait for me to answer; he barreled on as if I'd said yes. "We have a ritual we like to do around here on Saturdays. It's all about letting go of negative energy. Of course, Austin has heard all this before, but I'm not sure I trust him to explain it to you right."

Austin huffed.

"Honey, you gloss right over the heavy shit," Jim said to him. "Sometimes you've got to ponder more. You know what I mean, Paul." It wasn't a question. He'd simply declared that I understood and agreed with him.

I wished I'd had longer to *ponder* whether or not Jim was employing this charismatic style of speaking intentionally or if he was truly intuitive. But he continued. "Now what you wanna do is think about something you need to release. Some kind of stress, something you've been worrying about, something that's been holding you back." Jim leaned into my personal space. "A story that no longer serves you."

I raised my eyebrows. I was a little dubious to be honest, but Jim took my expression as encouraging.

"People tell us things about ourselves. They put labels on us. Sometimes they don't even realize they're doing it. But these projections are hurtful. They diminish our view of ourselves. We hear them, we take them in, we forget where they originally even came from, and we continue to tell ourselves these stories as if they're true, when a lot of them simply are not. Are you with me?"

I nodded. Was this man a therapist or some kind of psychic?

"So we're gonna call those stories out. Those labels. We're gonna name them, throw them in the fire, and send them back where they came from." Jim handed both Austin and me scraps of paper along with tiny pencils. "Namaste." He bowed. "My spirit sees your spirt." He walked away.

I didn't know what else to do, so I simply returned the bow and said, "Thank you."

I expected Austin to make a joke or say something to try to break the profound hush Jim had left in his wake, but he was already scribbling away, frowning in concentration. When he finished, he blew out a breath and started folding and refolding the paper into an impossibly tiny square.

"What did you write?" I asked.

"I can't tell you that!" He twisted his body away from me, clutching the paper in a fist against his chest like I'd asked to copy the answers off his pop quiz. "It's private."

"Understood." I held my hands up in a gesture of surrender. "Sorry."

"Psych." His shit-eating grin reappeared. "Nah, I usually just pick whatever thing I've been worrying about this week, like, needing to get a real job in the fall or feeling butt-hurt about nobody showing up for my class." Austin twisted his lips. "I try not to spend too much time thinking about what I *don't* want, though. I try to focus on what I *do* want. That's my only beef with this ritual. Otherwise I think it's pretty cool."

"I do too." I did.

It wasn't even that the stories *no longer* served me. They never had.

At the end of our relationship, Charles had thrown them at me like Molotov cocktails. *You can't write. And you can't even fuck.* Bombs of psychic poison. Intentionally weaponized insecurities. He'd known exactly what I'd been most afraid of.

The challenge for me in this moment was fitting all those words on a piece of paper the size of a fortune cookie message with a bowling alley pencil stub.

This was a naming spell. And the name of the thing that no longer served me was a story about...

Being blocked.

I couldn't write. I couldn't fuck.

I was... *impotent.* That was the word.

I wrote it twice, once on each side of the paper, once for each experience.

I couldn't remember if I'd said those words to myself before Charles had, but I believed them because it was easy to.

But even if they'd been true, I didn't want them to be anymore.

Austin was right. I wanted more than an absence of weakness, more than to simply *endure the world.* I wanted to be a great writer. I wanted to be a killer lover. I wanted to feel prolific and horny, able and empowered.

We joined the other men who ringed the bonfire and tossed our papers into the flames. We leaned back, following the sparks into the night sky. I hoped our silent wishes on the stars had greater power than the bullshit we told ourselves.

Together, Austin and I drifted away from the fire again. Without discussing it, we'd started walking toward the pool complex. It was close to the route we'd taken last night.

"Can I ask you something very blunt?" I said.

"Yeah. Sure."

"I want you to tell me the truth."

"Of course."

"Did you think the sex last night was... bad?"

"Are you kidding me?" Austin glanced over with an incredulous look on his face. "Fuck no. It was hot as hell. You're way too in your head about all that." I appreciated he hadn't given *all that* a name. "I bet that's more than half your problem."

I wanted to believe him. "My, uh... inability to perform has been a problem for others in the past."

Austin rolled his eyes. "There's *so* much more to chemistry than that."

"Like what?"

Austin laughed and looked at the ground. "You need a lot of reassurance," he muttered.

"It's a valid question. Why would a guy like you be into someone like me?"

"A guy like me? You mean, a hot dancer with a killer voice?"

I stopped walking. "Seriously. Come on. Look at you."

"Look at *you*," he said, studying me with a soft smile.

"With your ice-blue eyes and your thick beard with the reddish-gold in it. Your beefy chest and strong shoulders." In a lower voice, he said, "You're very handsome."

"I'm never going to have six-pack abs." Apparently, I was now blurting out random insecurities.

Austin scowled. "Are you hung up on body image shit? Oh my God"—his eyes went round—"do you think I am? I don't have a six-pack, and I'm hot as fuck. I love food. Plus, guys with six-packs aren't all that great to cuddle. It's like sleeping with a sack of clay. I like a man with a little belly. Muscles are hot, sure, but they're nicer with a little layer of softness over them. Like yours." He stepped closer and put his arms around my waist. "I'm a snuggle bear. Sex is easy to get. That cuddling, though..." He made a humming noise and pressed his lips to mine.

I gave in to the kiss, tasting sweet beer on his tongue, grinding against him until I had to come up for air. "I'm going to be blunt again. The ED medication worked really well. I mean, really, *really* well, as you can probably feel. And I would very much like to go back to my tent and..."

At the exact same moment I said, "Have a do-over," Austin said, "Do butt stuff."

"What?"

"Butt stuff."

"I heard you. I just can't believe you *called* it that."

Austin grinned. "Why? Do you have a problem with butt stuff?"

"I do not. I am, however, questioning how I feel about the *term*."

"I like calling it butt stuff."

"You do seem to be enjoying it."

"I always enjoy butt stuff."

"Oh my God! Shut up," I said through gritted teeth. "What the fuck is wrong with you?"

He laughed. "I'm just trying to make you smile."

"Well, you're being awfully aggravating." My tone was surly, but I couldn't help but reward him with the smile he wanted. I was going to get another chance.

As if he were humblebragging, Austin said, "Aggravation is my love language."

13

THE SHORTEST ROUTE TO MY TENT WENT THROUGH THE pool complex. The darkness at the edges of the field near the bonfire had given us some relative privacy, but a crowd was already gathering for another nighttime pool party.

I braced myself for a repeated onslaught of the socializing we'd experienced last night.

Austin grabbed my arm and pulled me close. The buzz of his low voice against my ear made me shiver. "Don't make eye contact with anybody. Keep your head down next to mine like this, like we're having a serious private conversation, and walk really fast."

I followed his lead. We made it around the pool without anyone calling out to us. Once we were past the cabana bar, Austin took off in a skipping run up the trail.

When I caught up with him, he was waiting at my campsite, giggling like we'd pulled off some great prank.

"Why are you running?"

"I didn't want to get sucked into talking to everybody."

"Isn't that part of your duties as Best Cub?"

His mouth dropped open. "Who the fuck told you I was Best Cub?"

"Um, like, at least twenty different people."

"Twenty people, my ass. You don't even know twenty people here." Austin reached for my hips. "Eric?"

"Eric might've been one of them." I kissed him, and he immediately opened his mouth, pushing his tongue against mine. He ran his hands under my shirt, and they were warm against my back.

A couple of guys stomped by on the trail, and we briefly pulled apart.

Austin's eyes were sparks in the dark. "Let's get in the tent," he whispered.

As I unzipped the door flap, I said, "It'll be easier if we strip out here while we're standing upright."

He nodded enthusiastically, and we raced to undress.

I took his clothes, wadded them up with mine, and tossed the whole bundle into a corner of the tent.

Austin chuckled. "Look at you being all *fuck the housekeeping.*"

I shrugged and crawled in first. Before following me, he arranged our shoes—my shoes—side by side on the mat outside.

I lay back on the cool fabric of the sleeping bag I was using as a duvet, wondering at the wisdom of getting naked all at once, but Austin covered my body with his warm bulk and kissed me again. Deeper, slower, sloppier.

I'd never been with a man I desired this much. Even when I'd first gotten together with Charles, when I was nineteen and I'd been fantasizing about him for weeks, the urgency had been... *polite* compared to this.

Austin spread his knees and slid his thick thighs to either side of my torso, cradling my hips and trunk as he rocked his cock against my belly, holding me in place as he ground his meaty ass against my gloriously hard dick.

He broke the kiss. "Fuck me," he said. "Stick that dick in me and fuck the hell out of me as hard and fast as you can."

His directness excited me, and his demanding tone stirred something powerful in me. Fucking a man had once been inherently aggressive. Nothing sadistic or dominating but a spark of power. For so long, I'd felt broken and apologetic. I'd entirely given up for years, and then, trying to find my way back, it had all been worrying and praying.

And whether it was the pill, the bonfire spell, Austin himself—or some combination of all of it—I felt powerful again.

I bucked against him, the move surprising him enough that he lost his balance, and I was able to throw him off me. I rolled him onto his back and shoved his thighs apart with my knees.

I repositioned myself over him, my legs between his, my lips hovering inches above his.

I was so hard I ached. "I don't mind if you want to beg for it. But I don't need you to tell me how to fuck you." I smiled to soften the words. "I'll fuck you how I want to."

He moaned.

I released more of my weight onto him, letting my belly fully relax against his. My cock pressed deeper into the furry crease beneath his balls.

He wrapped his arms around me and held our chests together.

I covered his mouth with mine, stifling both our groans, and he threw his legs around me, crossing his ankles, crushing me, trapping me, and his hands slid down to grab my ass as if he could pull me into him.

The head of my dick leaked against his hole, the tip sliding, catching, and almost slipping inside.

There was nowhere left for me to go but inside him. But first... "Let me go for a minute," I whispered.

He released me, and I reached for the lantern. I turned it on and brought it with me as I scooted down to the end of the mattress. I wanted to see the most secret parts of him. I set my feet against the floor of the tent, put my hands beneath his knees, and shoving with all my strength, I rolled him nearly in half. I ran my nose along his exposed taint. His scent was clean, still faintly shower damp. Repeated exposure to his body wash was quickly turning the citrus fragrance into an aphrodisiac, and his faint, natural musk was as potent as any drug.

I flattened my tongue against his hole and dragged it up to his sac. He cursed incoherently, grabbed his knees, and held himself open for me. With my hands free, I was able to hold his nuts out of the way. I pointed my tongue and drove it into him as deep as I could. I pulled back and spat on his hole, catching the moisture with my thumb, circling the ring of muscle, then pressing it into him.

The taste of him... Fuck. I could've stayed there forever, licking his hole, lubing him with my spit, and listening to the sounds he made.

I alternated tongue-fucking him and pulling him open with my thumbs until he was wet and ready, panting and begging for me.

I knelt on one knee and teased him with the tip of my cock. I'd wanted the light so I could watch the head of my dick disappear into him. I kept pulling out and putting it back in again, just the tip. He whimpered when I retreated, a bereft sound, and his hole stayed slack and open for me, the ring of muscle quivering.

"Damn," he gasped. "We gotta be making one hell of a shadow puppet, Prof."

I paused, listening to the footsteps and voices passing on the trail, mere feet from where we were. Were they watching us?

Don't think about it.

I shoved in again, deeper this time.

He sucked in a breath and clenched.

"Sorry." I froze. "Couldn't help myself." I waited, giving him time to adjust. I tried to revel in the sensation of his tight heat—being inside this gorgeous man was a big fucking deal—but waiting made me nervous. How long could I sustain this?

He finally nodded for me to continue. I pulled out halfway, but when I pushed into him again, the glide was more of a wobble. I was losing it and only barely managed to get back inside him.

I stayed there, not moving.

"Can you get yourself off?" I whispered.

He looked at me, realization dawning in his eyes.

"I want you to get off with me inside you," I said.

I held myself in place, silently willing him to hurry.

His muscles contracted as he jerked himself, threatening to expel me, and I prayed I could last long enough to at least give him this pleasure.

With a grunt, he came across his belly, and I slipped out.

I lay beside him as he caught his breath.

He glanced down at my softening cock and reached for me. "Do you wanna..."

I couldn't. Powerless to do anything else, I kissed him. "Not everybody has to get off every time, right?"

He smiled and stroked my cheek.

I would cling to the memory of him looking at me this way.

He sat up suddenly, rubbed his arms, and looked around for his clothes. "Brr. It's cold."

Oh fuck. No. Don't go. It was too soon, but how could I keep him?

"I could make us a fire," I said hopefully. "I brought some starter logs."

He grinned and kissed me. "Fire it up!"

I scooted my bag chairs closer to the fire pit, arranging them so they were closer together too.

Austin sat, huddled in another of my sweatshirts, watching me.

"Can I get you something to drink?" I pointed at the cooler, and rattled off a variety of beers, waters, and sports drinks.

"No juice boxes?"

"Shut up."

"You're such a total dad."

"Don't call me that."

"Daddy!" Austin cried in a high-pitched approximation of a twink in a porn.

"Oh my God! That's horrifying. Never do that again."

My mortification sent him into a fit of giggles. "Prof." He pointed at me and held his belly as he doubled over in silent wheezing laughs. "Your face."

"All right. Let's get this conversation out of the way." I knew the shift to my deep lecturing voice would play right into his schtick—or whatever it was. I honestly couldn't tell if he was kidding or not, but it couldn't be avoided any longer. "How old are you exactly?"

"I'm twenty-six." He sat up straight and smiled like a proud four-year-old.

I nodded. "Right. Okay." I remained standing, pacing back and forth in front of him. "I'm forty-two. I was sixteen when you were born. That's not a dad. That's an uncle at best."

Austin held up a finger in a point of order. "Sixteen's old enough to knock somebody up."

"You do realize that the *somebody* in that scenario would be your own mother, right?"

Austin grimaced. "Yeah. Okay. That sounds kinda gross."

I stopped pacing and faced him. "I'm afraid to ask, but how old *are* your parents?"

"My mom was my age when she had me, so she's fifty-two. My dad's a little older than her. He's fifty-nine, about to turn sixty."

I sighed, more relieved than I wanted him to know. "So he's old enough to be *my* dad too. That makes me feel a little bit better."

"It's all relative." Austin spread his hands in a gesture that said *everything's cool, bro*. "It doesn't matter."

"That's always the younger guy's line." I knew the mindset well. Charles had been eight years older than me when we'd gotten together, which was only half the age difference between Austin and me.

Austin reached for my hands. "What's my next line, then? Do I beg you to take me back to bed and make me your boy?"

I cursed under my breath. "Do you really want a daddy? Is that actually a thing guys your age are looking for?"

"Oh, I'm sure there's some who are. Some of the guys around here talk shit about hooking up with guests in the

Soggy Bottom—that's what we call this part of the campground—"

"Wait." I didn't know where he was going with this. "Have I unknowingly signaled something about my sexual preferences by camping here, or…"

"Nah, nah. It's trash talk. Locker-room banter about getting with the men who have money. The ones who rent the good cabins or the ones with nice RVs on Trailer Park Avenue."

I gestured to my site. "Seems like this would be considered the *real man's* camping though, no?"

"You're *way* butcher than any English professor I ever had," he said, swinging my hand. "But for the record, I'm not one of those guys. I'll figure out my own career, my finances, all that shit. I want to do something cool, and I want to be somebody in the world. I just want someone who wants me for me."

I looked away and cleared my throat. "You don't really give me *kept boy* vibes. And, besides, I heard that a man has to be really hot to warrant a tent fuck around here."

"It's true," he nodded gravely. "He has to be really worth it."

My back was to the fire so he couldn't see me blush. "Then I'm flattered."

"You should take me back to the tent and let me flatter you some more."

14

I SPOONED AUSTIN, BRUSHING MY FACIAL HAIR AGAINST THE back of his neck as he clutched our hands together beneath his chin.

"You can't go home tomorrow," he whined. "You have to stay for the fireworks."

Since so many people would be checking out on Monday, they'd do the fireworks on Sunday night. I'd paid through Saturday night—tonight—even though I hadn't intended to still be here.

I hadn't expected to meet him.

"I'll go pay Jim for an extra night," I breathed in his ear. "First thing tomorrow."

We drifted in and out of sleep, making out and humping, frotting, only half-conscious. I questioned how many more erections I could sustain. Austin said we should take it as a challenge and find out how far one pill could take us. We didn't try to fuck again, though. It wasn't a priority. Sometime before dawn, he woke me with a blow job and made me come so hard it almost hurt.

. . .

SUNDAY BREAKFAST FEATURED a parade of goodbyes. More than half the guests seemed to be leaving. A lot of people had long drives or wanted a day at home to decompress before going back to work.

I still planned to leave Monday morning. Austin said the staff would go into intense recovery mode around noon that day. I'd have to say goodbye sometime, and I didn't want to be in his way.

Ben and Eric headed out after Eric secured a promise from me to call and *tell him everything* when I got back to town. Ben said he'd come by my place on Wednesday to collect his tools.

If I hadn't stayed to be with Austin, it would have been depressing to be left behind after the party was over. With the majority of the crowd gone, the collective mood of the campground shifted. The vibe at the pool area mellowed. The satellite radio station was switched to soft classic rock. The Bloody Marys were still there, but needing to rehydrate, I turned them down. I vowed to stick to beer and water for the rest of the day.

Business at the cabana bar was thankfully sparse, which made it easier for Austin to steal moments with me. I camped out on a stool in the shade and kept him company all day as he worked. We mostly talked about inconsequential things—food and music and TV shows we loved—and he regaled me with the whispered backstories of dozens of people. His eyes lit up when he gossiped—not because he was mean-spirited but because he delighted in the colorful diversity and outrageousness of these men. He was proud to be part of this community.

In a lot of ways, it felt like I'd known Austin for weeks or possibly even longer. I honestly couldn't remember what the world had felt like before I knew he was in it. I had to keep reminding myself it hadn't yet been three days.

I tried to ignore the melancholy sense of a clock ticking.

I'd stayed so I'd have all these extra hours with him, but they were slipping by at a cruel pace. Time wasn't only distorted here; it was fickle. It could either speed up or slow down, and either way you couldn't control it. Bear Mountain Lodge wasn't so much a gay heaven as it was a kind of purgatory.

SUNDAY EVENING, as I ate dinner with my tent neighbors Grant and Rob, Austin hovered over me, only slipping away long enough to clear a plate or refill a glass, then come back. Jim gave him an admonishing look, but there was no conviction in it. Sawyer stared at us curiously, but he looked away when I caught him.

We were in a bubble, and it seemed like everyone around us could sense it, and nobody had the heart or even the ability to break our spell.

All the same people who had openly flirted with Austin now slipped silently by us like we didn't exist. Some spared us soft, knowing smirks, but they made room for us.

They parted around us.

After dinner, Austin and I showered together in Bathhouse Two. We kissed under the spray, and I didn't care who watched us.

Sunday night, we made out on a blanket in the bonfire field while fireworks went off directly overhead. Austin had been right. I couldn't have missed it. I couldn't have imagined this weekend without that moment.

We retired to my tent before eleven, and we stayed awake most of the night, talking, kissing, messing around, and talking some more, trying to squeeze every minute out of our last hours together.

I wondered aloud if we were only making our impending goodbye more torturous, but Austin shushed me and shook his head like I'd broken the gravest taboo.

For all the counting down I'd been doing in the back of my mind, the morning took me by surprise. In the thin, growing light, a sense of panic gripped my heart.

I hid it from Austin, careful not to infect him with it.

He had to leave to work breakfast. He kept stealing another kiss, which led to another, then another, all of them chaste and sweet. He delayed until he was definitely going to be at least fifteen minutes late, but he said it would be worth it, even if he got yelled at.

I watched him jog up the path in my red shoes. He looked back, waved, and almost tripped.

I decided to get a jump on packing up my site. I wasn't looking forward to it, but a daunting task would give me something to focus on other than how unprepared I was to say goodbye.

Grant and Rob invited me to walk up to the lodge with them. It was nice how quickly familiar rituals had emerged around meals, how comfortable I felt with these guys who'd been strangers only a few days ago. It wasn't only Austin I'd be leaving today. I would miss the sense of community and the company of other gay men.

Sure, I had Ben and Eric at home for the two or three times a year I could be persuaded to get a beer at a bar. I had no idea what things would be like now that they were together. They'd probably disappear into their own private world as couples did.

As for the university community, the English department was dominated by women—which was fantastic; I loved working with them—but I was only close to a few of them. They were undoubtedly allies, and they would've already fixed me up with any number of men if they could've convinced me to let them, but I didn't exactly talk to them about *butt stuff*.

And I hadn't seen them since I'd taken my sabbatical.

To *finally* write my next book, I'd taken personal time off for the spring and summer semesters, almost half of which I'd already squandered, and I'd be returning to my eerily quiet home office and the terror of the blank page on my laptop.

I understood why Austin might have wanted to take a job here and stay forever.

When Grant and Rob were ready to head out, I found Austin bussing dishes and stopped him long enough to tell him I was going to finish packing.

"Okay." He smiled, but his eyes were sad. "I'll come find you."

This time, I knew it was a promise.

BACK AT MY SITE, I let the air out of the mattress, took down the tarps, and started the painstaking process of folding and rolling lots of large things into the impossibly small packages they'd come in.

Alex, Noah, and Lance stopped by on their way back from having missed breakfast again. They'd managed to snag the last dregs of coffee and planned to check out a nearby diner on their way back to Edgewood.

"I was gonna say we should hook up back in town," Lance said, "but it's pretty obvious you and your muscle cub are..." He seemed reluctant to label it. I was caught between wishing he could and feeling relieved he didn't. "Anyway,

I'm not enough of a bastard to get in the way of that. See ya around."

I had everything arranged on the ground in the order in which I wanted it put in the truck when Austin showed up with a cold Gatorade. The drink was thoughtful in a surprisingly complex way. Not having the foresight, I'd already dumped the ice out of my cooler, and all my beverages were lukewarm.

Even though I was sweaty, Austin kissed me. "Looks like you got most of it done."

"I just have to cart it all to the truck."

"I'll help you." Austin hooked a thumb over his shoulder. "Lemme run over and turn the music on and make sure there's nobody waiting at the bar wanting something."

"I understand you're working—"

"We'll be walking back and forth right through the pool complex. It's okay." He pulled me in for another kiss. Which one would finally be the last? "I'll be right back."

He was gone longer than I thought he'd be. I was afraid he'd gotten sidetracked or pulled into something, and he wasn't coming back. Leaving without getting to see him would definitely be worse than having to say goodbye.

I grabbed a single item and set off down the path, hoping I'd run into him at the bar. I'd take my time until it happened.

Austin finally caught up with me in the parking lot, already apologizing. Guests kept stopping him.

With his help, carrying my stuff to the truck took fewer trips than when I'd arrived.

That shouldn't have been such a surprise, but it made it feel like I was leaving too fast.

I exchanged contact information with Grant and Rob.

They told me to keep in touch on social media and to let them know next time I planned a trip.

Austin stood by at a polite distance while I hugged them goodbye. It was bittersweet.

I cast one last look at the site, ostensibly to confirm I wasn't leaving anything behind but really to commit as much of it to memory as possible.

"You got lucky, you know," Austin said.

Boy, did I ever. "What do you mean?"

"With the cursed campsite."

"Oh, yeah. You never told me why it was cursed."

"I thought I did."

"You didn't."

"All the things that make this spot so ideal—the shade, the carpet of moss, the soft soil, the lack of rocks... This is the floodplain for the creek. And *this* particular spot—you see how the trail runs down through here? That path's not worn by foot traffic. It's actually carved out by water runoff. When it rains heavily, even before the creek floods, the path becomes a parallel stream. And your campsite is right where the trail and the creek both bend. The water doesn't bend, though, it heads straight for the creek, so..."

"The entire holler floods down through this campsite."

"Bingo."

"Why would you let me risk that?"

"What's the worst thing that could happen? I mean, don't get me wrong, packing up a wet campsite can suck—"

"You think?"

"There was this one time last year when it fucking *poured* right on the day everybody was trying to pack up and get out of here. Your only option when that happens is to pack *under* your tarp and take it down last. The night before, everybody heard the forecast but not every site has the right tree cover for hanging a tarp. The tents were packed pretty close together of course, so once it really started coming down, somebody got the idea to just start connecting all the tarps, and it caught on. Everybody was pitching in, and it became this big group engineering project. It was cool. It was weirdly kind of a blast. The sense of being in it together, not only man against nature but a team of guys all on the same side making it happen. I don't know if it would have gone down the same way on the first day. You like to think there's a sense of community the minute you set foot on the property, but after a whole weekend of partying together, it was a moment of, like… spontaneous democracy. Socialism, maybe? I can tell by the look on your face I'm not using the right terms. But you know what I'm saying, right? Brotherhood."

I nodded. I did. Or I had a pretty good idea. Now.

"Anyway, we ended up with this one huge tarp, like a patchwork ceiling over the entire camping area. And everybody was crammed in under it, packing. Some people fled as soon as they could, but they left their tarps behind for the cause. And a lot of guys stayed working until everybody who needed to got out with their shit as dry as possible."

"That's very cool."

"*But* the dude who was in this spot? Fuck. Yeah. His shit was trashed."

"You're telling me this *now*?"

"I knew you'd be okay. There wasn't anything in the forecast. When you get lucky, it's a sweet spot. You got lucky, Prof."

I'd never felt luckier.

. . .

As we reached the pool complex on my last trip to the truck, Austin suddenly stopped walking. "Shit. We don't even have each other's phone numbers."

"I wasn't gonna leave here without exchanging details."

"Fuck. I don't even have my phone on me. I always leave it in the bunkhouse."

"You can just give me your number. I promise I'll text."

"Hold on." Austin ducked behind the cabana bar and returned with a permanent marker.

"Do you have a piece of paper or—"

"No." He held out his arm. "Write it on me."

"Seriously?"

"Yeah. I don't wanna keep up with a scrap of paper. I'm afraid I'd lose it." He rotated the pale skin of his forearm toward the sun. "Brand me, Prof."

I walked him into the shade of the bar so we could lay his arm on a stable surface. My hands trembled as I tried to figure out which direction to write and how big to print the numbers. I could read it from this angle, but could he? This was permanent ink. There was pressure to make it neat and legible. And as I was juggling all those thoughts, I had a flash of forgetting my number or writing it down wrong.

God, I was a mess.

He watched me, smiling as if he could hear my thoughts.

When I finished, he read my number back to me, then asked for my phone. Watching him create a new contact with his name and number, I felt a mixture of hope and relief. I wouldn't be fully relieved until I'd heard from him, but for now, it was enough to believe it wasn't over.

"Oh! Selfie." Austin grabbed me and pulled me against him before I could think too much about it and snapped our picture together. I wished I'd had more time to prepare, to smile more, maybe even take a few alternates and keep the best one. But he handed the phone back to me.

"Text me whenever you can," I said.

"I'll hike out to the road this evening where I can get a good signal." Austin took my hand and swung it between us as he walked me to my truck.

I tossed my backpack into the passenger seat and stood with the door open.

Austin squinted. "This part sucks." The sun was in his eyes, so I couldn't tell by his expression if he was frowning or wincing in pain.

How many times had he lived through a similar scene? It was entirely novel to me, but surely he'd had to say goodbye to other men he'd met and felt a connection with.

I didn't know what to say. I had no words for this. "I didn't expect much coming here. But it was better than I could've imagined... *You* were. You are."

Austin nodded. His throat worked, but he didn't say anything. Maybe he couldn't.

I pressed my forehead to his. "Thank you."

He stared at the ground, probably oblivious he was still wearing my shoes.

I didn't say a word about it. I didn't want him to take them off.

Austin took a deep breath. "Okay, I gotta dash." He spared me a quick glance, and I saw the same panic I'd been feeling all morning reflected in his eyes—fear, that it felt wrong to leave, that something might happen and we'd never see each other again, that it was going to hurt. He kissed me hard. This was the last one. There was no good way to make it more special than the others. "Don't be mad, but I'm gonna walk away really fast, and I'm not gonna look back because I will totally fucking boo hoo, okay?"

"Okay."

I watched him in the rearview mirror until he was out of sight.

As the gate rolled closed behind me, I thought, *Yeah, this part sucks.*

15

I SAT IN MY TRUCK IN MY DRIVEWAY TRYING TO COMPOSE THE perfect text message to Austin.

With this much time and effort, I could've produced a fucking haiku. *That* had a formula. I had no prior experience with personal communication in this particular scenario. I had no template for this.

I'd rewritten the text a dozen times, stripping away anything I thought sounded pretentious, overwritten, too desperate, or too casual. I'd finally whittled it down to the polite, functional, and completely dry as fuck: *Home safe. Thanks again for an amazing weekend.*

A strong first sentence was important, but there was a chance Austin might never respond, and this thread would become yet another manuscript I'd started that never went anywhere.

I shook the thought away, cursing myself for being negative and for clinging to stories that no longer served me.

Attempting to give it some enthusiasm and optimism, I added a smile emoji after *Home safe*, changed the second period to an exclamation point, and attached the selfie he'd taken of us.

Was the pic too much?

Before I could back out or start another revision, I hit Send and shoved the phone into my pocket.

Arriving home usually felt more satisfying than this, but I was exhausted. Cumulative sleep deprivation, alcohol consumption, and sun exposure had caught up with me. I dreaded having to unload my gear, especially having spent most of my morning getting it all into the truck. I dragged my backpack with my toiletries and clothes off the front passenger seat and left the rest to deal with tomorrow.

I loved my house. It was a Craftsman built in 1929. I'd purchased it as a fixer-upper, locking myself into the professorship I'd accepted at Edgewood University.

I'd hoped there would be follow-up bestsellers to eventually secure my freedom, but in less than three months after publication, my second novel had all but disappeared. It languished on bargain tables in brick-and-mortar bookstores for months, and my publisher opted to release me from my contract.

Thanks for playing. We don't need a third book after all.

Besides my degrees and my novels, remodeling this house had been my single greatest accomplishment. It was definitely the bigger source of satisfaction.

Ben was known in Edgewood as something of a miracle worker when it came to carpentry in old houses. I'd hired him first to help me restore the main staircase. I hadn't wanted someone to do the work *for* me. I'd wanted to get my hands dirty. I'd been surprised when he said he was cool with my assisting, and we'd gotten along really well. The first few times he casually mentioned his sex life, I'd wondered if he might have been flirting with me. I'd later come to realize he'd been trying to let me know he was gay. He eventually introduced me to Eric, and for the first time, I'd had gay male friends near my own age. When Charles and I had been together, we'd socialized entirely with the university faculty he'd wanted to impress, which was mostly a lot of older, married, straight people.

Over the last several years, Ben and I had gone from one project in my house to the next, gradually restoring everything to historically accurate appearances with some well-hidden modern improvements. Last week, we'd completed our final project, the upstairs bathroom. The renovations were done.

With my sabbatical disappearing at an alarming clip, I'd joked that if I couldn't get a manuscript written by the end of summer, Ben would have to go into business with me flipping houses. I was seriously considering buying a rental property or a vacation home just so I'd have a new project.

Why couldn't I give up writing and focus on this other creative outlet? I loved it, and I could probably make more money at it. Unfortunately, writing was a *calling*. It sounded pretentious, but it felt like it was what I'd been put on this earth to do, and I couldn't ignore that.

Even if I were successful at another career, I'd still have a serious writing hobby.

I made myself a half-ass, dry turkey sandwich—a piece of bread folded around a slice of deli meat with no condiments—and ate it standing at the island in my perfectly staged kitchen. The hum of the refrigerator and the ticking of the vintage schoolroom clock seemed ominous.

I slipped my phone out of my pocket to check the thread I'd started with Austin.

Of course, there was no reply; it had been less than ten minutes.

He didn't have his phone on him, and he was working. Although business at the bar might be a little slower today because of the holiday, he'd be helping to set up and serve a poolside cookout for dinner.

It would probably be hours before he had a chance to check his messages.

I washed my sad lunch down with a few gulps of milk straight from the carton and headed upstairs. I looked forward to showering in my own bathroom without an audience or having to wear flip-flops.

While I waited for the water to get hot, I stripped in front of the vanity mirror. I tried to see myself the way the men from this weekend might have seen me. The way Austin might have seen me. Lance had complimented my body, and I had no doubt that Austin found me attractive too. I'd always liked older guys myself, especially when I was their age, but a dad bod was easier to appreciate on someone else.

Maybe it was that I looked different, that I'd changed from how I'd thought of myself for so long.

Right now, I mostly looked *red*. My shoulders and forehead were sunburned, my cheeks were flushed. The medication had surely worn off by this point, but my blood pressure was probably a little elevated from lack of sleep.

My lips looked like I'd been doing a lot of making out and sucking dick.

My dick was sore, nearly raw from overuse, but, at the thought of all that Austin and I had done to each other, it began to swell.

I spat on my fingertips and stroked myself off into the sink basin in record time. I couldn't believe I'd manage to come *again*. It hurt a little, and the size of the ejaculation was minuscule. I was well and truly spent. This was beyond record-breaking for me, even taking into account my freshman year of college. Those first few months away from home, I'd been insatiable. Until I'd met Charles.

I stood under the spray for ten minutes until I almost fell asleep on my feet. I should have toweled off and gone straight to bed, but I hoped I might hear from Austin.

I checked my phone again, not really expecting a reply. It was still early. They wouldn't even have served dinner yet. I put on some basketball shorts and a clean T-shirt, padded back downstairs to the living room, turned on the TV, and flung myself onto the sofa.

The last thing I remembered was the hypnotic murmur of talking heads on cable news.

I OPENED my eyes to a darkened room with window-shaped blocks of amber-colored streetlight on the walls.

I lunged for my phone.

It was quarter past midnight, and there were new text notifications.

I swung my feet to the floor and sat up straight, simultaneously overjoyed that Austin might have texted me back and shattered that I had missed it. I swiped open the screen and found messages from hours ago. One from my sister, Veronica, wanting to know if I'd made it home okay, and three from Eric that were only progressively growing strands of question marks.

Nothing from Austin.

Was *I'll message later* another form of *I'll swing by*?

I was disappointed, embarrassed, and annoyed that I'd hung my hopes on someone who was probably at a nighttime pool party or in a bathhouse full of naked men.

There might've only been a small crowd left, but they'd still number in the dozens at least.

I trudged upstairs and flopped onto my bed. My real bed. I burrowed into my down pillows hoping their cool familiarity could drown out the images of Austin with the *dozens* of men who'd been biding their time all weekend, waiting for me to leave...

I AWOKE to full morning sunlight. Shocked I'd slept so long, so hard, so late, I tapped my phone to check the time.

There were five new messages.

One from Eric demanding I call him when I got up.

And four from Austin Fox.

16

I STARED AT HIS NAME ABOVE THE MESSAGES, AFRAID IF I blinked *Austin* would resolve itself into another similar name.

Glad you made it home safe!

I'm really glad you came! Smiling devil emoji. Face with hearts emoji.

I love this pic!

The first three texts were time stamped twelve forty-five a.m., but the fourth had been sent at one twenty:

You probably crashed early. Sleep well!

The flush of joy—*he'd texted me back!*—was chilled by an immediate stab of regret. I'd missed the chance to respond in real time.

But he'd taken his phone and hiked all the way out the front gate to the main road not once but twice. He'd thought of me explicitly on at least two separate occasions, and it was entirely plausible he'd been thinking about me for an extended period of time.

Of course, there was no way I could know for sure how he might have spent the two intervening hours...

I shook my head. It was too early in the day—and too soon in my knowing him—for this much emotional whiplash.

Since he probably wouldn't see my reply for hours, I figured I could take my time and compose something thoughtful. Something quirky and sexy that didn't sound overthought.

Even though I was definitely going to overthink it.

I'd already read his messages twenty times before getting out of bed, and I'd spend the rest of the day dissecting them.

While the coffee brewed, I pulled up the selfie of Austin and me. I centered and cropped it around his face and assigned it to his contact information.

He looked adorable of course, although a little goofy and cross-eyed because he'd stared at the wrong part of the phone instead of directly into the camera. My smile was a shy grimace, and my hair was sweaty from packing and hauling gear, making it appear even thinner than it was. Due to foreshortening, I appeared small next to him.

I was strung between treasuring the picture and feeling slightly mortified by it.

I didn't look like I could be his *dad* though. Surely nobody would think that.

I considered sending it to Eric with a message in all caps that screamed *HE TEXTED ME BACK! #Paulstin.*

But then, it might never happen again. Austin was too nice a guy to ghost me. He might've replied out of politeness.

I didn't want Eric to pity me later. Plus, once I replied, he'd text me at least twenty-five more times. I'd be committing myself to an hour of back-and-forth—or worse, he might *call* me like someone from the twentieth century.

I'd need to be caffeinated for that.

My sister, Veronica, was a similarly rabid communicator. She sent me a seemingly innocent text about my niece's upcoming birthday party, but I could feel her waiting to pepper me with invasive questions about the campground. Since she'd gotten married and had kids, she wanted to live vicariously through my sex life. As if I had one. I had to be the most disappointing single, gay brother a woman could have.

She'd also ask me how the book was coming—she *always* asked me how the book was coming. She romanticized my author career too. I'd been lying to her about my progress for months.

Today, I needed to take action that honored the bonfire spell. I needed to shift my energy away from guilt and failure to what I wanted. I needed to get out of my own way.

I replied to Veronica's message, letting her know I was home safe, a little hungover, and would catch up with her later.

I swiped back to the picture of Austin and me. *I wonder what his social media looks like...*

No.

I'd promised myself I'd take the weekend, maybe get a little action, see if that helped shake loose some ideas—*get my groove back*—and when I returned, I'd get to work banging out words.

And that is exactly what I intended to do.

As soon as I put away my camping equipment in the attic above the garage.

It was truly one of the most justifiable reasons for procrastinating I'd encountered in a while. I regretted I could only use it today.

I'd also vowed—in a dramatically pagan ceremony, now

that I recalled it—to let go of the stories that no longer served me and the labels other people had given me.

Despite my agent constantly advising me to refrain from checking reviews—*reviews are for readers*—I'd read them all. The comments about my first book had been glowing. It had been an author's dream come true. I'd been so high on the accolades, even the few trolls who'd left one-star reviews— just to shit on something thousands of others had already lauded—hadn't brought me down.

I'd thought I was doing a pretty damn good job processing criticism in a detached, constructive way.

Until it had come from Charles during our last screaming fight—about him cheating on me *again*—when he'd said I couldn't write.

I'd known he was trying to wound me.

He'd been in the wrong. Everyone had known he was in the wrong. He'd known it. But he'd lashed out like he was the one being attacked.

It had been guilt expressed as aggression.

He'd also said I couldn't fuck. He'd *confessed* it like it was a burden he'd been carrying. Never mind that any armchair psychologist could've diagnosed my inability to get it up for him. He'd cheated on me for years when I'd been away working on my master's, then my doctorate.

Charles had loved my writing. He'd been the one who'd convinced me to keep going when I'd felt stuck or blocked. After *Boy* had been published, he'd introduced me at readings and stood by my side during signing events, beaming with pride like it had been his book too.

And it had been. I'd thought of him as my partner in all ways. My successes had been his.

When I'd looked back on all the times he'd supported me, I'd known his praise had been genuine. But the nasty look on his face when he'd read me for filth on his way out of my life...

It had played on a loop in my mind. For months, I hadn't been able to make it through a day without reliving it.

It wasn't only a story or a label that he'd flung at me; it was like he'd called up a demon to attack and possess me. Somewhere, in some deep vault, in some cage within my heart, it had continued to rage.

Charles hadn't been a random anonymous keyboard warrior on the internet. He'd been my first love and my first reader.

There were some things that certain people had the power to say or do that you simply couldn't forget.

I couldn't unhear it.

I knew—intellectually—that he'd only been projecting, and that it couldn't have been his real opinion.

But that hadn't kept his poison from doing its worst.

I'd wanted to let it go, but deep down, I'd feared he'd known some truth about me that no one else could see.

Still, I'd written the second book to spite him.

Divining Virginia had been powered by sheer rage.

Impotent rage.

And when it had launched with a thud, my biggest fear had been confirmed.

Charles had been right.

Now I imagined Jim asking, *Why does he get to be right?*

Jim's message at the bonfire ritual had spoken to me. And Austin had given me a glimpse of how quickly things could change.

I could see a way forward. It was banal and obvious and awfully unexciting compared to fire magic and tent sex, but the strategy had worked for me in the past.

I was a devout believer in the power of proprioceptive

writing, what Julia Cameron called "Morning Pages" in *The Artist's Way*. You simply wrote whatever came to mind without judgment.

I'd sworn that when I returned from camp, I would write every day.

Even if it meant sitting down and writing *I don't know what the fuck to write, I don't know what the fuck to write, I don't know what the fuck to write* over and over again.

Eventually those pages of word vomit and blather would stray into actual ideas and fragments of prose I could use.

When I'd taken the sabbatical at the beginning of the year, the goal had been to write a book before the end of the summer. I was willing to settle for a first draft or at least a strong concept and a working outline I could pitch.

I'd already wasted five months. Half my time.

But the actions required hadn't changed. I still needed to show up every day and write something.

Anything.

Starting today.

I sat at my desk, took a sip of my tea, set a timer on my phone, and started writing.

About Austin.

Because the thing I most wanted to think about wasn't my work, and it definitely wasn't Charles.

Memories of the weekend flowed out of me.

And that was okay.

The rules allowed for anything that wanted to come through.

My experience with Austin had been significant. It deserved to be documented.

Some part of me still judged it, but maybe if I got it all down, it would free up the mental bandwidth for something real to emerge.

Because this couldn't be *real* writing—the first time I'd laid eyes on Austin; us rolling around in my tent; the recurring fairy tale shoes that had the misfortune of being true and yet too on the nose for serious fiction.

But.

This was more than I'd written in one sitting in years. It felt good just to *type* this much.

The alarm went off.

I scanned the document.

I cringed thinking what my editor—former editor—would think of it. I almost deleted it, but it felt too much like I'd be erasing Austin. He'd probably love it. I pictured his crooked smile and him calling us *hot.*

Writing had been so hard for so long, but writing about Austin was easy. And if it was only valuable as a form of therapy, so be it.

I swiped open my phone, thumbed to the picture of us, and zoomed in on Austin's face.

I needed more images of him. I had a few dummy accounts for lurking on social media. If he were to look for me online, he'd find my dormant author profiles with my headshot from ten years ago when I hadn't been much older than he was now. I hoped he wouldn't compare it to our selfie and wish he had met me sooner.

I searched "Austin Fox Best Cub," and found him within seconds—@musclecubfox—one of those accounts with less than fifty original pictures posted and one hundred fifty thousand followers. He'd been tagged *#musclecub* in tons of photos by other people. I recognized the backgrounds. They'd invariably been taken in front of the lodge or in the parking lot between the pool complex and the front gate. There were dozens dated yesterday and the day before. While I'd been packing and waiting on him, guests had been stopping him to take selfies with him before they departed.

I went back to the solo selfies Austin had personally uploaded and saved screenshots of about twenty of them. That was all I'd come for. I hadn't been expecting the rest, but now that I saw glimpses of his life when I wasn't in it, I couldn't stop looking.

And overthinking.

All those men with their muscled, tattooed arms casually draped around his shoulders... The more I scrolled, the more their selfies started to look like trophies.

How many of them might have also fucked him?

In a few days, another batch of men would arrive at Bear Mountain Lodge. Hundreds of naked men who didn't have performance issues.

I couldn't compete with them.

I opened the pictures of Austin I'd saved. *I should go ahead and delete them now. Start the process of reversing my infatuation.*

When the phone rang, I startled and almost dropped it.

He was calling me.

17

I FUMBLED TO HIT ACCEPT, AND CONSIDERING THE circumstances, managed a preposterously cool, "Hello?"

"Prof! Didya miss me?"

"I didn't miss that nickname," I lied, sure the smile in my voice betrayed me.

"You love it," Austin teased. "What're you doing?"

"Uh... writing." I jumped up from my desk and started to pace. "Trying to anyway. You?"

"Turning this campground over. Recovery days are no joke. I just jogged out here to see if you'd texted me back."

"Are you at the pole?" When I'd left camp yesterday, I'd seen a guy out there on his phone. It was a bit of a hike.

"I'm literally hanging on the pole." He giggled. "Maybe I should audition for Big Richards."

Big Richards—no apostrophe—was a famous male strip club in Atlanta. "You expect me to believe that's never occurred to you before? With moves like yours?"

"I'm not sure the masses are ready for all this thick, juicy *beef* coming at 'em. It's a little too *Kung Fu Panda*, you know?"

"What the hell are you talking about?"

"The shot of Panda running in slow motion? Don't tell me you haven't seen that movie."

"The *cartoon*?"

"The Oscar-nominated animated film, sir." He enunciated each word in a snobbish, locked-jaw voice. "Anyway. Dancing could be a year-round gig, but..."

"Still not much of a long-term plan," I finished.

He huffed, but there was affection in his voice. "You're such a total dad."

"Don't say that."

"You hate it, don't you?"

"I really do."

"So you don't want me to call you"—here came that horrendous porn-twink voice again—"*Daddy*?"

"Oh God!" I could've kicked myself for snickering.

"You're laughing," he taunted in a singsong voice.

I growled.

"Fine." He sighed into the phone. A loud, fake, wistful sigh. "*Prof* it is."

"Perfect," I deadpanned.

"I'm coming to town for a gig tomorrow."

"Oh?"

"Yeah, we're usually off on Wednesdays. That's when we go into town, do some shopping. Buy a shit ton of snacks for the bunkhouse. Go to a bar we don't work at. We can ask off for other times if it's something important. But this week I picked up a substitute teaching spot at Blue Ridge CrossFit."

"That's awesome."

"So you'll come?"

"Um." I was glad he couldn't see my panicked expression. "To the CrossFit gym?" There were always legions of Hemsworth lookalikes and Captain America clones going in and out of that place.

"Yeah. To my class. You said if I subbed in town, you'd come."

Oh, Dear God. What the fuck could I say? At the bonfire, he'd teased me about not coming to his Morning-After Drill, but maybe he really had been disappointed.

"I'm not implying you need to work out," Austin said, misreading my hesitation. "You don't need to change anything about yourself at all. You'd be helping me out. Fitness classes are all about body counts. I'm already gonna lose a bunch of people when the regulars find out their usual trainer's not gonna be there. And if I want to pick up more classes or get on their schedule permanently, it's gonna depend on how many people I can draw."

"I can't imagine you wouldn't be able to draw a lot of people." I really couldn't. Especially not after having seen all the selfies he'd been tagged in.

"Well, the lumberjacks from camp have all promised to come." He paused, waiting for me to say something. "You don't have to be a member or even pay anything. Just tell the front desk you're my guest." His voice went soft. "I really want to see you."

Well, that did the trick.

I tried to think of a scenario where I could see him under less potentially mortifying circumstances, like grabbing a beer afterward or meeting for dinner, but I didn't want to risk saying no to the class and then find out he already had other plans. How many more Wednesdays might go by before I got another chance?

"Okay," I said.

"Really? You'll come? Oh my God. Thank you so much! You have no idea how much this means to me."

"Would you like me to see if Eric and Ben can come too?

I mean, I know Eric has a membership there, and if you need more people..."

"Yes! That'd be amazing."

"I'll ask them."

"Fantastic! I'll bring Dorothy and Glinda."

"Who?"

He laughed. "Your shoes. I named them." He dropped his voice. "I'm wearing them right now."

A week ago, I would never have believed a guy commandeering my shittiest pair of sneakers and naming them after queer movie icons could make my dick stir, but —*fuck*. Austin had an unnerving ability to be ridiculous and sexy at the same time.

"I've been wearing them constantly," he said. "Ever since the morning after."

I wasn't sure if he was talking about the Morning-After Drill or the morning after being with me, but either way, it rendered me speechless. I grunted a wordless curse.

He chuckled. "You don't need them to work out, do you?"

"No, no." Other than camping, I couldn't have imagined wearing those ratty things in public. "I have some new ones," I lied. I'd had no occasion to buy sneakers in a long time, but Austin didn't need to know that.

I heard another faint voice on his side of the line.

"What?" Austin said to whomever it was.

There was a pause while the other person spoke again, but I couldn't make out what they were saying.

"We're only two weeks into the season, bro." Austin's voice was too loud to have been talking to me. "Nobody's that big of a ho." He apologized to me, and said, "Some jackhole just asked me if the number on my arm—your phone number—was a tally."

"Who was it?"

"Ryan." He spat the name with a mixture of fondness and fake disgust. "I'm right behind you," he yelled to Ryan. To me, he said, "Sorry, Prof. I gotta run. But I'll text you the details, and... I'll see you tomorrow."

Tomorrow.

I GROUP-TEXTED Eric and Ben to see if they were available.

Ben sent a thumbs-up emoji.

Eric replied, *Unfortunately, I have to work, but TELL ME ABOUT AUSTIN!*

I'll only be sharing those details with those who attend the class with me.

Eric sent a wow face and a middle finger emoji. *It's not like I don't have ways of getting Ben to talk.*

Fine. I'll tell you over lunch tomorrow if you go shopping with me.

Makeover!

Calm down. I just need new shoes.

I SPENT the evening feeling restless and distracted.

For three hours, I tried to watch the same forty-minute television episode, pausing every five minutes to scroll more of Austin's social media feed.

I ran across an article he'd shared that claimed the basic fitness level of a man over forty was defined by his ability to do fifty consecutive pushups without stopping.

After barely making it to thirty, I stared at myself in the mirror from a variety of equally disappointing angles before finally accepting that tomorrow was not a test I could cram for.

Still tired from the weekend, I gave up and went to bed.

THE NEXT DAY, as soon as the waiter had taken our order, Eric said, "Okay. Tell me *everything*.

"Honestly, it was pretty incredible," I started.

But that was as far as I got.

Eric launched into a half-hour account of the life-changing twelve hours he and Ben had spent alone in their cabin the night before I'd arrived at the campground. "I mean, it was like no time had passed. It was exactly like it'd been when we were in college only with this *urgency*. He spat on it, and—"

"Okay." I sat back in my chair and raised my hands. "Lemme stop you right there. Ben's coming over this afternoon to pick up his tools, and if you go any further into this blow-by-blow, I'm not gonna be able to look him in the eye."

Eric grimaced. "Sorry."

"It's okay. I'm really happy for both of you."

"Thanks. I'm..." Eric paused, trying to find the words. "I can't describe it. It's like I'm watching my life from outside it, you know? Like the past week happened to someone else."

I nodded. "I can relate."

Before going to the shoe store, Eric insisted I check out a nearby shop that sold mostly upscale yoga wear. On the short walk down the block, Eric asked me again about Austin, promising this time he wouldn't interrupt.

I confessed that there had been a surprising connection. That I hadn't expected Austin's intelligence and wit.

I knew Eric wanted salacious gossip, but I wasn't going to share the kind of details I'd been writing about for the past few days. I'd woken up early this morning with words pouring out of me. I'd brought my laptop to the kitchen island so I could get it all down while the coffee was brewing.

I did tell him that Austin had made me laugh more in three and a half days than I had in the last ten years. I heard myself gushing. The more I tried to describe how easy it had been to be with Austin and how nervous I was about doing his class, the more I knew I sounded like I wanted it to *go* somewhere.

Eric stopped on the sidewalk in front of the shop. "It's a big deal to take it outside the campground, especially for a guy who works there. But Austin's initiated this whole fitness-class scenario. He obviously didn't even have it booked in advance or he would've mentioned it to you before you left. I wouldn't be surprised to find out he called every trainer he knows in town and begged them to let him sub for them just so he'd have an excuse to invite you."

"He could've just come to see me. I would've said yes to coffee. I would've invited him to dinner at the slightest hint. Why does it have to be a *high intensity interval training class*. Dude, what the fuck? That's not my life."

"Ahh, but it's his. And it's him in his element. Maybe he wants to shine for you. Show you he can do more than crack open beer cans and flirt."

It was a better theory than thinking the universe was testing me or that Austin would end up judging me for being too old for him, too out of shape. Unable to keep up. Unable to perform.

I caught myself. I was enduring life again and focusing on what I didn't want to happen.

It *was* more likely that Austin wanted to show off for me. I'd denied him the chance at the campground.

Eric opened the door. "Whatever Austin's motivation is, you need to look cool. At least expensive."

The shop workers were all dressed in dark, monochromatic, synthetic clothing that somehow managed to be flowy and tight at the same time. They looked like a modern dance company of hybrid hippie-goths, and they all spoke in the same breathy voice.

I recognized a pretty guy who'd been the only male-identifying student in a Women's Studies seminar I'd led last fall on *A Room of One's Own*. Hogan. He was evangelically vegan. The amount of times he'd managed to work veganism into a discussion about a feminist essay written nearly a hundred years ago was a fucking masterclass in having a consistent platform and talking points.

He'd asked for an extension on the final paper because of a conflict with a once-in-a-lifetime opportunity to attend a tantric weekend. I'd allowed it, partly because he had bewitching lichen-green eyes and it made me nervous to be alone in my office with him, and I'd wanted him to hurry up and leave.

Hogan was very attentive to me and Eric, running back and forth to the fitting room with alternate sizes as I kept going larger and larger to escape the *skinniness* of the clothing's construction. I had nice, muscular, grown-man thighs. I'd thought Hogan had been taking pity on my middle-aged fashion crisis until I found myself at the cash wrap with well over five hundred dollars' worth of merchandise he'd smoothly convinced me I needed.

"This is way more than I need for a single class," I muttered to Eric. "And we haven't even made it to the shoe store yet."

"Austin'll probably want you to work out more with him

in the future. I wonder if you'll get a special membership rate if you're the trainer's significant other?"

The cashier rang up Eric's two hundred dollars' worth of underwear, and he handed her a store credit card.

"You have an account here?" I asked. "Do you even *do* yoga?"

Eric twisted his lips. "I wish I could say yes, but no. I just love their boxer briefs. Plus, we get a company discount."

I was incredulous. "For a record label?"

"They sell a ton of basic pieces in black stretch fabric." He said it like that explained everything.

I stared at him.

"It's the music industry."

I still didn't get it.

Eric rolled his eyes. "Remember the cover art I showed you for the new Black Star Crown album with the pic of the lead singer? Dude's wearing a women's ballet shrug that one of our in-house photo stylists bought here and artfully shredded the shit out of. They fall apart when he takes them off, though, so he's gonna need at least twenty of them for the live tour. Just one example. I could go on."

"Huh. I thought he was doing that move where you put the front half of your T-shirt behind your head so you don't get cum on it."

Eric nodded. "Exactly. Which is why it's the cover."

18

BEN FOLLOWED ME INTO THE LAUNDRY ROOM.

I'd thrown my new clothes into the washing machine while we argued about which tools belonged to him. There were several that neither of us could confidently claim after floating around my house for years and mixing with my own. Ben swore he'd bought duplicates for other worksites, but he ended up giving me more than he took.

I thanked him, but I didn't know what else to say.

Remodeling this house with Ben had saved me during those critical years after Charles had left and the second book had failed. He'd evolved into a sort of construction therapist, but expressing how much working with him had meant to me was outside the realm of our usual rapport.

We talked shop—Ben with as few words as possible— and never about our feelings.

When I pulled one of the shirts from the dryer, Ben spotted the logo and raised his eyebrows. "Fancy."

"It was your *boyfriend's* idea." I enunciated the term to acknowledge his new status with Eric.

Ben chuckled—he might have blushed, but I was careful

not to look at him—and that was our entire conversation about their relationship. "You ready to head to the gym?"

The question saved me from feeling obligated to comment on his last official visit to the house as my contractor. It wasn't like he'd never be back as a friend again, but it was the end of a chapter.

I cleared the lump in my throat. "That'd be cool."

"Sure you don't want an epic deck?" It wasn't the first time Ben had suggested it. He said that every time he went to the campground and saw the lavish outdoor spaces on Trailer Park Avenue. He always came back with an urge to build one.

I always turned him down. I had a beautiful, tiled patio that was original to the house, mature shrubs and trees that had taken decades to mature, and a backyard that was too small for a deck. "Why don't you build one for someone at camp?"

Ben sighed. "Everybody's already got one."

WE ARRIVED at Blue Ridge CrossFit twenty minutes early, which was fortunate because the guy at the front desk handed us clipboards filled with personal information forms and liability waivers. He directed us toward the far end of the counter so we wouldn't obstruct the actual members waiting to scan in.

We changed in the locker room and found the class in a huge room with high ceilings, mirrored walls, and a structure resembling a black jungle gym. Dumbbell and kettlebell racks flanked a basketball-court-sized open space.

About twenty people, more than half of them women, were scattered around the space, stretching and talking to one another in small groups of two and three. It looked like a casting call for a superhero movie.

Some of the men were familiar faces from the campground—Gunner, Hank, and a couple of other guys whose names I couldn't remember. They looked different out of their staff uniforms and disco drag.

Gunner wore white basketball shorts, a white tank, and hot-pink high-top sneakers with a matching terrycloth headband. His boyfriend, Hank, provided a preppy contrast in plain gray basketball shorts and a navy Edgewood University T-shirt.

They called out to Ben and me and waved us over. I awkwardly negotiated their fist-bumps—failing on the first three pretty miserably but nailing the fourth—and they seemed genuinely happy to see me.

And of course, there was Austin. I'd sensed him the moment I'd entered, but I'd tried to play it cool. Seeing him again for the first time in a completely different environment was faintly surreal like a celebrity sighting.

Austin looked covered up—for him—in a bright-yellow crewneck T-shirt and long, gray basketball shorts. Only his kneecaps showed above tall, yellow-striped tube socks and a pair of classic black-and-white Adidas.

I understood why he hadn't worn my crappy red Nikes, but I would've been lying if I'd said I didn't feel a twinge of disappointment. However, my phone number was still visible on his arm.

Austin read aloud from a tablet screen to a tall woman, who taped signs around the room defining workstations with different equipment groupings—weights, ropes, wooden boxes, and yoga mats.

He glanced up. When he noticed me, he stopped talking to his assistant.

My face flushed.

Austin's lips curled into a smile, his eyes flashed, and he up-nodded. The whistle around his neck gave him a sexy, coach/referee vibe.

I gave him a tiny, dorky wave.

Austin thanked everyone for coming and asked us to spread out.

I dashed to the back of the room, the safe haven for reluctant students in any class. Ben came with me. The location allowed me to check everyone out without their realizing it. I could always justify people-watching as character inspiration.

I'd expected there to be a bunch of younger fitness model types in this group, but the *bodies*... Jesus. The woman directly in front of me had the nicest legs I'd ever seen on anyone of any gender. She was lean and muscular, without an ounce of extra body fat, and she was also pregnant. Very pregnant.

Ben and I weren't the oldest people in the room. A man in the first row with a silver military buzzcut had to have been in his late fifties or early sixties. He reached to scratch the back of his neck, and his biceps were so enormous he could hardly complete the motion. He was definitely not your average papaw. That a man his age could be so fit encouraged me and filled me with a sense of hope for my future. But of course he'd probably gotten that way as a result of doing classes like this.

I leaned close to Ben and muttered, "I'm afraid I'm about to make a fool of myself."

He pulled a face and shook his head.

"All right, listen up!" Austin's *coach voice* sounded affected, even compared to his *bro* speak, but it was commanding, capable, and shockingly hot.

If I'd never had a gym teacher/coach fantasy before, I definitely had one now.

As Austin led us through a series of stretches and calisthenics, I couldn't decide which was more distracting—dissecting his vocal performance, trying to watch him while also attempting to follow the movements, or getting winded five minutes in.

I kept glancing at the clock, wishing I'd asked how long the class was supposed to last.

At thirty minutes, Austin blew his whistle, called for everyone to stop, and told us to grab a sip of water.

That hadn't been so bad.

I was thinking—naively—that I could do that every day when Austin said, "Now that we're warmed up, we can move on to today's workout."

Oh shit. That was the warm-up. I whispered to Ben, "What the fuck have I done?"

He tilted his head and grimaced. "Pace yourself."

After a five-minute break that felt like it lasted ninety seconds, Austin asked everyone to line up along the mirrored wall. He divided us into five groups of four and told us to choose a station.

Ben and I ended up with the pregnant woman, who introduced herself as Ashley, and her friend, Mary Beth. They were perfectly lovely. Neither of them appeared to have broken a sweat. Since they were clearly our superiors, we followed them without question to the station labeled *Dead Lifts.*

All the groups had erupted into conversation, and Austin allowed it to go on for a few minutes before whistling for everyone's attention. He announced we would be doing something adapted from *Spartacus.* "It's based on part of the official training regimen used by the actors on the TV series." Austin's eyes gleamed. He loved this shit. This was his element.

I'd never watched the show, but I could see several people there portraying gladiators with the right costumes.

The woman who'd been assisting Austin with setting up the stations rotated through each of the exercises, slowly performing the movements as he explained them. He talked us through the proper form, the goal of each exercise, what muscle groups it was intended to isolate, what *not* to do, pitfalls to look out for... He also suggested alternate movements for anyone with medical limitations without calling out anyone in particular.

In most of the fitness classes I'd ever been to, or with videos I'd tried following online, I usually flailed around for a bit, spending too much time and energy trying to figure out what the hell was going on.

I appreciated how much detail Austin shared. He was evidently incredibly knowledgeable, not only about the content but also about how to teach it. He'd clearly been professionally trained, but as with any subject, he had a passion that couldn't be taught.

I often felt guilty that I didn't have more passion for teaching. I had a love for *literature*. I enjoyed reading, writing, and discussing books. It was easy to see why my parents and teachers had always told me I'd make a good professor. For a lot of writers, teaching was something you did to pay the bills. It was the expected career path, the only one anyone in graduate school ever talked about.

Most authors didn't make a living from book sales, and almost none of us had a bestseller right out of the gate.

I'd never expected that. I'd been prepared for the opposite to happen—to languish for years producing work that would go unnoticed and would make a few months' worth of income compared to my teaching salary if I were lucky.

So I hadn't been surprised when lightning hadn't struck a second time. I'd tried not to let anyone see how disappointed and embarrassed I was by my second book's performance, and I'd simply gone on teaching.

I'd gone on *enduring* it.

Austin was not enduring this class. He was living for it.

He was a natural coach.

I'd been in boot-camp-style classes before, where some action-figure lookalike yelled at everyone like we were in some kind of basic-training hell.

Austin may have bellowed with the volume and the energy of a drill sergeant—and he definitely made suggestions to a few people to improve certain aspects of their form—but as I listened to him calling out individuals, I noticed something telling about him.

The content of his yelling was mostly encouragement: "Killer intensity, Mary Beth! Way to get after it, Xena! You got this, Scout Master!"

For a substitute, he sure knew a lot of people's nicknames. I had to wonder if he might be making them up on the fly.

I hoped he wouldn't single me out, but when he finally did, it was positive. "That's a real nice deep squat, Prof. You're making it look easy!"

I was surprised by how much his praise affected me. If my face hadn't already been so flushed from exertion, he might have seen my blush.

I went from just wanting to survive—to endure this—to wanting to impress him.

Even still, when Austin blew his whistle, I was damn glad it was over.

I'd done it. I hadn't crapped out, I hadn't let him down, and I hadn't made a fool of myself.

"Okay, that was round one, guys," Austin said, applauding us. "Three more rounds to go."

Wait. What?

In response to this bombshell, some people whooped and others clapped. I groaned.

Austin flashed a wicked smile. "The actors on the show do this every day, y'all. Imagine how freaking ripped you'd be, right?"

What the actual fuck?

There was no way in hell I was going to make it through a second round. But then, I thought the same during the one-minute break—that felt like five seconds—before the third round started.

Through some miracle of time or the haze of endorphins, that round ended too.

I kinda felt... capable.

I kinda felt strong.

And by the halfway point of the fourth round, I thought, *Maybe I can do this.* The repetition of the exercises had cured a lot of my initial awkwardness. I knew what to expect. I could anticipate and steel myself. I knew where I might falter, how many reps I'd managed before, where to dig in, when to access that extra strength that came from my will— from my *soul*—not from my body.

Ben didn't seem to be faring much better than I was. Sure, as far as the weights were concerned, he had the physical strength from his years of construction work, but the real challenge was the cardio aspect.

Even a few of the lumberjacks were suffering.

Papaw Silver Fox was breathing hard, but he was

standing proud and tall, looking pumped like he might want to tear a phone book in half.

Ashley looked dewy and glowing.

For the record, I was barely keeping up with the pregnant lady.

"One more exercise," Austin called out. "Sixty seconds. You can do anything for sixty seconds!"

Could I?

My group had been ending every circuit on box jumps. These were wooden boxes on the floor, at about knee-height, that you had to jump up onto, stand straight and tall, step down, and immediately do it again. You repeated this over and over, as many times as you could manage, until time was called.

On the first round, the box had slid out from under me a little bit. I learned quickly to get high enough that I was coming down on top of it and not clipping it from the side.

"Five seconds!" Austin was right behind me, speaking directly to me. "Come on. You got this. Give me one more!"

One more? Really? I was pretty sure that had been my last. *Ever.* For the rest of my life.

Austin leaned in, his voice close to my ear. "Remember when you were a little kid and you got new sneakers and you were convinced they made you run faster? I see you got some new Altras, Prof. I bet you can *fly* in those fuckers."

The desire to impress him was a tiny bit stronger than my self-doubt. I swung my arms for leverage like Austin had shown us, and even though I felt ridiculous, I heaved myself up like a giant, gay, middle-aged frog.

But the last jump was exactly like my first, only worse. I didn't clear the top at all. I caught the edge with the toes of my new shoes and basically kicked the box out from under me.

Before I pitched face-first toward the ground, Austin was beside me. With one hand on my chest, he stopped my forward motion, and with the other on my arm, he hauled me upright at the last second.

He pulled me against him. "You all right there, Prof?" His beard scruff tickled my neck. I was both turned on and embarrassed.

Unable to speak, I nodded. Everyone had stopped and was looking.

"He's good!" Austin yelled, setting me on my feet and releasing me, and everyone applauded.

What the fuck was it with people *applauding* me?

Oh. Wait. Austin was walking around the room clapping, obviously for everyone having made it through the workout. They were applauding him, each other, and the end of the class.

Ben and I met in the corner where we'd left our water bottles earlier. We paced in tight circles, sipping, catching our breaths, neither of us capable of speaking yet.

Austin stood near the door fist-bumping, high-fiving, and thanking people as they exited. Ben and I, along with the lumberjacks, were the last to leave.

Austin beamed at us. "Thank you so much for coming, guys."

Ben clapped him on the shoulder. "Kicked my ass, man, but it was great."

We all headed to the locker room to shower. The private stalls removed the temptation to gawk at Austin. I lost sight of him when he went to change—his locker wasn't near ours —and then I rushed to catch up with him.

But I needn't have worried. A couple of the lumberjacks had disappeared, but Gunner, Hank, and Austin were waiting for me and Ben in the lobby.

Austin had changed into what I supposed were his *street clothes*—a plaid button-down shirt with the sleeves ripped off, cut-off denim shorts, and work boots. I'd only ever seen him in a devil costume, a staff uniform, and his workout gear. "You guys want to grab a bite somewhere?" he asked.

"Sure," I said. Now that the hard part was out of the way, I was eager for a chance to talk to him.

Gunner and Hank shared a look. Gunner muttered something about them meeting up with Albie and Kevin, and with a quick goodbye, they were out the door.

"I'm gonna head out too," Ben said. "I gotta get home to Eric."

"Dude." I spread my hands. "You drove me."

Ben smirked. "I'm sure Austin'll give you a ride home."

Austin smiled. "Guess it's just us, then."

19

AUSTIN SUGGESTED THE RESTAURANT NEXT DOOR. "DO YOU ever eat here?"

"Yeah. My mom actually loves this place."

"Is she vegetarian?"

"No. She's a lady who likes to pick at salads when she eats in public."

He chuckled. "Well, I'm a man who likes to destroy a cheeseburger with or without an audience. But I feel like I'd be a shitty trainer if I didn't encourage you to eat something clean right now."

I opened the door for him. "You're definitely not a shitty trainer."

"A glowing testimonial. Promise me you'll leave a review online." When we got in line to order, Austin caught my eye. "Thanks again for coming."

"Of course. I'm embarrassed to tell you how long it's been since I've done anything like that."

Austin shrugged. "No worries. We all go through periods where we fall off, and then we get back into it. It's a choice to get strong. To *be* strong. You said yes, and you showed up."

Austin bumped my shoulder with his. "You looked great out there too. In your fancy workout duds and your new kicks."

"I tried to keep up with my pregnant teammate. But holy shit, did she make me feel out of shape."

Austin chuckled. "Few can keep up with Ashley. We call her Xena."

"Are the nicknames an Austin thing or…"

"It's a CrossFit thing too. Originating in military culture. For the record, I'm a lover and a pacifist."

"Well, I appreciate that you didn't yell at us. My ego couldn't have handled it."

"I believe in positive motivation. If negativity worked, we'd all be our best selves already. You did great."

"Well." I blushed again under his simple praise. "It almost got a little bloody there at the end."

"My bad for not warning y'all about the boxes on the polished wood floor."

"No, you explained everything very thoroughly. You're a good coach. Thanks for saving me."

"My pleasure." Now Austin was the one blushing.

The cashier interrupted. "What can I get you guys?"

I touched the small of Austin's back, urging him to go first.

He was already staring up at the menu board, so he didn't see the once-over she gave us. I wondered how we must look together—Austin with his ripped clothes, guns blazing; me in khaki cargo shorts and a V-neck T-shirt, trying to suck in my stomach. Charles and I had been one of those couples who dressed alike.

Austin ordered a veggie lasagna, black bean burger with avocado, mushroom risotto, and a stuffed bell pepper.

"Student ID?" the cashier asked. Most establishments offered a discount to university students and employees.

Before he could answer, I flashed my faculty badge. "This is together. Add a falafel wrap and two drinks, please."

"Thanks, Prof!" Austin smiled.

The cashier shot me another cool, appraising look as she passed our empty cups across the counter along with a numbered sign to set on our table.

We filled our drinks, and I followed Austin to a booth in the far corner next to a group of young women wearing Tri Delt T-shirts. They ceased talking as Austin approached. He said hello to them and slid onto the bench with his back to them.

When I sat across from him, I caught a brunette fanning herself with her hand. I couldn't help but smile. *Same, girl. Same.*

Austin picked up our conversation. "So about you feeling out of shape. Most people, when they hear terms like 'working out' or 'getting in shape,' think 'strength training.' I saw you picking up heavy shit, no problem. But if your heart rate's jacked up, and you're having a hard time catching your breath, that's not about muscles you can see." He was *cute* in lecturing mode. "You want to focus on building some cardiovascular endurance. Nothing major to start out with. Take a walk. Once a day, preferably outside, not on a treadmill. Alternating speeds is actually most effective for conditioning, so you could also jog intermittently."

I made a skeptical noise and sipped my tea.

"Whatever pace feels doable. You're a writer. Call it a walking meditation. Staring at the sky and communing with trees also helps with accessing the creative flow state."

I lifted my brows. "I'd be willing to try anything that might help with that."

Austin studied me. "Writer's block?"

I twisted my lips, reluctant to confess another *issue.*

"Some people claim it doesn't exist, but when it's happening to you, it's all too real."

"Walking every day religiously for thirty or forty-five minutes will totally help. Do it for three months, and I promise you, you'll start to feel all kinds of things shifting."

I liked Austin's serious, earnest side. The laugh lines at the corners of his eyes had almost disappeared, but his furrowed brow was every bit as charismatic as his smile.

A thin, harried guy appeared, carrying a heavy tray. He randomly but evenly divided the plates between us because he didn't know where to put everything. Austin thanked him and dragged most of the dishes to his side of the table after he left. "Have whatever you want," he said.

"I'm good with my wrap."

We chewed quietly for a few moments. I'd forgotten how good food tasted after a hard workout. "Obviously, I'm not a trainer, but I've taught for a while, and I know what it takes to motivate people. You have the unique ability to be both commanding and likable. You build people up and inspire them to be better."

"I don't know about all that." Austin looked down at his food, a shy smile on his face. "Working out's the one thing that's given me a sense of purpose this past year. It's something I can control, that doesn't depend on anyone else, that helps me feel strong physically, mentally, and spiritually. A lot of jocks end up teaching gym because it's the one job you can count on to be connected to sports programs, but I got my bachelor's in health and physical education because I wanted to teach kids how to access that strength earlier in life."

"That's... a worthy purpose."

He sighed. "Unfortunately, some people don't want somebody like me teaching their kids."

I frowned. "You said you'd burned a bridge..."

Austin waved dismissively. "It's a long story. I'll tell you about it some time."

I waited in case he wanted to say more, but I didn't press him.

"You know, I made a rule this summer," he said, "that I wasn't going to try to keep anything going outside the campground." He took a bite of lasagna.

Damn, that was an abrupt change of subject. I raised my eyebrows. "Okay."

He took his time swallowing and wiping his mouth. "I hooked up with a guest last year. I thought it was more than a vacation fling, and... I was wrong. I made a total fool of myself. Got my heart fucking *crushed*. And clearly, I suck at rules because I'm talking about an ex on our first date."

Our first date. I shouldn't have been surprised he'd said it so casually, but my heart raced.

"But what can I say?" He sighed. "I'm a hopeless romantic. If I feel something, I gotta find out what it is, even if it turns out to be nothing. The way I see it, one day there'll be a spark, and then it'll keep going, keep becoming more. If you take a forever love story and a weekend fling and lay them out side by side, those first few days—those first few chapters—are gonna look awfully similar, right? In the beginning, you can't tell the difference. The spark has the potential to turn into something more until it doesn't. When I meet the love of my life, then later look back on the story of how we met—just being honest, here—it'll probably look a lot like my other hookups. I can't imagine being with somebody I'm not attracted to from the jump. People think it's a game or a hunt, but for me, it's a search. I keep finding guys who are dicks, but I only need one who's not. I'm compulsively hopeful. So when there's a spark, I blow on it."

He chuckled, amused by his own choice of words. "And I intend to keep blowing until it either catches fire or goes out."

I snorted softly and smiled. If this wasn't a spark, I didn't know what was. "Then why make a rule this summer?" I asked quietly. *Why break it for me?*

He bit the inside of his cheek. "Moment of weakness, I guess. Fear. I thought maybe it'd be easier." He narrowed his eyes, but they still twinkled. "Turns out, it was impossible."

I shifted in my seat, and my foot bumped his. I surrounded his shoe with both of mine and squeezed. "Should we get out of here?" *And see where this keeps going?* I forced myself to hold his gaze and not look away.

He slowly and emphatically nodded.

I slid out of the booth and offered him my hand. Even after he stood, he kept holding it, right there in the middle of the busy restaurant, both of us grinning like fools.

"Thanks for dinner," he said.

"My pleasure."

Austin's smile softened, his gaze shifting to something— or someone—behind me, and I turned to see who it was.

It was my mother and her friend Honey.

20

"Mom."

"Paul." Her eyes slid to Austin.

"I'd like you to meet Austin Fox." Since I was still holding his hand when I introduced him, it felt like I was presenting him. "Austin, this is my mother, Catherine Carter."

Austin tilted his head. "Miss Catherine." He pronounced it Miz. "It's so awesome to meet Paul's mama."

I cringed—I didn't call her my *mama*—and *sweet Mother of God, he's going in for a side hug.*

My mother was not a hugger, especially with someone she was meeting for the first time. Last month, at Mother's Day brunch, I'd received a rare awkward pat, and prior to that, I couldn't remember the last time we'd physically touched.

Austin had draped his heavy arm over my mom's shoulders and was pulling her against his side like a stiff doll. The size of his biceps next to her head might've been comical under other circumstances and with an entirely different person. But at least with his head pressed against hers, denting her immaculate blonde bob, he couldn't see her grimace. No one could have mistaken it for a real smile.

I grinned for Austin's benefit and tried to send Mom a telepathic message: *Be nice. He means well.* He was coming from a good place, but he was coming on Austin, which meant coming on awfully strong in Catherine Carter's book.

I would never have entertained him meeting her like this. Not only were we nowhere close to that stage, but I would've prepared him beforehand, given him some pointers. Unfortunately, most of them would have been to *not* do the things he was doing right now.

He probably wouldn't care about making a bad first impression, but she would. And I did.

I rushed to introduce her companion, who was watching the interaction with amusement. "And this is Honey Dean."

"Oh my God!" Austin released Mom and shifted his attention to Honey. "You're the prom lady!"

Honey's personality was the polar opposite of Mom's—she was ogling Austin like she hoped he'd grab her too—but I didn't want him to diminish her work. "Honey's the founder of Youth Alliance, the organization that hosts the inclusive prom events every year."

Honey shrugged and smiled. "I'm the prom lady."

Austin grabbed Honey in a full-frontal embrace, lifting her onto her tiptoes. She giggled and squeezed him back, sticking her tongue out over his shoulder at me and Mom.

Austin set her down and took hold of her hands. "I've heard so much about you. I work at Bear Mountain Lodge. We do a fundraiser for you in the summer."

"I know, sugar. I've been trying to convince y'all to let me come to the Bear Run for two decades."

I imagined Honey gliding through the pool complex in a floaty caftan and parking herself at the Bloody Marys' table.

If there were any woman they'd make an exception for, it would be her. Those men would worship her if they didn't already.

I doubted my mother even knew the campground existed. If she did, she'd never picture me there.

Austin said, "I was Best Cub last summer."

Honey put her hands on her hips, bracelets jangling. "You're the one who didn't show up to the party," she scolded. To my mother, she explained, "We have a little cocktail hour at Peter's. They let us use their private room in the back." If Mom only knew what other kinds of private events they held in the back room at Peter's... "The boys from Bear Mountain Lodge come and present us with the money they've raised. And this one right here was a no-show, and everybody kept wondering where he was."

"I'm so sorry I missed it," Austin said. "I had to go out of town last minute."

Honey playfully slapped Austin's shoulder. "Well, you better come this year."

"I will. If I keep my title."

"Come anyway. Tell Jim I said so." I pictured Jim Savage and Honey Dean in the back room at Peter's, volleying *honeys* and *sugars* back and forth.

"Can I tell y'all something funny?" Austin looked back and forth between Honey and Mom. I appreciated him making an effort to include Mom in the conversation, but I doubted she'd be amused by whatever he was about to confess. "Now keep in mind, I only moved here about a year and a half ago, but for the longest time, when I saw your event posters and your ads on social media and stuff, I thought you were a drag queen."

Mom looked to Honey for a cue as to how she should react. Honey cackled. "Sugar, you're not the first to think that, and you won't be the last. I take it as a compliment. I'm built like a linebacker. You shoulda seen me in the shoulder pad era." Honey was a tall woman. She looked like a cross between Jean Smart from *Designing Women* and Dolly Parton.

Mom gave Kelly Bishop from *Gilmore Girls* vibes. If Emily Gilmore had been a Southern blonde. She tittered now, noticeably uncomfortable. I'd often wondered how open-minded my mother would be if it hadn't been for Honey's influence. Honey's son was gay, and she was rich as God. Even though this was a small college town in a conservative part of the state, Honey made being a queer ally a requirement for all the women who hoped to participate in local "society." The country-club set loved to gossip about Honey's having married for money—and she let them; it was part of her larger-than-life persona—but with charisma and charm that would've terrified them in a politician, she bent them to her progressive will.

Mom asked Austin, "Are you one of Paul's students or..." She glanced at me. I saw her gears turning, worried what the answer might be.

Not wanting her to misconstrue, I jumped in. "I'm actually one of his. Austin's a fitness instructor. We came to grab a bite after his class next door."

"Philip's a member there." Honey always brought up her son in conversation and assumed everyone knew who he was. Philip was an *influencer* and the original poster child for her organization. For years, I'd thought she was trying to fix me up with him until I'd realized she was only constantly promoting him.

The food runner showed up with their dinner. Mom and Honey apologized for standing in the middle of the busy restaurant and dutifully moved to sit in the nearest free booth.

I took it as an opportunity to say our goodbyes, hoping Austin would follow my lead.

"Will we see you at Sadie's birthday party?" Honey asked.

"Yeah... Of course I'll be there." I looked at Mom, but she didn't meet my eyes. To Austin, I explained, "My sister, Veronica, is having a cookout for my niece. It's Sadie's eighteenth birthday, and she also just graduated from high school."

Austin smiled. "Sweet."

Mom glanced at me and said to Austin, "You're welcome to come if you'd like."

She'd only asked him because it would've been rude to talk about it in front of him and not extend an invitation. *Like bless your heart, you should come* was a Southernism with multiple meanings.

"Thanks. I'll see if I can get off work." It sounded like one of Austin's noncommittal yeses. He wasn't likely to show, and my mother wouldn't miss him.

On our walk to the parking lot behind the gym, Austin gushed about meeting Honey.

I took his hand. "I can't believe you told Honey Dean you thought she was a drag queen to her face. I'm probably going to get a call from Mom about that tomorrow."

Austin chuckled. "Straight talk is how I keep it one hundred. Besides, Honey liked it. She's a glam girl. Your mama's pretty too. Very classy. She's a little reserved, though, huh?"

"You need to approach her less directly. Let her come to you."

"It was a bit like hugging a cat."

"She's definitely not a hugger."

"So that's what's wrong with you."

"What's that supposed to mean?" I said in mock outrage.

"Just psychoanalyzing you." His expression was pure mischief.

"I'll have you know, my dad's a hugger."

"Hmm. That might be more fun to unpack."

I wasn't surprised to discover Austin drove a yellow Jeep. It was exactly the type of vehicle I would've chosen for him if I were writing him as a character. People who drove yellow cars were said to be joyful, sunny, and young at heart. Not afraid to be noticed.

I was always researching that kind of psychological trivia.

Once I'd climbed in and buckled my seatbelt, Austin pointed to my red sneakers on the floor behind the driver's seat.

"Dorothy and Glinda, I presume?"

"Aren't those names perfect?" He was way too pleased with himself.

I shook my head, unable to suppress a grin.

Austin plugged a media cable into his phone, and while I gave him general directions to my place, he started scrolling through a music app. "This is for you." He grinned and peeled out.

I braced myself for the country playlist he'd threatened to make for me, but I recognized the familiar opening guitar riff. The volume was deafening—I could feel the bass in my lungs—but it was an old song I loved and hadn't heard in a while. With the windows down, the breeze blowing across my skin, and the endorphins from the workout still buzzing in my veins—not to mention the high of being with Austin—the part of my mind that observed the story content in everyday life said *this* was a perfect moment.

The second song was another favorite, one I always turned up in the car when it came on. I could've sworn he'd accessed my own streaming account.

I told him to take the next turn, and asked, "When did you have time to make this playlist?"

"You like it?"

I nodded.

"I made it a few years ago for my dad."

I shot him some side-eye.

"What? You guys like the same shit."

AUSTIN PULLED into the driveway behind my truck. "Wow," he said, peering through the windshield. "I freaking love Craftsman houses."

"Yeah? It was built in 1929."

"It's awesome."

I'd had a rule for years that I didn't bring men to my house. On the few occasions I'd hooked up with someone, I always insisted I couldn't host. If things in the bedroom didn't work out, I didn't want to find myself in the position of having to get rid of someone. I preferred being able to leave when I wanted.

Austin had broken his rule for me, so I invited him to come inside.

I left my shoes in his Jeep. I'd remembered they were there, but I preferred him having them. At least for a while longer.

As he followed me up the walk to the front door, he said, "I can't believe I met your mom on our first date."

"Me either. I think I may need to process it with my therapist." I unlocked the door. "And for the record, we spent three nights together, so I'm not sure this qualifies as our first date."

21

"PROF." AUSTIN TIPTOED INTO THE FOYER, HIS VOICE HUSHED and reverent. "This place is so cool."

"Thank you. My ex always said old houses were *depressing money pits*." Even if Charles wasn't there to hear it, I still gloated. "He said my love of them was *maudlin*."

Austin sneered. "Who the fuck even talks like that?" He walked over to the staircase and touched the banister. "This woodwork is amazing. Is this all original, like, from back in the day?"

"We had to replace some of the wood, but we tried to restore everything with as much historical accuracy as possible." Conscious of having used the word *we* so soon after mentioning my ex, I hastened to clarify. "Ben helped me with the restoration."

"Ben, like *Eric-and-Ben* Ben?"

I nodded. "That's how we became friends. This kind of carpentry is his specialty."

"Right on."

"We just finished our final project, the upstairs

bathroom. You'll have to check it out. No one else has seen it yet."

Austin turned toward the living room. "Holy shit!" He bounded over to the fireplace and stared up at the framed print of Van Gogh's *The Starry Night* hanging above the mantle. He pointed at it, mouth hanging open, looking to me as if he wanted me to confirm he wasn't imagining it. "I have this same painting! I swear to God. I could drive you over to my apartment right now and prove it, but I have a buddy that's kinda subletting, and it's a total dump compared to your place, so I'm not sure you'll ever be allowed to see it now."

I laughed. "I believe you."

"Mine's just a poster, though."

"Oh, that's a print. Obviously." I chuckled. "The original is hanging in the MoMA. Fifth floor if I remember correctly." I sounded like a pompous know-it-all. "Have you been?"

"No, but I'd love to see it." His eyes lit up. "We should go."

"Okay." I wasn't sure how serious he was, but thinking about us taking a trip in the future left me flustered.

If he'd noticed, he didn't let on. He leaned in toward the print, hands behind his back as if he were in a museum. "It looks so good in an actual frame and everything. Mine's kind of a raggedy mess. I've had it since high school. It was one of the only things I brought from home when I left for college. It's been in every dorm room and shitty apartment I've lived in since. And it's always been stuck on the wall with double-sided tape. I'm such a tacky bastard. But no matter where I live, not counting the bunkhouse, that poster is the one thing that makes me feel at home." He turned his dark eyes on me and smiled like I'd hung it there as a gift for him.

His presence in my house was ordinary but also surreal. A week ago, I hadn't even known he existed. "I've had mine since high school too. It wasn't always in that frame. The first time Charles—that's my ex—saw it on the wall in my dorm room freshman year, he called it *juvenile*."

Austin pulled a face. "He kinda sounds like a dick."

"Oh, he's definitely a dick."

With my advance from *The Boy Who Didn't Come Back*, I'd put a down payment on a modern, new-build condo Charles had fallen in love with. I'd had the print framed, but Charles insisted the image simply didn't *go* anywhere. Neither had I.

We'd had our own dressing rooms in parallel wings on either side of the en suite bathroom, enormous walk-in closets with windows, skylights, and cedar-paneled walls. Since it was the only space with anything remotely resembling cozy woodwork and since it was bigger than any bedroom or office I'd ever had, I put a small desk and Chesterfield armchair in mine, and I hung the print where Charles would never have to see it. He'd had few reasons to come into my dressing room, and it became my sanctuary.

I'd been ashamed for anyone to know that a closet was my only space in a property I'd paid for with my own money.

Later, when I'd first peeked in through the front windows of this house before the realtor had arrived to let me in, I saw the mantel and envisioned *The Starry Night* there. The day I'd moved in, I'd hung it right away before I'd carried in the first box of my other possessions.

I didn't have to defend loving it to Austin. "What a crazy synchronicity."

I let Austin wander wherever he wanted and followed him. He commented on architectural details—which pleased me, considering how much expense, effort, and thoughtfulness had gone into them—and he complimented the decor, which I humbly accepted. My furniture was mostly practical and a little on the sparse side.

He also noticed unique items among my favorite things —an Eveready flashlight from the 1920s, the elevation maps of local mountain ranges hanging in the dining room, the Amish table and matching hutch. He even pointed out the dovetails and box joints.

Surprised and excited by his frame of reference, I started to babble, sharing stories about where I'd discovered certain treasures, how in some cases I'd rescued them from thrift shops and garage sales, paying small token amounts that made them all the more precious.

When we reached the kitchen, I offered him something to drink, and we stood sipping bottles of water with the island between us.

Austin looked around and sighed. "If somebody could build the dream home in my head, it'd be just like this. You have stories about your things. It's like your life is an ongoing treasure hunt, and your house is your own personal museum." Austin picked at the label on his water bottle. "I'd love to have a place like this someday. I thought I would've been a little closer by now."

His view of my life humbled me. "You'll get there. I've had a bit more time to work on it."

"Still, I bet when you were my age, you had your shit figured out."

I huffed. "By the time I was your age—God, I can't believe I just said that—I'd already been living with Charles for years. We were never technically married but close enough. When I look back on that time, it feels like I wasted my twenties. I definitely didn't have my shit figured out. I still don't. I didn't really start putting any of this together until after we'd broken up. This house was the first major asset that was mine alone. I shared the renovation work with Ben—platonically and professionally, of course—but this was my first project without any input from Charles. Now I'm the one talking about an ex," I muttered. "If it makes you feel any better, I bought this place in my midthirties. I had a mattress on the floor, one set of plain white CorningWare dishes I'd bought at a big box store, the Van Gogh print, my books, and my clothes."

"At least you already had a career." Austin walked over to my office door and leaned against the frame, peering into the room as if he sensed it was haunted. My daily dread and feelings of failure must have started to linger like the stench of cigarette butts in an ashtray.

With more windows than walls, the office had originally been a small sunroom. It was austerely furnished with a Shaker desk and hanging baskets of philodendron. The usual clutter found in offices and studies that most people considered charmingly *professory* gave me anxiety. I couldn't stand the distracting visual chaos of overstuffed bookcases, and I didn't want anyone's work—including my own— taunting me while I tried to write. I'd hung covers of my novels, along with my degrees, in my office on campus where they could impress those who would be impressed by such things. No one would have ever seen them here anyway.

Austin wouldn't find any evidence of my doctorate to undermine his nickname for me. If he found out, he'd undoubtedly start calling me *Doc,* and I wasn't sure I could endure that. I preferred students address me as *Professor* instead of *Doctor*.

Austin nodded toward the open laptop on my desk. "How's the new book coming?"

I joined him at the door, mirroring his pose, leaning in and looking around as if I might miraculously spot an answer on the floor like a forgotten wad of paper. "Who are you, my agent?"

Austin shifted position to face me, his weight on one leg, the other hip cocked. "I bet I'd make a killer agent. You said yourself I'm good at motivating people, and I'm even better at harassing them."

I rolled my eyes. "I believe it."

"I could specialize in working with surly male authors." He laughed at my glare. "Jody Summers was kind of a crabby old bitch, but he loved me. He was always asking Jim to send me to his place to do random chores."

"I'll bet he was."

"Nah, it really wasn't like that. Most of the time, he wanted somebody to listen to him. He made a lot of diva demands, but I could usually convince him he didn't want whatever it was he thought he did. I was the only one on staff who thought he was funny. He'd go off on a rant, and everybody'd avoid making eye contact with him and try to scurry away. I just laughed at him. He pretended to be offended, but he loved it."

Who wouldn't have loved it?

Austin folded his arms across his chest. "So are you gonna tell me what your book's about?"

I sighed. "I wish I could. That's the million-dollar question sitting at the center of my world, and I have until the end of summer to find an answer. I took a sabbatical for spring and summer terms, but I've squandered half the time with absolutely nothing to show for it."

"Did they already pay you an advance?"

"No. Thank God. It's proven to be a mixed blessing. I originally had a three-book deal, but after the second book took off like a flightless bird, they canceled my contract."

"Harsh. Can they do that?"

"Oh, yeah. They can. So my *cool career* is pretty much back at square one. I still have an agent. Technically. Maybe. If I can pitch her something really good in the next few months."

Austin unfolded his arms and hooked a finger through one of my belt loops. "It's a sophomore slump. It happens to bands all the time." He pushed off the wall, planted his feet, and grabbed another belt loop with his free hand, the weight of his arms pulling our hips together. "You still have muscle memory. Your talent's still there. All your practice and experience. You just gotta get out of your head and into your body and let instinct take over."

"Believe me, I'd love nothing more than to be able to do that. I sit at that desk and stare out those windows, waiting for inspiration to come, but—" I shook my head. Why were we even talking about this? I should shut the hell up and get him upstairs.

"I can help you brainstorm," Austin murmured, brushing his lips against mine. "I come up with movie ideas all the time. Ask anybody."

I hummed. "I didn't invite you in so we could *brainstorm*." This would be the first time I ever kissed someone in this house.

"Maybe I can help you with something else." He covered my mouth with his and immediately parted my lips with his tongue. The deep, hungry kiss left me unbalanced on my feet when he pulled away. "But first I need to pee. Show me this new bathroom."

I directed Austin upstairs and followed him, staring at his butt and marveling at his calves. On the second-floor landing were doors to two bedrooms on either side and one large bathroom directly ahead. Houses from this era usually didn't have designated primary bedrooms with private en suites, but there was an additional door connecting my bedroom on the right.

The room was small, so I leaned against the sink counter while Austin admired the traditional hexagon-patterned black-and-white floors, the white subway tiles on the walls, and the original clawfoot tub.

"This is the prettiest bathroom I've ever been in," Austin said, whipping his dick out over the toilet. Where I could see it. He watched me watching him as he pissed, but it was more casually intimate than erotic. When he was finished, he shook himself off, handling his cock more than was necessary. He tore off a few squares of toilet paper and buffed the rim clean in a comically fastidious manner.

I chuckled at his performance.

"Excuse me." Before I could step out of the way, Austin reached for the faucet, brushing his arm against mine. He washed and dried his hands while making eye contact in the mirror.

It reminded me of watching him remove his horned headdress and makeup in the bathhouse the night we'd met. But in this moment, I did what I'd wanted to do then. I stepped behind him, slipped my arms under his, and encircled his belly. I nuzzled his cheek, my facial hair tickling his ear. "I jerked off into this sink thinking about you the other day. Right after I got home." I studied our reflection. "I can't say I love watching myself, but..." I pressed my crotch against his ass.

He covered my hands with his and gave me a filthy smirk. "I didn't think I'd want you to take me from behind because I like looking at you, but"—he pushed his ass back against my crotch—"this is kinda working for me." He turned in my arms and cupped my face. "But we'll have to come back to it. I gotta do something else first." He dropped into a deep squat so quickly I had to grab the edge of the vanity to steady myself.

I watched as he unbuttoned and unzipped my shorts, slipped his fingers into the waistband of my boxer briefs, and yanked everything down to my knees. My half-hard dick bounced out, and he caught the head between his lips.

He kept his mouth loose, warm, and wet with almost no suction at all. With his hands on the backs of my thighs, he pulled me into his throat. The sound of him trying not to gag was almost as hot as the sensation of the muscles spasming around the head of my cock.

He held me there. I caught myself holding my breath along with him, only I could never have lasted as long. Just as I began to worry he might asphyxiate, he pushed my hips away, dragged air into his lungs, and grinned up at me.

He swiped away the rope of spit connecting my dick to his lips and used it to wet my shaft, his loose fist making obscene squelching noises. The sensation was incredible.

Austin stopped to stand and pulled his shirt over his head.

I took mine off too.

He unlatched his belt buckle and attempted to drop his shorts, but they got hung up for a moment on the thick hook of his erection. He wasn't wearing any underwear, and once he'd freed his hard cock, he stepped out of his shorts, naked except for his Adidas.

"God, you look so hot like that."

He twisted his lips in a wry smile. "The one time I'm not wearing yours. I'll remember for another time."

Another time. It had crossed my mind that it might have been nicer to lie with him in my bed—it was less than twenty feet away—but there would be other times. Hopefully, this was only one of many.

I shoved my shorts and underwear down to my ankles, but unlike him, it was as far as I could go without taking off my shoes. I was hobbled. But we were eating one another's mouths with our cocks sliding together, and I didn't want to interrupt any of that.

Austin fumbled for my open dopp kit on the counter. For once, I'd been lazy with my unpacking and thankfully hadn't put everything away yet. He found the lube bottle and flipped open the top.

He broke the kiss. "Did you want to do this, or... can I just move things along?"

"Sure," I spluttered, not sure my dick would stay hard long enough to fuck him.

Austin reached back to lube himself, biting his tongue and making a silly face, and then he flipped around to our original position and pushed back against me.

My spit-slicked cock slid up the crease of his ass. The sensation was staggering, but I was already getting in my head wondering if there still might possibly be some ED medication in my system.

Austin's expression shifted. It was subtle, but he'd detected the worry in my eyes. "You're not going all the way in yet." His tone was nonchalant, cocky and confident. "Trust me. This'll be every bit as good."

He reached back and angled my cock down so I was encased between his thighs in a tunnel of hairy flesh. He crossed his ankles and clenched his leg muscles, tightening around me. He was a few inches taller than I was, the perfect height for an interfemoral fuck.

I wonder if he knows that word... Not the time for a vocabulary lesson, brain.

I pushed and then dragged my cock through the sticky, hairy tunnel between his ass, his taint, and his thighs, the head nudging his sac.

Damn. This *was* almost as good as fucking, and I didn't have to worry about how hard I was.

Austin grinned at me in the mirror, and as if he'd read my mind, said, "Right?"

"You feel incredible," I panted, clinging to his hips and thrusting, watching him—watching *us*—in the mirror.

Austin stood up straight and leaned back against my chest.

I opened my mouth and sank my teeth into the muscle at the base of his neck. I looked like some kind of predator. I wanted to bite him hard. I wanted to eat him alive.

He stroked himself over the sink basin, his balls pressed against the edge of the vanity, forced down and away from his cock. I loved the way that felt, a surprise benefit of the new, taller counter height.

"You think you can come?" he asked, his voice ragged.

Fuck, I was close. "Yeah."

"Do it."

His goading flipped a switch in me, and my legs started to tremble with my impending orgasm.

Austin stroked himself faster, his hand a blur.

I came hard, shuddering, my mouth open in a silent

expression of shock. Almost losing my balance, I hung on to him.

Austin cursed as his cum flew across the sink, one blast glazing the faucet, a few more disappearing against the white porcelain, the last of it coating his knuckles.

His gaze found mine in the mirror, he smiled, and I had no words.

22

WE HAD TO TAKE TURNS SHOWERING BECAUSE THE CLAWFOOT tub and circular curtain couldn't safely accommodate two grown men.

I'd never regretted a historically accurate design decision more.

"Do you wanna stay and"—I was so nervous to ask, my throat clicked—"hang out?"

"That'd be nice."

Austin had left his gym bag in the Jeep, but I assured him I could find some comfortable clothes that would fit him. I liked seeing him in my things.

Charles had never worn anything of mine, other than the few times he borrowed a jacket off the hook by the door to run out and grab mail in the rain.

My drawstring sweatpants clung to Austin's ass and cock even better than I'd hoped. He chose a ribbed white tank that showed off his muscular shoulders.

"Snacks and TV?" I asked.

"Sounds perfect." Austin kissed me. "You got any popcorn?"

"I have a popcorn cabinet," I bragged as I led him downstairs. "Well, it's a shelf in a cabinet, but it's the *entire* shelf."

I rarely had guests. Even when my mom or my sister stopped by, I followed them around with mild anxiety, trying to anticipate their every move or requirement, then felt relieved when they were gone. Despite the noticeable hush they left in their wakes.

I liked watching Austin move through my space. He inhabited my kitchen without reticence, opening cabinets until he found the drinking glasses, filling them with ice, and pouring us sodas. All the while chatting like he'd been here a hundred times before.

Where did you come from? I thought. *How are you here?*

His presence was both magical and gloriously mundane. Like he belonged here.

The thought was so recklessly hopeful I had to cover for it by mansplaining how best to microwave the popcorn. "A minute and nineteen seconds."

Austin ignored me, punched in two minutes on the clock, and hit Start.

"What are you—"

He lifted his chin. "You're supposed to listen and stop it when there are two full Mississippis between pops."

"Which, I am telling you, sir, is exactly one minute and nineteen seconds."

He lifted his chin. "We'll see."

I scowled, and he mimicked my expression with cartoonish exaggeration until I finally gave in and laughed at him.

As the timer neared the optimal number—which I'd perfected from countless attempts—I reached for the touchpad, but he batted my hand away. He cocked an ear, listening.

I crossed my arms and glared at him. *Stubborn fucker.*

He punched Stop at one minute and twenty seconds. "Perfect."

I rolled my eyes. "Oh, please. We both know I won that round."

I USED the room at the front of the house next to the living room as a den. It had originally been a bedroom, but we'd removed the door so it felt more like a passthrough.

I told Austin to sit wherever he liked, to make himself comfortable, but he insisted I claim my usual spot first.

I put my drink and the popcorn within reach on the coffee table and sat in the corner of the L-shaped sectional. Austin arranged a few pillows so he could lean back against me with his legs stretched out. He grabbed the cashmere throw folded over the back of the couch, sniffed it, and sighed. "Smells like you." He covered himself with it from feet to chin, and once he was settled, I draped my arm over his shoulder with my hand resting on his chest.

I smiled against his hair and clicked the TV remote.

Reno 911 appeared on the screen.

"I love this show!" Austin said excitedly.

I smiled. "I do too."

"Really? I figured you'd want to watch *Masterpiece Theater* or a documentary."

"I like those options fine, but I also particularly love a mockumentary. You wanna hear a confession?"

He tilted back his head to look up at me. "Always."

"I have a crush on Lieutenant Dangle," I whispered. "The one who always wears short-shorts."

"Yeah, he's cute, but I'm partial to Travis Junior." He sighed. "I swoon for a good mustache."

For years, I'd contended that one of the benefits of being single was not having to compromise on TV choices, but finding something to watch with Austin hadn't required a single second of negotiation.

Halfway through the second episode, he'd gone quiet. His chest rose and fell beneath my hand. Every few moments, he shifted, fighting sleep. I loved that he felt comfortable enough to fall asleep in my arms, but the electricity of his presence kept me awake.

I gently kissed the top of his head. "You wanna stay the night?"

He sat up quickly and turned to search my eyes. "You want me to?"

"Yeah." I kept my voice casual, even though my heart pounded so hard my eyeballs throbbed.

"I have to make it back to the lodge by nine. I'm terrible about sleeping through my alarm."

"I'll set one for you on my phone too. And I'll get you a new toothbrush."

We dropped off our dishes in the kitchen and headed upstairs.

"Do you have your own dental care cabinet?" he teased.

"No, but I do have a dental care storage tub." From the linen closet I produced a plastic container filled with all the swag I'd collected from twice-yearly cleanings. "What color do you want?"

"Red."

We stood side by side at the sink brushing our teeth, watching each other in the mirror. Compared to the last time we were there, the scene was comically wholesome.

"That was really hot earlier," he mumbled through a

mouthful of toothpaste. "The..." He spread his legs and thrust his hand between his thighs.

I spat and rinsed. "Intercrural coitus."

"It's an actual thing?"

"It's also called interfemoral sex. Thigh fucking."

"Femur. Leg bone. I get it." Austin nodded. "Bet nobody wants a thigh gap now, am I right?" He held up a hand.

"I'm not high-fiving you."

"Why not?"

I grinned. "I have to deny you something."

He shrugged. "I'm hard to say no to."

Austin followed me into the bedroom and helped me turn back the covers. Even though we'd already slept together, I was nervous about officially having him in my bed. But once we'd both climbed in and he'd snuggled against me with his head on my shoulder, it felt like the most natural thing in the world.

Austin slid his arm across my chest. "Do you usually sleep naked when you're home alone?"

"Honestly, never. I'm sure that's not the *hotness* you were hoping for."

"Stop." He nuzzled my jaw. "Trust me. I've found the hotness." He pressed his cock against my hip, kissed my neck, and purred softly against my ear.

I clutched his arm, holding it tight to my chest. "I don't want you to be disappointed, but"—I cleared my throat —"after the past several days, and the workout, and then the—"

"Intermural corsage?"

"Frottage." I chuckled. "I'm not so sure about my ability to go again."

Austin shushed me like he was soothing a cranky infant. "It's all good, Prof. I'm here for the cuddles, no matter what."

He exhaled a contented sigh. "This right here was my entire reason for coming to town."

More bluntness. So direct and yet so terrifyingly sweet. "Really?"

"I paid the trainer who usually teaches that class a hundred dollars to let me sub for her."

"You didn't."

"I did."

Well, Eric had nailed that. "Why the hell didn't you just ask me if I wanted to do this instead of making me fucking exercise?"

He laughed. "You loved it."

I hummed skeptically. "I wouldn't use the word *loved*. So you trying to get in at the gym was an elaborate cover story?"

"No, not at all. I'd like to work there as much as possible. But there's a... situation that could get messy." He paused, but I waited for him to go on. "I slept with the owner last year."

I gay-gasped.

Austin either missed the sarcasm or chose to ignore it. "Yeah. And I also slept with his husband."

I snorted.

"Separately, for the record. And, until today, I was completely unaware they were even together. Apparently, they're one of those couples who get off on cheating on each other and having a bunch of drama about it. They both approached me tonight, again separately, asking me to keep our last encounter on the DL, but while also hitting me up again. I don't know if it's a game, if they really don't know, or they're pretending they don't. I mean, I understand spice and cuckold kink or whatever, but with them it feels toxic. My gut says they're doing it wrong, you know? It's so unnecessary. I bet if they'd talk about it, they could have a healthy open marriage."

"You think open marriages are healthier?"

"Not necessarily in general. I'm sure it depends on the couple. But it has to be better than lying to your husband." He threaded our hands together on my chest. "Like, I'd want it to be just us, at least for a while. Not some arrangement where we're essentially roommates in competition to sleep with tons of guys behind each other's backs. I mean, I'll never say never to bringing in others for fun times because I'd do whatever to make my partner happy. I just... I guess I'm kinda old-fashioned when it comes to marriage. It's hard to explain. But for me, it's more about loyalty than sex."

He used us *as an example.* Was this emotional safety? I exhaled. "Charles fucked my teaching assistant, Jasen. I call him *Jasen with an e* because that's the way he introduced himself. It started off as a fond, teasing nickname, but it ended up as a bitter, petty insult."

Austin squeezed my hand.

"Anyway. Jasen was like a little brother to me. Looking back, I was probably inappropriately close to him. I was the one who included him in our lives, invited him for meals with us, and suggested he stay and sleep on the couch when we'd been drinking. I knew people whispered about us, the gay couple with the younger guy in and out of their house. I'd been Charles's student when our relationship started, so I'd learned to tune out the faculty gossip.

"One night, after the three of us had split five bottles of wine, Charles had to put me to bed. I'd sensed something was going on between them, and I'd drank more than usual. He'd tucked me in with a bottle of water and some Tylenol —suspiciously nurturing for him—and then he'd said he didn't want to leave our guest alone.

"I knew what was going to happen. I blurted out, 'Please don't fuck him.'" Charles told me to stop being paranoid and to go to sleep. And then he'd gone downstairs and done it. Done him. Jasen with an *e*.

"A week later, he left me for him. Blamed it on my ED and my weight gain. Four months later, they were married. Something Charles had maintained he never wanted. He'd said gay marriage was unnecessary. And he'd always referred to it as *gay marriage* too as if it were a different institution. Almost as if he agreed with those who opposed marriage equality."

"Prof," Austin whispered. "He wasn't the right person." He didn't offer any other platitudes or commiserate with a tragic relationship story of his own. He just listened.

I sighed. "No, he wasn't." Keeping hold of his hand, I turned beneath his arm and he assumed a big-spoon position against my back. "You know, cuddling in my bed is a damn good upgrade from the tent."

"Hell yeah, it is." He pushed his knees deeper into the space behind mine, sealing the contact along the entire length of our legs. He even flexed his feet to hold my soles. "But shout out to the air mattress with the headboard."

I smiled.

Knowing he had to get up early and head out, I lay silently replaying our conversation about marriage.

I reveled in the simple reality of lying next to him—his scent muddled with the smell of my body wash, the sound of his breathing, the gravity well of his body on the mattress.

The writer in me wanted to catalog every aspect of this experience and commit it to memory. I hadn't written about anything like this before because nothing like this had ever happened to me. I didn't know when or if it might happen again, but I couldn't help but imagine what it might be like if this were every Wednesday night.

Oh, romantic fantasy, you fucking drug.

I'd assumed Austin had already drifted off, so I startled when he spoke. "What's your first book about? *The Boy Who Didn't Come Back.*"

"It's set in the early eighties. It's about an eleven-year-old kid named Eddie who goes missing for a few days and returns claiming to have found a doorway into another world. Eddie insists that his father, who disappeared years before, is there. Nobody believes him, of course. But his teacher, Mr. Kirkwood, recognizes details about the world Eddie describes that correspond to a series of obscure British fantasy novels written in the early twentieth century. Eddie's determined to return to the other world and bring back his father. Mr. Kirkwood follows him, thinking to protect him, and he discovers that Eddie's been telling the truth. The other world is real. And Mr. Kirkwood is faced with his own choice to stay or return."

Austin's silence compelled me to go on. "When I was a kid, I always wondered why Dorothy wanted to go back to black-and-white Kansas so badly. And why was Aslan such a bastard, kicking the Sons of Adam and the Daughters of Eve out of Narnia and making them go back to postwar England? I wanted to challenge that particular trope in portal fiction, that the protagonist always wants to go home." I wasn't sure if I'd lost Austin entirely. "You know what I mean by *portal fiction*, right?"

I felt him nod against the pillow. "I've never heard the exact term before, but yeah. Why's it set in the eighties?"

"Because it's also a story about a gay man who has the chance to escape the AIDS epidemic at a time when there was no escape. My kindergarten teacher died of AIDS very suddenly a few years after he'd taught me. He was my favorite teacher of all time. The book was my way of trying to save him."

"Wow. That's really sweet. Heavy, but... What's the other book about?"

"*Divining Virginia* is about a grad student who's researching Virginia Woolf's diaries and discovers she has the ability to channel the author's spirit through automatic writing. Or she thinks she does. I played with the boundary between belief and delusion."

Austin sighed. "Can I be honest with you?"

Oh, God. You never want to hear that. "Of course."

"Your books sound"—he made a skeptical noise —"kinda gloomy."

"*Gloomy?*" I repeated more defensively than I would've liked. I'd told him Charles called my love of old houses *gloomy.* Had the word stuck in his subconscious, or was he fucking with me?

"Yep. Way too fucking gloomy."

I huffed. "Thank you so much for that candid feedback. It's really valuable coming from someone who hasn't read a single word of either of my books."

"That's just it." Austin propped up on his elbow behind me. I felt him looking down at me, but I didn't turn to meet his eyes. "I don't have to read it to know if I'd *want* to read it. The people who haven't read a book yet are the ones you have to convince to buy it, right?"

Fuck me. He had a point.

"Think about movie trailers. You watch two minutes of highlights and you're, like, 'Damn, bro. I wanna see that.' Or, like, you hear an elevator speech and you're like 'I'm in.' You know what I mean?"

I did. But I didn't need him to mansplain it to me. "It's called a pitch. An elevator pitch."

Austin snapped his fingers. "Right. Okay." He kicked off the covers and sat up. "Lemme pitch you a couple of story ideas off the top of my head."

I repositioned the pillows so I could lean against the headboard. "This should be interesting. Go for it." *I may have to kill him if he comes up with something genuinely good.*

Austin spread his hands. *Picture this.* "This guy has the hots for his roommate's dad. He's been lusting over him and fantasizing about him for months, and then—boom—the power goes out at the dad's place. Or something happens with the plumbing. It doesn't matter. Anyway, the dad has to come sleep over at his son's apartment, and the roommate accidentally-on-purpose runs into the dad getting out of the shower—"

"Okay, wait. Let me stop you right there." My knee-jerk fear that Austin might prove to be a literary savant had clearly been a moment of insanity. "Is this a story-story or a jack-off story?"

"It's a love story," Austin said like it should have been obvious.

"At what point does the romantic element become a driver of the plot? Are we talking in the first few chapters, near the twenty percent mark, the halfway point, or—"

"Nah. Later. Closer to the end."

"Hmm." I tilted my head. "That sounds very sexually focused to me. No disrespect to authors of erotica—there are gorgeous examples of craft to be found among erotic works—but I don't really think that's the right lane for my brand at this particular phase of my career."

"Really?" Austin looked genuinely shocked. "I'm already

dying to read this story. Are you sure I can't convince you to write it for me?"

"I really don't think you could." At least I'd found something else he wanted that I could say no to.

"You could write it for shits and giggles. You know, like, post it on a blog somewhere for free. That way it's more likely to go viral."

I pinched the bridge of my nose. "I really don't think you understand how publishing works."

"Or"—Austin ignored me, bulldozing on—"plot twist. The younger guys are a couple, and the dad's a serial killer who's been stalking his son's boyfriend, the guy."

"Can we give him a name other than *the guy*? Or maybe call him Guy?"

"The son's gone to sleep, and *Guy*'s getting out of the shower when the dad sneaks up behind him and garrotes him with a piano wire."

"Should I be worried about inviting you to sleep here? The verb *garrote* is really specific. Where the hell did you even pick that up?"

"True crime shows. Here's another one. This young guy —we'll call him Toby—is staying at a cabin he found on Airbnb, this big blizzard hits, and he gets snowed in with no power. He burns all the logs in the fireplace and all the ones stacked on the hearth, and he's outside trying to split more wood. He's really struggling, it's getting dark, and he's starting to panic."

"Wait. Hold up. Why can't he chop wood?"

"He's a little college twink. Like a book nerd with no upper body strength."

"Excuse me, *sir*. Why can't Toby be a literary type who happens to be strong from doing lots of carpentry and renovations on his house?"

"Mm." Austin pulled a regretful face and shook his head. "No. He doesn't have a house. He still lives in the dorms. He's a student, remember? He hasn't reached his daddy phase yet. Suddenly, this sexy, older lumberjack dude shows up. Frank. He lives in the woods nearby, and he's been spying on Toby. Frank goes over to check and see if Toby needs anything, and Toby asks him if he can help him split firewood. Frank takes off his shirt, and he's enormous, beefy, hairy, and he looks really hot chopping wood—like, it's shot in slow motion and shit"—I didn't bother to interrupt him with the crushing news that there is no *slo-mo* in books —"and of course they end up having sex in front of the fire."

"Of course."

"But then—twist—we find out Frank's been hiding out in this remote area for years because he's wanted for murder. One he committed with an ax."

"And how do we find that out?"

"Toby sees a story about it on the internet."

"I thought the power was out."

"He sees it on his phone. And he's like"—Austin shifted his voice to an impersonation that sounded even more *bro* than usual with a touch of Kardashian vocal fry—"'Oh, no. I've already fallen for this sexy lumberjack daddy, and now I have to kill him in self-defense.' But he has no choice. It's the only way he'll get home alive."

"Back to the dorm in time for winter term to start," I added.

"Right." Austin was immune to my sarcasm. "And his friends all start to worry about him. He's not the same. He's tormented—no, *haunted*—by everything that went down over break. He keeps thinking he sees Frank everywhere. It turns out, the lumberjack may not really be dead after all but stalking him forever more."

"So it's dark erotica/instalove romance/psychological thriller/horror?"

"Yes! Suspenseful. Like *Gone Girl* but gay. And with a ton of sex."

I grimaced.

Austin rattled off another implausible premise that began with *a ton of gay sex* and ended in a murder-suicide. When I asked if all his ideas started out like porn from the pre-internet era, he said, "Sex sells."

"Okay, but why all the surprise murder?"

"People love love stories. And they love murder. I'm thinking, combine the two... Boom. Brilliant."

"You don't consider all this gore to be a little on the gloomy side?"

"No, because they're crimes of passion. People get off on that way more than the emo shit you discuss with your therapist."

"I think *you* might need to discuss *your* shit with a therapist," I muttered.

"They're killer ideas."

"Literally."

"All right off the top of my head."

"You plucked them right out of thin air. I was here."

"Imagine what I could come up with if I stared out the window for several hours every day."

"Oh, fuck you." I launched a pillow at his face. "That was a low blow. For the record, you typically don't kill off main characters. Especially not in a love story. Audiences don't like that."

"Ah-ha, but see, that's why it's so cool. It's totally unpredictable. People will sit in the theater stunned for like ten minutes as the credits roll."

"I am a novelist, not a filmmaker."

"Maybe you should aim higher. If you write more exciting stories, they'll be more likely to get made into movies."

"Wow." I didn't know whether I should be fuming or laughing. I had no comeback.

"Email my pitches to your agent and see what they say." Austin karate-chopped the pillow I'd thrown at him and lay down with a satisfied sigh. "I don't mind if you pretend they're yours. I've got tons of them." He turned onto his side and curled away from me.

"Well, putting aside the problematic graphic content, I can tell you with certainty she'll say that this kind of mixing of genres makes it impossible to sell a book. It's too difficult to market."

"You gotta stop coming from a place of no, Prof." A yawn distorted his voice. "Choose to be positive."

"You're right. They're fantastic ideas," I said woodenly. "For another author."

"I forgive you for being ungrateful." He cracked an eyelid to peer at my reaction, failing to hide a grin. "Now shut up and spoon me." He reached back and grabbed my hand, pulling my arm around him like I was a blanket.

I lay beside him, matching my breaths to his, basking in his presence in my bed.

I'd known him less than a week—barely five days—but it felt like we'd been doing this for months.

It wasn't a holiday anymore, just an ordinary Wednesday night. And even though he knew fuck all about story craft, I could get used to this.

23

IN THE EARLY MORNING, WHILE THE SKY WAS STILL DARK, WE rolled around in a tangle of sheets making out until the alarms we'd set went off. Rushing to get Austin out of the house on time for work distracted me from having to say goodbye to him again.

I'd always thought of my home as a sanctuary, but it felt too quiet in his wake. I bore the evidence of our hours together in sore muscles and chapped lips. As I poured a second cup of coffee, I glanced at the clock, already calculating how many more hours it might be before I heard from him. Part of me was certain he'd text later, but a small voice whispered, *What if he ghosts me?*

I shook my head. Obsessing over him was a manifestation of resistance, a diversion from writing.

Despite the late-night brainstorming session with Austin —or maybe because of it—I spent the rest of the morning filling the pages of an untitled document with fragments of interfemoral sex and details of sharing my bed with him. My inner critic nagged and berated me about the futility of the exercise, but I clung to a small fierce faith in the power of practice.

At noon, my phone pinged with a notification. I snatched it up to find a long text from Austin with another rambling story idea. This one featured a runner who hooks up with a person on a dating app marked as less than a hundred feet away. One morning, the guy comes back from a run to find his neighbor waiting for him in his house face down, ass up.

I responded, *Since I assume this is a precursor to horrific bloodshed, I decline to be turned on.*

Smiling like a purple devil emoji, I abandoned my office to make a sandwich and banter with Austin about common foreign language terms for various sex acts until he had to go back to work.

I lost the afternoon to procrastination cleaning and scrolling Austin's social media.

I FELL asleep on the couch watching TV, trying to stay up until he called.

Finally, a little after midnight, the phone rang.

"Sorry. It took me forever to get out of the Hole. I was hoping since it was Thursday night after a holiday weekend, everybody'd knock off early, but Sawyer doesn't want us to close if there's so much as one guest in there. And that guy was a talker. Did I tell you Sawyer's booed up with Luke?"

He had, but happy to hear his voice, I listened as he rattled on about the relationship between the campground owner and the young musician. Having been distracted by my own adventures over the weekend, I hadn't been fully aware of how captivated the staff were by this workplace affair.

When he wasn't trying to pack a story with the shock and awe of improbable violence, Austin was pretty entertaining. Although his segues could use some work. Out of nowhere, he said, "It's our one-week anniversary."

"My longest relationship in years." Taken off guard, I'd reached for a quip, but when I heard his forced laugh, I regretted making light of it. "Quite the milestone, huh? Although *anno* is Latin for *year*, so it's not technically an *anniversary*." I could've kicked myself for being such a know-it-all. I tried to soften it with some humble ignorance. "I know it's called a *mensiversary* when it's been a month, but I'm not sure what the equivalent is for a week."

Austin let out a long-suffering sigh. "Way to kill my weekiversary boner, Prof." He chuckled. "What have you been up to?"

Writing four thousand words about having sex with you and stalking your selfies online. "Oh, you know, going through the motions of my writing practice."

"Awesome!"

"Well, it's nothing I can really use."

"It's not nothing. All practice is progress."

"It would be if I were practicing on an actual project."

"Why don't you write about a handsome, nerdy professor who goes to a naked campground and meets a spunky younger man?"

"One that starts with a string of sex scenes and ends with them butchered in a tent by a serial killer?"

"Damn, Prof. You can be so fucking *gloomy* sometimes," he teased. "It's a love story. An MM romance. That stands for *male-male*."

"I know what MM romance is." My sister Veronica was a voracious reader of the genre and brought it up every time I mentioned writing. I could only imagine what would happen if the two of them ever put their heads together and decided to gang up on me.

"Remember when I was telling you about Jody Summers, and I said there was another author who came here too? Well, he writes romances set at the campground. Of course, he changes all the names and stuff, but we all know it's about us. I'm definitely gonna buy the next one and see if he put me in it."

"But are you going to read it?" I deadpanned.

"Har, har. I'm gonna read the sex scenes. Out loud. To you. Over the phone."

"Please do. That'd be priceless."

We chatted for almost two hours, most of it silly, dueling banter about everything and nothing. At one point, he pretended to argue that adaptations began as movies and TV shows, and if they were popular enough they were made into books. Eventually, we both agreed to get some sleep, and I reluctantly said goodbye.

I DIDN'T REGRET HAVING SPENT the time with him, but I was exhausted the next morning. No amount of coffee could've forced meaningful words from my brain. I convinced myself it would be a good day for admin tasks.

I responded to a few emails I'd been avoiding from the English department about the classes I was scheduled to teach during the fall semester. The looming end of my sabbatical depressed me.

I checked my phone for the hundredth time, but there was no response to my text wishing Austin a good day.

I tried to take a nap, thinking it'd be easier to pass the time until I could talk to him again if I were unconscious, but my mind raced. I read for a bit, but I resented the author for having inspired ideas and polished prose. I even broke down and listened to a guided meditation that purported to help release creative blocks, but the narrator's simpering tone grated on my nerves.

With a burst of manic motivation, I decided to take Austin's advice and go for a walk. Exercising again would be the quickest way to work through the soreness in my muscles. I put on some of the new workout clothes I hadn't worn yet, grabbed my wireless earbuds, and before I could change my mind, set off down the street.

Choosing the hottest part of the day was a total rookie move, but I'd already waved to two of my neighbors, so I couldn't exactly turn around without looking like a fool. I felt on display like the occupants of every car that passed were thinking, *Oh, good for him. He looks like he needs it.*

Impostor syndrome and performance anxiety even affected my ability to walk down the fucking street.

When the health app on my phone reported I'd gone a mile, I turned around and headed back. I hadn't expected an instant transformation, but it was every bit as daunting as writing—one tiny turn of a hamster wheel that would require days and weeks and months of sustained discipline to produce any results.

But there was one reward—being able to tell Austin I'd done it and hearing his praise.

I passed the rest of my Friday grocery shopping, making myself dinner, eating it alone in front of the TV, and incessantly checking my phone.

Eric texted wanting *the scoop* about Wednesday night. Mom and Veronica both sent reminders about Sadie's birthday party the next day, but still nothing from Austin.

. . .

I MUST HAVE ANSWERED the phone in my sleep because Austin was already talking. "I thought of the perfect song for you."

"What?"

"Well, I'm kinda debating whether it suits your voice or mine."

"What time is it?"

"Lemme sing it for you, and you can tell me what you think." Austin brayed the chorus to "Wonderwall" in what he must have believed was a Mancunian accent.

I held the phone away from my ear and glanced at the time. It would have been torture to hear anyone sing that song at one in the morning, let alone him. I chose my words carefully. "You... killed that."

"Thanks, Prof!" Austin said without a trace of irony. "Now you try it. It's an audition. Whoever sings it best gets to claim it."

"I'm not singing."

"Why not? Nobody's gonna hear you but me."

"No way. It's not happening."

"But it's such a great song for karaoke."

"Is it? I'm not sure anyone should be sustaining vowels for *that* long in public."

"You have a great voice. Even listening to you talk turns me on." He hummed. "I wish I had enough bars out here for us to video chat. We could jack off together." His breaths sounded like gusts of hot wind.

"Are you *playing* with yourself right now?" I teased.

"I can't help but play with myself when we talk on the phone."

I pictured him standing out on the road with his shorts pushed down around his thighs, pulling on his cock. "We were on the phone last night for almost two hours."

"Well, it wasn't *the whole time,* just part of it. Until I got off."

My voice went up an octave. "At what point did that happen?"

"When we were talking about you writing a book about us. If you wrote some sex scenes, you could try them out on me."

What would he say if I pulled up the pages I'd written about him? I chickened out, blaming it on my laptop being downstairs. "I'm not sure I can handle any more feedback from you about my writing." I also didn't love the thought of all the men who might be watching him. Men who were right there at the campground, steeped in the collective sexual ambience, riding the edge of arousal for days. Men who were on the hunt and available while I was here. "Put your dick away. You're gonna get mosquito bites in places you really don't want them."

Austin laughed. "Yeah, the light on the pole is the only one for miles. I'm kinda asking for it. I need to go take a shower anyway."

Austin showering at the campground surrounded by easy opportunities was worse than him putting on a show at the pole. I tried to sound nonchalant. "Go shower."

"I will. I'm buying some time. There were a few staff groupies lurking around in Bathhouse One earlier, up by the bunkhouse."

"Well, that's bullshit." It was one thing if he was getting attention because he wanted it, but it was another situation entirely if he didn't.

Austin hummed. "It kinda goes with the territory."

"You still have a right to privacy."

"Yeah, but it takes a lot of energy to be pissed off all the time. I don't care if people look. Hugs and pats don't bother me as long as they don't cross a line."

I got out of bed and started pacing. I was fuming. "Is management aware of this?"

"Calm down, Karen. Sawyer and Jim have our backs. If guests don't act right, they will throw their asses out. The first weekend I worked here, right in the middle of dinner service when my hands were full with iced tea pitchers, this dude got on his knees in front of me and tried to unzip my shorts. Sawyer saw him, yanked the motherfucker off the floor, dragged him out of the dining room, and screamed at him in the lobby for five minutes. He told the dude's friends he could stay in his cabin and sleep it off, but he'd be checking out first thing in the morning. Sawyer can be scary as fuck."

"Well... good." As long as someone was looking out for him.

"Listen, I chose to work here. And up until a week ago, I was ready to go all in on the debauchery. You heard the guys. They totally outed me in the pool that night."

"I don't want you to miss out on anything." A part of me did.

"The only thing I'm missing is you."

Fuck. I wanted to see him again, and I didn't want to wait until Wednesday. I wasn't exactly dying to introduce a guy I'd known for a week to my entire family—there was no telling how *that* would go—but... I wanted to keep this going.

"Prof? You're awfully quiet over there. You beating off?"

"No," I scoffed. "I was thinking. I'm not sure if you were serious about coming to my niece's birthday party tomorrow, but... do you want to go with me?"

"Ah, damn!" Austin laughed.

My heart sank. "It's cool if you can't. If my mom asks, I'll tell her—"

"I was gonna surprise you! I asked off. I have to be back in time for dinner service tomorrow, but yeah. I'd love to come."

"Yeah? Okay. Cool." For emotional safety, there sure was a lot of whiplash.

24

"TA-DA!" AUSTIN STEPPED THROUGH MY FRONT DOOR wearing a red-and-white gingham button-down with the sleeves ripped off, tight denim cut-offs, and work boots. "I wore my picnic shirt."

"You did." When I pulled him to me for a kiss, I noticed he'd also doused himself with extra cologne.

"You said it was a cookout." His lips twisted. "Too hoochie?"

"Not at all," I lied. *Jesus Christ, he's going to meet my entire family dressed like the Dukes of Hazard's gay cousin.* "You look great."

"You always look handsome," Austin said, adjusting the collar of my polo shirt. "I didn't know if I was supposed to bring anything or if there'd be alcohol, but I've got a twelve-pack of Blue Moon in the Jeep. I was gonna pick up some flowers for your sister, but I didn't know what her color story might be, and all they had at the convenience store were some sad-looking bouquets of carnations with baby's breath." He grimaced.

"That was very thoughtful. The beers'll be great.

Veronica's having barbecue catered. I'm sure a few people will bring sides and other drinks, but I usually pick up extra bags of ice on my way. That's my go-to for family gatherings. I've managed to keep their expectations of me pretty low."

Knowing we wouldn't have many private moments, I stole a few kisses before we headed out and a few more in my truck after we'd stopped for ice.

Pulling into Veronica's neighborhood, I experienced a cold flash of nerves. I glanced at the pale skin at the tops of Austin's thick, tanned thighs, where the tips of his pockets were peeking out of his denim shorts. He caught me looking.

"What?" he asked.

I shook my head, *Nothing*.

He reached over and pinched my knee. "Don't worry. They're gonna love me."

I hummed skeptically. Other than my mom, I'd only seen him interact with drunk horny men on vacation, jocks at a workout class, and Honey Dean, Queen of the Edgewood Gays. "Well, if you could refrain from assigning people nicknames they're not already aware of, that'd be great. And, for the love of God, don't hug my mom this time."

"Women love my hugs."

"She didn't."

"Everybody loves my hugs."

"Just... trust me about her, okay?"

"Can I hug your dad, then?"

He was aggravating me. I hoped.

"What?" His innocent expression did little to hide the mischievous gleam in his eye. "You said he was a hugger."

I groaned. "Don't make it weird."

. . .

VERONICA'S DRIVEWAY was full of cars, and I had to park along the street a few houses away.

As soon as he jumped out of the truck, Austin cocked his head. "What's that?"

I listened, hearing distant music and someone singing. I recognized the voice as belonging to my brother-in-law, John.

"Is that what I think it is?" Austin's eyes lit up with excitement. He hoisted a bag of ice onto each shoulder the way I'd seen him do at the campground and headed toward the sound. "How could you keep this from me?"

With a sinking feeling, I recalled a few years back when there'd been a singing competition show on every network and platform. John, who'd been in bands in high school and college, had become obsessed with the idea of Sadie auditioning. My niece had a pretty voice, but she'd always been extremely shy. She hated getting up in front of people. As a little kid, she'd cried when we sang "Happy Birthday" to her.

I wouldn't have put it past John, but... surely not. "Don't get your hopes up," I told Austin. "My niece and her friends just graduated from high school. I'm pretty sure people their age would rather die than sing in front of their family."

In a singsong voice, Austin said, "When they get to college, they're gonna wish they'd practiced."

"Hey. I managed to obtain three degrees from three separate institutions without ever having performed a power ballad for a wasted crowd of my peers."

"And yet, you swear you don't have issues." Austin frowned with mock concern. "I believe you believe that."

When I opened the door in the tall wooden privacy fence, we were hit with the full force of unmistakable karaoke—my brother-in-law, John Meier, belting John

Mayer's "No Such Thing." I wondered how many of the guests were capable of appreciating that choice. Austin would've been over the moon if he'd known.

I held the door for him. He paused as he stepped past me, his face close enough we could've kissed. "*This* is why you always have a song ready." He waggled his eyebrows. "They're really gonna love me."

I groaned. I prayed he wasn't going to try too hard. When Mom detected someone trying too hard, she got a look on her face like she was smelling raw sewage.

We headed for the tables set up on the lower-level patio. Balloons, paper lanterns, and streamers hung from the trees and the gazebo in the middle of the lawn that John had transformed into a stage.

I smiled and nodded at the familiar and unfamiliar faces watching as we approached—Veronica and John's friends, a few people from my parents' country-club set, and my aunt and uncle from Stone Mountain. Thankfully, Aunt Corinne was sitting too far away to speak to. She'd made it known years ago that she disapproved of the profanity in my books. My niece was holding court with a group of teenagers on the deck above the patio as far away from her father's mortifying entertainment as they could get while still technically being present. My eleven-year-old nephew, David, and some kids his age appeared to be lighting a starter log in the firepit.

Austin said hello to Mom, who greeted him with a convincing smile and helpfully directed him to the drink coolers. Once he'd dropped the bags of ice, I introduced him to my dad, enunciating the name *Robert*. To his credit, Austin did not call him *Bob* or *Bobby*. Dad smiled warmly and shook Austin's hand.

John's song ended, and encouraged by the smattering of

polite applause, he announced he was going to "take it down a little bit" with his next selection, "Crash."

Austin cupped his mouth and whooped loudly. He turned to my dad and confessed what a great song he thought it was, and Dad—who probably had no idea who Dave Mathews was—agreed with him wholeheartedly.

I left them alone long enough to shove a few beers into the cooler. It was a little surreal—and only a little cringe-inducing—to watch Dad in his linen button-down and khakis, seemingly unfazed by Austin's quintessential *bear bro* outfit, chatting about music. Austin shared a love of nineties grunge with his own father; he had no way of knowing Dad's last CD purchase was Rod Stewart's *The Great American Songbook*.

Dad laughed at something Austin said, and I released a breath I hadn't realized I was holding.

Honey appeared in a cloud of perfume, squeezing my arm briefly with her manicured, bejeweled fingers before gliding past to greet Austin with a hug. Austin complimented her on her red jumpsuit, and she gushed about how they were *matching*. They clung to each other like long lost sorority sisters until my sister interrupted.

I introduced Austin to Veronica. He thanked her for having him and told her how stoked he was they'd rented a karaoke machine.

"You know, we didn't actually rent it." Veronica shot me a look. "John had to *buy* one." The edge to her voice told me this was an ongoing argument that would continue long after their guests were gone. "Now it gets to live forever in the garage apartment with all the other musical equipment he hoards."

"Really?" Austin grinned like this was great news to him. "I should go say hi while he's between tracks." He started walking toward the gazebo, but I stopped him. "What?" He looked back, eyebrows raised innocently.

"We just got here." In my mind, I pleaded with him. *Begged.*

Veronica intervened with a dismissive gesture. "Let him go. John hasn't been able to get anybody else to play with him."

I couldn't have stopped him anyway.

Veronica headed inside to check on the food but declined my offer to help with anything. Mom told me I could refresh the ice in her gin and tonic. She murmured her thanks, staring toward the gazebo where John and Austin stood with their heads together, grinning and chatting over a large binder.

I handed Mom her cup. "I wouldn't normally bring someone I just met, but since you invited him..."

"I thought maybe you'd brought him to make Charlie jealous."

"What? No. Why would you—wait. Please tell me you didn't invite Charles."

She held up a hand, defensive. "*I* didn't invite him. Veronica and Sadie ran into Charlie a few days ago, and Sadie asked him to come. He's her uncle too."

"He's *not* her uncle." This wasn't the first time I'd had to correct her about this.

"Well, she thinks of him as an uncle. You were together the whole time she was growing up."

"We broke up when she was eleven."

"Those were very formative years." She smoothed her hair. "Charlie and I still message on Facebook, you know."

Yes, I knew. She was forever repeating the story of how Charles had sent her a friend request, and how she couldn't have said no.

From the moment I'd brought Charles home to meet my parents, Mom had been charmed by his pretentiousness. When Charles and I had split up, my mother had pouted. She'd tried to convince me that Charles had simply *strayed*, that it happened *all the time*, and adults didn't end relationships over an *indiscretion*. She'd told me a story about one of her girlfriends whose husband had cheated and how they'd *worked through it*. The implication being that not only was it somehow *my* fault I'd been cheated on, but by refusing to forgive him, I was acting irrationally.

Now she leaned closer, her voice low and purring with gossip. "Their divorce was finalized last month."

I rolled my eyes. She'd kept me apprised of every increment of Charles and Jasen's break-up. I didn't care so much that she and Charles communicated, but it bugged the fuck out of me that she kept bringing up their marriage without ever acknowledging how he'd refused to even consider marrying me. Once, when the topic had come up with my parents at dinner, Charles had lectured us about how *embarrassed* he was for same sex couples seeking heteronormativity.

Mom took a prim sip of her drink. "I always predicted their age difference would prove to be too significant." Realizing she'd put her foot in it, she fluttered her lashes.

I watched her trying to calculate the age difference between Austin and me. Had she gotten anywhere close? Austin had a baby face, but facial hair tended to throw off people of my parents' clean-shaven generation.

In the gazebo, John and Austin high-fived, and John handed him a microphone.

Oh shit.

I recognized the opening bars of Leanne Womack's "I Hope You Dance." Austin had claimed it as one of the top three country ballads in his wheelhouse. At least it wasn't "Wonderwall."

Mom took the opportunity to walk away, leaving me standing alone in the middle of the yard. With everyone sitting at the tables on the patio and the deck behind me, I couldn't see anyone's reaction when Austin started to sing, but I *felt* them watching.

A bark of laughter escaped from the vicinity of Sadie and her friends. I closed my eyes, silently begging her to forgive me, then tried to arrange my features into a supportive smile for Austin's sake.

He sang to me the way he'd danced at me the night we'd met. When he danced, his skill was obvious, but when he sang...

He was so committed to the performance, so completely unselfconscious, I felt ashamed for caring what anyone else might think of him.

Veronica's voice startled me. "Please don't take this the wrong way. He's really cute, but his voice is..."

I completed her thought so she wouldn't have to. "Fucking terrible." I tried to sigh, but it turned into a laugh.

"Is he *pretending* to be that bad?" Veronica's expression was confused and hopeful.

"You couldn't *pretend* to sing that badly if you tried. No. He is completely and utterly tone-deaf." I slowly shook my head. "And yet, he feels compelled to sing in public."

"Maybe he does it to be funny." Veronica cocked her head and watched him with a fond expression. "It's kind of adorable." She always talked about what a dork John was, and she never apologized for him. "He's not your... student, is he?"

"No!" I didn't mean to snap. "He's not. He never was."

"And you didn't... *hire* him to come with you?"

"Really?" My mouth dropped open. "You think I'd bring an *escort* to my niece's birthday party?"

"I just thought maybe since Charlie was gonna be here..."

"I had no idea you'd invited Charles. Thanks for the heads-up, by the way. I wasn't even sure Austin was going to come. We ran into Mom and Honey the other night. Honey brought it up, and Mom invited him in that half-ass polite Southern lady way that's not *really* an invitation. And to anyone else, Austin's usually like 'Sure, bro, let's hang later,' even though he doesn't mean it. But apparently, this time..." I gestured at Austin crooning on the gazebo stage.

"He likes you."

Austin had reached the bridge in the song. He was *rocking out* with his bottom lip between his teeth, confusingly sexy and mortifying at the same time.

"You like him."

The way she looked at me, there was no point in denying it. "I do, but... he's twenty-six. I'm sixteen years older. Look at him. Why would a guy like that be into me?"

Veronica scowled. "Older men are hot. Aren't you, like, a daddy now?"

"Okay. First of all, eww. I don't like being called that, especially by my sister. And it's really not like that with him and me. I don't want people thinking it is."

"Who cares what anybody thinks? He's obviously really into you." Onstage, Austin had reached the dramatic conclusion of the song. He held out the notes on each refrain while John lent background vocals. "He's singing to you. Perfect song choice for the record. He clearly gets you. Don't overthink it."

As if that should have been so easy for me.

Austin's song finally came to an end. Veronica cheered

so loudly that, for a moment, it didn't register that other people were clapping too. I glanced over my shoulder—no sign of Charles yet—and everyone was smiling. Apparently, they judged Austin's terrible singing charming.

Maybe it was the outfit.

Or his body in the outfit.

Austin spent too long bowing and thanking his audience before finally exiting the stage. He handed the mic back to John, clasped John's shoulder, and slapped him on the back in an affectionate *dude bro* kind of way.

Veronica shouted John's name to get his attention, pantomimed eating, and John announced that everyone could head into the kitchen and make themselves a plate.

Austin bounded over to me. I tried to think of something nice to say, but he preempted me, breathless with excitement. "Did you know John used to be in a band in college? He invited me to come back and let him record me in his studio." Austin grabbed my beer and took a deep pull. "He has autotune."

"Cool." Honestly, I could picture them becoming bros, and it made me smile. "That'll be perfect for your Cher-does-Abba numbers."

Austin gasped. "You remembered!"

I rolled my eyes. "You kinda spoke about it at length the other night."

Austin's smile tightened, and he nodded to someone behind me.

Before I turned around, I knew it was Charles.

With his hands on his hips and a smug grin on his face, my ex stood looking back and forth between Austin and me. He wore a polo identical to mine except for the color. Even though he was eight years older than me, his hair was as thick as it had ever been and almost completely silver. He'd never worked out a day in his life, yet he was perpetually lean and muscular. He was more handsome than he had any right to be. I had a hard time believing in karma.

"Paul." Charles greeted me with the same plastic, camera-ready warmth he displayed whenever we ran into each other on campus. He desperately wanted everyone to believe we'd remained friends. Which was fine. Being perceived as a source of gossip didn't serve either of us.

"Charles. This is Austin Fox. Austin, this is Charles Tollett, Dean of the College of Arts and Sciences."

"Charlie," he corrected me, shaking Austin's outstretched hand. "That was quite a performance up there." For someone who knew him as well as I did, it wasn't an entirely convincing compliment, but Austin took it as genuine.

"Thanks, bro," Austin said, throwing his heavy, muscled arm across my shoulders. I couldn't deny that the possessive gesture thrilled me. "I've been wanting to sing that one for Prof."

"Oh?" Charles lifted his brows feigning casual interest. "You're a student of Paul's, then?" He was *so* fucking eager to catch me being a hypocrite.

"No, no." I chuckled to keep from grinding my teeth. "Austin graduated from the University of Georgia. In Athens."

Austin smiled. "Phys ed."

"Ah." Charles lifted his eyebrows in a way that came across as more patronizing than impressed. "Coach Fox."

"Austin's also a fitness instructor during the summers." I hated myself for needing to elevate him in Charles's eyes, but I also wanted Austin to hear himself defined in a more empowering way. "At Edgewood CrossFit and at..."

"Bear Mountain Lodge," Austin said.

Charles's smirk returned. "Well, I can definitely picture that." His gaze roamed over Austin's body, and then he glanced at my belly a half second too long. "Good ol' Bear Mountain Lodge. I've made some memories there."

"You've been?" The question fell out of my mouth before I could think better of it.

Charles looked me in the eye. "Jasen and I went together a few times." He shifted his focus back to Austin. "But, you know, I've never been as a single guy. I might have to check it out again."

"You should." Austin squeezed me against him in a side hug. "Look how lucky I got." He walked me toward the house, his arm around me the whole way.

After we'd filled our plates, I chose the empty seat beside Mom so Austin could sit across the table from me next to Honey, but he didn't stay put for long. He spotted Veronica struggling with a tray of drinks and jumped up to help her deliver them to the kids' table. He asked if he could grab anyone anything else from the kitchen, and one request led to another. Before I knew it, he was serving the entire patio like he was working the dining hall at the lodge.

Austin didn't know who any of these people were or which ones were related to me, but it didn't seem to matter. From the few snatches of conversation I overheard, he seemed to be equally at ease chatting with kids, teenagers, and adults.

My aunt and uncle had apparently discovered that Austin had grown up in the Atlanta suburb where they'd lived for thirty years, and they'd lit up with excitement. They started calling out every business, church, and tree in Stone Mountain, and Austin matched them by naming other establishments they would know. He'd found more in common with them in three minutes than I had in a lifetime.

When Austin finally sat down to eat between John and Honey, John started describing his workout routines to Austin in exhaustive detail. Austin listened patiently, nodding as he chewed and repeatedly saying, "Right on," between mouthfuls.

My dad jumped into the conversation to share that he'd been his fraternity's arm-wrestling champion in college. "Were you in a fraternity, Austin?"

"Um..." Austin cocked his head and twisted his lips, appearing to think hard before answering. "Not in the way you're thinking, no."

I could see Dad's brain buffering as he tried to imagine what *other* ways one might be in a fraternity, but he abandoned the thought process and challenged Austin to a match.

Forced to abandon her seat so Dad and Austin could relocate to the corner of the table, Mom rolled her eyes.

Who physically wrestles with his gay son's boyfriend the first time they meet? Not that Austin was officially my *boyfriend*, but Dad didn't know that.

Their impromptu competition attracted a group of spectators and escalated from two-out-of-three to three-out-of-five. Austin made Dad work for it before letting him win. I assumed. Dad was in his late sixties, and Austin had discreetly winked at me while loudly lamenting the loss. I was grateful. I'd stopped indulging him in this sport by the age of twelve. A little red in the face, Dad grinned from ear to ear.

While I helped Veronica clean up, I overheard Charles holding court at a table in the corner, blathering on about his approach to *managing teams of intellectuals*. I'd never heard so much humblebragging in my life.

Maybe I'd missed it, but I hadn't witnessed him saying two words to anyone in my family, including Sadie.

Austin, on the other hand, had infiltrated the young people's table and was fiercely whispering with my niece and her friends. I sidled over under the pretext of presenting Sadie with her birthday money, and they all went quiet. Sadie thanked me and gave me a hug, but since I'd clearly killed the vibe, I made an excuse to go inside.

Austin came with me. I asked him what they'd been talking about.

He rolled his eyes. "Who we have crushes on. Duh."

"Oh really?" I wanted to ask if he'd talked about me, but I repressed the juvenile impulse. "Is Sadie dating?" If she was, Veronica didn't know, or she would have told me.

"I'm not telling you. I can't betray my girl like that!"

When we entered the house through the sliding glass door, we almost stumbled over a half dozen of the younger kids sprawled across the floor and the sofa of the sitting room area of the open-concept kitchen and dining room, watching David and another boy playing a video game.

Austin stopped and leaned toward the TV with his hands on the back of the sofa. "I love this one," he breathed reverently with the same glazed expression as the kids.

On-screen, sword-wielding gladiators in loincloths and sandals clashed against a backdrop of the Coliseum, their musclebound bodies rendered in graphic detail. It was a dissertation on homoeroticism and body dysmorphia waiting to happen.

"I can see why," I muttered too low for anyone else to hear me. "Did you want me to show you where the bathroom is?" I was hoping he'd take the hint so we could steal a few moments alone.

My suggestion broke his trance, and he grinned. "Yeah, sure. Lead the way."

At that moment, David's opponent apparently won because several kids started yelling and the winner stood on the sofa in a victorious pose.

A woman who was helping Veronica in the kitchen snapped, "Oliver! Get down!"

"You guys," Veronica said wearily. "You're being too rowdy. David, we talked about this. This is an outdoor event."

The other mom pointed. "Oliver. Addison. Outside. Now."

"One more game?" David whined.

"No." Veronica pointed at me and Austin. "Our guests can't even walk through here. If you wanna yell, go... sing with your dad."

David looked revolted.

"You guys wanna do some real gladiator training?" Austin asked.

David sneered. "That's not a real thing."

"David!" Veronica said. "Don't be rude."

Austin crossed his arms. "Uh, yeah, it is. I teach it. Professionally."

David narrowed his eyes at Austin, a spark of interest warring with skepticism. David glanced at me as if for confirmation.

I nodded gravely. "He does. I went to one of his classes a few nights ago. It was brutal. Kinda dangerous too."

Nothing appealed to David more than a warning that someone could get hurt. *Sold.* He was off the sofa and out the door in seconds, and the others raced to join him.

Veronica clasped her hands as if in prayer and mouthed to Austin, "Thank you."

Austin followed the kids, glancing back at me and whispering "Sorry." It clearly wasn't the time or place to get him behind closed doors, and I could tell he was every bit as excited as they were.

Once they were gone, Veronica said, "Paul, will you turn that off? Just hit the power button on the remote. We took the console out of his room so he wouldn't turn into a shut-in, but honestly, the noise of it is driving me freaking nuts."

After a quick trip to the bathroom, I returned to the backyard to find Austin walking the kids through a set of movements I recognized. "Sixty seconds," he called out while setting a timer on his phone. "Go!"

I sidled up to Austin. "The *Spartacus* workout, huh?"

Austin arched an eyebrow. "With some equipment-free modifications and a little bit of the Morning-After Drill."

He managed to keep them focused for about ten minutes before they increasingly started doing their own thing, but he brought them back to attention by announcing a new challenge called "Gladiator Poses."

Midway through warrior two, a girl with an awfully chic bob for a child called him out on it. "This is just yoga."

"*Just* yoga? Can you do this?" Austin went up on one foot in a shaky tree pose, and they all copied him. "What about *this*?" He dropped into a one-legged squat with the other leg straight out hovering parallel to the ground, and everyone who attempted it ended up sprawled on the grass.

While leading them through more increasingly absurd contortions, which I doubted belonged to any formal fitness discipline, Austin had also drawn a crowd of adult spectators. Charles among them. When I caught his eye, he smirked and shook his head, amused.

Honey clucked her tongue. "There's nothing like a man who's good with kids, is there, Cathy?"

Unable to disagree with Honey, Mom responded with a vague hum.

Austin finally left his new followers lying immobile in starfish positions on the ground and joined the adults.

"What have you done to our kids?" one of the moms quipped. She'd obviously intended it as a joke, but Austin flinched, and his smile fell.

Veronica said, "You must teach us this witchcraft at once." A few of the other parents chuckled.

Austin recovered his usual happy expression and shrugged. "Shivasana. It works on all ages."

Honey put her hand on Austin's arm. "Did I overhear you telling Charles you're a gym teacher?"

"Well..." Austin shoved his hands deep in his pockets and drew his shoulders up near his ears. "Technically..." I could tell he was struggling with how to answer.

I jumped in to speak for him as I had with Charles, spinning what little I knew. "Austin recently obtained his degree and certification. He's looking for the right position for his talents. He's very passionate."

"Wonderful." Honey said. "We have a new program at YA that I think you'd be perfect for." She pulled a phone from the pocket of her jumpsuit and held it out to Austin. "Why don't you give me your number, and I'll text you later."

"Yeah. Sure." Austin chuckled nervously. "Excellent." He entered his digits and handed the phone back to her.

Missy, my mom's Shih Tzu, appeared in a blur of movement at our feet. She could be obnoxious around crowds, but Mom adored her more than any living thing on the planet. She couldn't stand to leave Missy home alone, so she usually confined her to a guest room. Having escaped, Missy was beside herself with excitement. She sniffed Austin's boots before deciding to climb his legs.

"Missy! Get down!" Mom impotently admonished her. "Leave him alone."

Austin lifted Missy into the crook of his elbow and allowed her to lick his face.

"I'm sorry, Austin." Mom reached to take Missy from him.

"Ahh. No need to apologize." Austin scratched Missy's ears. "No such thing as a party that can't be improved by a small enthusiastic dog."

I could tell Mom was pleased he was indulging her little monster.

"Did you just make that up?" I was prepared to be impressed.

Austin shook his head. "Nah. Saw it on the internet."

Veronica interrupted, calling over the karaoke mic for everyone's attention. She made a teary-eyed toast to her daughter, and then, as Sadie shrank in mortification, John took over the mic to lead everyone in singing "Happy Birthday." One of Veronica's friends brought out a cake alight with candles, and Sadie blew them out.

We all clapped, and Austin executed an ear-splitting whistle with two fingers in his mouth.

John persuaded David and some of his friends to sing a song of their choosing as a group while the cake was being cut. I didn't know it, and they didn't sound too terrible. What they lacked in talent they made up for with shamelessness. Austin's performance had apparently reset the bar. He cheered them as if he were at a music festival.

I checked the time on my phone. "Shit. We should head out."

"We haven't had cake!" Austin protested.

"Well, we can take some with us. But if you're gonna make it back to the lodge in time for dinner, we need to go."

I typically liked to leave a gathering by ducking out before anyone even noticed, but Austin had to make a great show of saying his goodbyes. A casual observer would've thought they were *his* family. He had a final word, a laugh, and a hug for almost everyone.

Except for Mom. Since she was holding Missy, Austin opted for sloppy dog kisses. Mom gave his arm a little squeeze and a pat.

"Did you see that?" I whispered to Veronica.

Her shocked expression mirrored my own. "Wow."

"She *touched* him. Like, actual physical affection."

Veronica sighed dreamily. "Well, it's official. Everybody loves him."

Could it be that easy?

I'd hoped to at least escape without having to speak to Charles again, but waiting for a container of cake had slowed us down. He ambushed us near the gate.

"Maybe I'll see you guys at the campground," Charles said.

"Yeah, bro." Austin slung his arm over my shoulders. "You should come to the Bear Run next weekend. Have you ever been?"

"I haven't."

"It's the biggest event of the season."

"I might have to check it out." Charles said. "It was a pleasure meeting you, Austin."

"You too, Charles."

As soon as we were out of earshot, I said, "He hates being called Charles, you know."

Austin grinned. "I do."

25

As I drove back to my house, Austin wolfed down birthday cake. "Here," he said, feeding me a chunk. "You have to eat at least one bite. It's a curse on Sadie if you don't."

I allowed him to feed me, licking icing off his fingers.

"That was fun," he said. "I really like your family."

"Everybody loved you. Even Mom warmed up at the end."

"Thanks to Missy."

"Missy's her favorite child."

"See? I'm actually very family friendly."

"I can tell how much you like kids."

"I dig people that age. Ten, eleven. Still young enough to play, not quite old enough to be emo yet." Austin put the lid back on the cake container. "I taught sixth grade. Briefly."

Recognizing his confession-blurting tone, I stared straight ahead at the road, encouraging him to go on by saying nothing.

"I did my student teaching in Athens, and then I got a

job at North Crest Middle. I moved here eighteen months ago and started right after the winter holiday break."

I thought for a moment that was all he was going to give me, but after a pause, he went on. "The thing you gotta know is, I've always been out—as a student, as a student teacher, even when I interviewed for the job. Representation is a big deal to me. I didn't want to be closeted. Not with how vulnerable queer kids are, especially at that age."

"When did you come out?"

"When I was seventeen. I was *outed* actually. I was the only male cheerleader at my high school, so everybody *called* me gay, even before they *knew* I was. I never personally doubted it. I'd been in love with our next-door neighbor, Chris, for as long as I could remember. He was a year older than me, same age as my brother, Grayson. They were best friends all through school. I mean, from kindergarten to high school. Chris had a weight bench in his garage where they worked out, and I was always trying to hang out with them. Grayson would try to run me off, but Chris would always tell him to let me stay.

"The summer before my junior year—their senior year —Grayson got a part-time job. He wasn't around much, but I still hung out and lifted with Chris. The vibe was pretty intense when it was just the two of us. I went over there every freaking day hoping something would happen, obsessing over whether or not I should make the first move. And finally, right before school started back, I couldn't take the suspense anymore. I kissed him. And he kissed me back.

"We were totally making out, and this girl, Staci, walked in on us. We heard someone at the door, and we jumped apart, but she'd already seen us. Staci was a senior. She cheered with me, and she was really into my brother. She liked both Grayson and Chris. People were always making jokes about them having three-ways.

"Anyway, she immediately turned around and left without saying a word. Chris took off after her, and he never came back. I waited for like two hours, pacing his garage, before I finally gave up and went home. I found out later that Chris and Staci had hooked up. That day. I guess he was trying to prove he was straight, or maybe he thought he could keep her quiet about what she'd seen. I don't know. But the first day back at school, Chris and Staci were officially dating. My brother was pissed. He was either really into her and mad that his best friend had stolen her, or... I wondered if maybe there'd been something going on between Grayson and Chris to be honest. But they totally fell out. It was some serious drama.

"And then, right in the middle of all that, a rumor started going around that I had made a pass at Chris. Of course, I assumed Staci was the one telling everybody. I didn't feel like I had any choice but to embrace who I was, so I just owned it. I was like, 'Yeah, I'm gay.' Nobody ever questioned Chris's sexuality because he got Staci pregnant, and they ended up getting married before they even graduated.

"Grayson was a fucking mess the whole year. He blamed me for all of it. I didn't find out 'til way later—from Chris, actually—that Grayson was the one who'd told everybody at school about me."

"Wait. *What?* Your *brother* outed you?"

"Yeah. Apparently Staci did tell Grayson about seeing me and Chris together, but Chris swore she liked me and that neither of them would ever have done that to me. It was all Grayson."

"Austin. Jesus."

"That year—and my senior year, after they were all gone

—were hell. I was bullied constantly. Every class I was in. And none of the teachers really intervened or stood up for me."

"I'm so sorry you went through that. My God. How are things between you and your brother now?"

"We're fine. I forgave him a long time ago. But that whole experience was a big part of why I wanted to be a teacher. By the time I was in college, open representation was starting to be seen as an asset by some school districts. Even in fucking Georgia. Of course, shit has more recently started swinging back in the wrong direction, but I digress... When I was hired at North Crest Middle, I was welcomed as an out teacher. Embraced. On paper, it was the perfect job for me, a combination of PE classes for students who identified as male and coed health and wellness instruction for everybody. I was gonna make a difference. What happened to me was not gonna happen to my students. I had a safe space sign on my door and a rainbow flag above the chalkboard. There was already another gay teacher who'd married her wife a few years back. Everybody was cool with it. Well, not everybody. There were a few dickhead teachers —there's always a bigot or two—but most of the faculty were allies."

We arrived at my house, and I pulled into the driveway. I didn't want to interrupt his story, and he didn't make any move to get out of the truck. I put it in park and left the engine running so we could keep the air conditioning going.

"So anyway, there was a trans boy in my health class. He'd come out several months before, at the beginning of the school year, and started asking everybody to call him Tucker. The principal and the school counselor were aware of his situation. They were supportive. They talked to me about it. Of course, I intended to acknowledge him as he wished. The first time I called roll, I asked if he preferred Tucker or Tuck. And instead of having everybody say 'here' or 'present,' I asked them to share their pronouns, so he—or anybody else for that matter—would be comfortable sharing theirs without feeling singled out. There a couple of kids who snickered and rolled their eyes, but the vast majority handled it in a low-key way. I was really proud of them. I felt hopeful. But... I'd unintentionally made things worse for Tuck."

Austin plucked at the fraying threads on his shorts. "The students had our school email addresses that they used for turning in assignments and forms and stuff. Over spring break, Tuck wrote to ask me if I could refer to him in class as Andy, a gender-neutral version of Andrea, the name his parents had given him at birth. He said it would make things worse for him at home if I continued to identify him as a boy. He said he was afraid of what his dad might do to him. It broke my heart, but more than anything, I was afraid for him.

"He reached out to me because he trusted me, and I felt like I was betraying him, but we're legally obligated to report suspected abuse."

"Then you did the right thing," I said softly.

Austin stared out the window. He shook his head, either in regret or because he was unconvinced. "I had a college professor tell me I was in the wrong profession for *one of my kind*. The vice-principal at my first student teaching position told me he was *watching me*. And there was always some fear in the back of my mind that a student could make up a malicious lie about me. I'd discussed that scenario with people. I'd thought a lot about it. I was prepared to defend that. But I truly believed this was my purpose, and being closeted wasn't the answer for anybody.

I was advised to operate in full daylight, to leave no room for shade.

"I never communicated with Tuck in secret. I'm just gonna call him Tuck. I refuse to erase him. Every word of our email correspondence was shared with my superiors. They assured me I'd done the right thing. But shit still hit the fan.

"I came in on Monday after spring break, and somebody —Tuck's dad—was raging in the principal's office. Screaming, demanding to talk to me. I assumed he'd read Tuck's email. He was threatening to call the police and the media if they didn't bring me to him right then and there.

"To be fair, nobody really threw me under the bus. The principal tried to keep me out of it, but it was obvious the man was going to track me down. Better here than in the parking lot at my apartment or something. I thought maybe if I just talked to him, face-to-face, I could defuse the situation. I thought I could help. I thought I could make a difference."

Austin blew out a breath and glanced at me. "It was not pretty. That man spat fire and brimstone at me, literally spitting at a few points. He hurled every self-righteous Bible verse you've ever heard. He accused me of grooming his daughter and brainwashing her into thinking she was a homosexual. There was no acknowledgment of the term *trans*, just *homosexual,* pronounced like it was the nastiest word in the English language."

I cursed under my breath. "What did you do?"

"Nothing. I couldn't get a word in edgewise. And his rage scared me. My principal told me to leave. I walked out the door, went home, got into bed, and I stayed there for a week. The principal emailed, texted, called, and left voicemails checking on me. He said he didn't want to fire me, but they couldn't hold my position. He suggested I take an unpaid leave of absence pending either my return or my resignation, so I agreed. I didn't want to deal with it. Ryan said he could get me on at the campground. It was the beginning of the season, and I'd been wanting to check it out. It was the perfect escape. Somewhere to get some space and to think. Or to not think."

Shit. I'd been torturing myself over my next book, whining about having to start over, but at least I knew I was a writer. I knew there'd eventually be another book. Worst-case scenario, I had a fucking *job* and a home. Austin's entire life plan had imploded. His identity was at stake.

I reached for his hand and rubbed my thumb across his knuckles. "Did you ever hear from Tuck again or find out what happened to him?"

"No. I haven't talked to anyone at the school for over a year. And it wouldn't be appropriate to try to contact him." His brown eyes welled up with an unfamiliar sadness. "I really failed him." He sounded shocked by the realization.

"*You* didn't fail him," I said firmly, willing him to look me in the eye.

Austin shook his head, but he smiled. "Sorry. That was a lot. I would've told you the other night, but we were having such a great time."

"I understand. It's okay. Have you been able to talk to anyone else about this?"

"Jim. And a little bit with my parents. Mostly my mama."

"Your parents have been supportive, then?"

"They have. But I've been kind of avoiding them for the past year. They keep wanting to know what my *plan* is. Last summer wasn't long enough to figure out what the hell I'm supposed to do with my life, but I was able to save a lot of what I made. I came back to Edgewood, got a few personal-training clients, worked out a lot. Now I'm back for another season, and I still don't know what I'm gonna do when summer's over."

I smiled sympathetically. "Our education system perpetuates the myth that we can choose a path when we're teenagers and never change course, and that if we don't have our shit figured out by our midtwenties, we've failed. You know, if you even have an inkling of who you're supposed to be in the world, you're ahead of everyone else. You have a true north to navigate by at least." I hesitated before asking, "Do you see yourself going back eventually?"

"No." Austin shook his head, his voice adamant. "Definitely not there or anywhere else like it. Things aren't getting better fast enough. In some ways, they're getting worse. Teachers aren't only unappreciated; they're under attack. Queer youth are targeted. You know enough about me to know I'm not a pessimistic person. I'm positive about almost every aspect of my life. But this? Not anymore. I love the kids, but I don't think a person like me can make a difference within the constraints of the public school system."

"There are private schools."

"Conservative, rich-people schools? Religious schools?" I'd never heard him sound bitter. "It's too big a fight. I'm not a fighter. At all. I'm a cheerleader."

"Well, what about an organization like Youth Alliance? Honey started out as a pissed-off parent whose son was told he couldn't take his boyfriend to prom. So she hosted an alternative prom. And then she grew it into an enduring, successful nonprofit. She pretends to be a flaky socialite, but she's very adept at politics. She's been fighting bullshit in this state for over twenty years, and she serves the same kids you're trying to reach. She said she has something you'd be perfect for."

"You think she'd hire somebody with *my* employment history?" In his eyes, hope warred with skepticism.

"Hell, I think she might try to *adopt* you. I've known her a long time. She really likes you." It pained me to see him, of all people, doubt himself. "It's at least worth a follow-up."

Austin looked at the dashboard clock. "Oh shit. I hate to drop this bomb and run, but I'm late."

"Hey." I stopped him before he got out of the truck. "Thanks for telling me everything. I'm glad you felt like you could."

"I trust you." He kissed me. "I'll call you later. Oh! Do you want the rest of this cake? Talking about feelings is so draining. I think my blood sugar might be low."

I laughed. "Take it."

26

It hadn't been a great place to leave a conversation like that. I spent the evening reconsidering who Austin was and where he was in life. He wasn't some twentysomething fuck boy with no sense of purpose. He wanted to change real people's actual lives. How did my obsessing about fictional characters even compare to that?

Later that night, when he called from the pole, I tried to bring it up again. I thought maybe since he'd opened up, he'd want to talk more, but he deflected.

"That's why they're called thoughts and feelings, Prof. You're supposed to keep them *inside*. If you talk about them, they become words." While I reeled from the nonsensical semantics, he asked, "So you're coming next weekend?"

"To the... Running of the Bears?"

Austin snorted. "The Bear *Run*."

"What the hell is it? Naked men racing down the trail and stampeding between the tents in the Soggy Bottom?"

"Oh, wouldn't that be fun? Nah. It's a huge gathering of guys who come from all over. There's a theme night..."

"How is that different from any other weekend?"

"It's... *more*. It's like the difference between a home game and homecoming."

"Is there a court?"

"Kinda. There's a contest. People vote."

"Oh, yes, the man pageant. I guess you'll be passing on your crown."

"The hell I will! I'm gonna win again. And I want you to be there. I've arranged special accommodations for you."

"Uh-oh. What does *that* mean?"

"It's a surprise. All you gotta do is say yes."

"Well, I guess I fucking have to," I said as if I could've said no, "since you invited *Charles*."

Austin laughed. "It's sold out. The only way he's getting in last minute is if he's willing to tent camp. He doesn't look like the type."

I hummed skeptically. "He's not."

"Forget about him."

"Trust me, I have."

SUNDAY MORNING, I awoke from a dream that I was spooning Austin. I jacked off remembering holding him in my bed.

I caught myself mumble-singing "I Hope You Dance" in the shower. On impulse, I belted a few lines. Maybe I did have a good voice.

Sundays were usually my rest days, but since I'd taken off yesterday and was now planning to be away next weekend also—fuck. The last thing I needed was another vacation as an excuse to procrastinate. I had to get some writing done. Austin might continue visiting on Wednesdays, and I'd need to rearrange my schedule to accommodate that on a regular basis. I was probably getting ahead of myself. Maybe I could use it as motivation, a way to mark time until I could see him again.

By my second cup of coffee, researching the Bear Run online had overridden my good intentions.

Okay. I'll start strong and go hard tomorrow. That's what Mondays are for.

Like old-school circuit parties or big city Pride events, bear runs moved around to different locations at different times of the year. They were like conferences, opportunities for the greater community to gather beyond the usual bars, camps, and clubs.

A run typically featured tournaments—beer pong, billiards, darts, rugby, volleyball—and a euphemistically titled *contest*, where winners were awarded titles by category.

According to the Bear Mountain Lodge website, there would be an additional entrance fee and a bear market to help raise money for Edgewood Youth Alliance.

I called Eric, and he assured me they wouldn't be auctioning off actual men at the bear market. They sold T-shirts, leather gear, and high-end underwear.

I asked if he and Ben wanted to come. I told him I'd miss having them there, but he said they were enjoying their *alone time*. I heard the air quotes. Before he could go into detail, I blurted out that I'd taken Austin to meet my family.

After I'd filled him in on the events of the past few days, he said, "Damn, dude. You've gone and got yourself a full-on boyfriend."

"Please." I scoffed at the term, but Eric couldn't see my smile. "Calm down."

"I don't think you'll miss us at all." Eric sighed loudly. "I hope you dance."

"Fuck off."

. . .

When Austin called that night, he told me he couldn't come to town on Wednesday. Due to the extra preparations required for the upcoming weekend, the staff wouldn't be able to take their usual day off. "It's a good thing I requested the half-day to go to Sadie's party, or I would've ended up working three weeks in a row without a break." He sighed. "I don't think I could go that long without seeing you."

"Me either," I admitted. I was disappointed, but knowing he'd intended to come was some consolation.

"Five more days," he said, his smile evident in his voice.

I started the week strong. I went for a three-mile walk, did fifty pushups, ate grapefruit for breakfast, then took a long shower, hoping to invite the muse.

Apparently, my muse was Austin. He was all I could think about.

I made a pot of tea, sat down at my desk, and thought, *Fuck it. Maybe I am writing a book about him.*

This time, I went beyond the gilded descriptions of the veins that corded his arms and the ever-present glint of mischief in his warm brown eyes. I attempted to dissect how he'd charmed my family despite his cheesy fashion choices and his shameless vocal stylings. How he cloaked his worries in the joy he channeled for others.

Even though the words flowed, his charisma evaded my vocabulary. I transcribed his jokes, but I failed to do them justice.

My inner critic sneered at the pages and declared them *self-indulgent*, but it felt good to write them. Like singing in the shower.

I logged the word count anyway and vowed to keep going.

I wrote through the hours until he called and counted the days until I could see him again.

WEDNESDAY MORNING, I received a work email with a schedule of the department meetings coming up in August ahead of fall semester. Writing about Austin's motivation to teach, I questioned whether I deserved to be called a professor. Austin's passion humbled me. I couldn't recall a time when teaching had been more than a job to me or if it had ever been more than an aspiring author's backup career.

I marked the email as unread. I'd come back to it.

Taking a lunch break in the kitchen, I couldn't get "Wonderwall" out of my head. I shouted at the smart speaker on the island to play something random from my general Likes playlist, and "Bouncing Off Clouds" filled the room.

Listening to Tori Amos and writing about a boy in your diary.

A bark of laughter escaped my mouth. *Busted.* Someone with a deeper faith—someone who believed in magic— would've felt seen by the universe. I felt...

What did I feel?

I felt fucking *happy*.

As a high concept, happiness was difficult to define. As a personal experience, it was a total distraction. Terrible for discipline. Happiness didn't give a fuck about the novel I was supposed to be writing, not when a real-life love story was an option.

. . .

AUSTIN SOUNDED EXHAUSTED that night on the phone. He said he was bummed he hadn't been able to come see me.

"Two more days," I said, mimicking his usual cheery countdown. I listened for the sound of his smile, and when I didn't sense a shift in his mood, I said, "I miss you."

He hummed a low sweet sound and sighed. "I miss you too."

BY THURSDAY MORNING, Austin's enthusiasm had returned.

I had just sat down at my desk to work when I received his text: *It's Bear Run Eve!!!*

It's 9:15 in the morning.

What do you call 9:15 a.m. on December 24?!!

I smiled, closed my laptop, and fired off a few tips about exclamation point usage.

I'd known the risk. Aggravation was his love language. For the rest of the day, he sent me sexually suggestive messages with an ever-increasing number of exclamation points.

What he likely intended as playful promises, I processed as expectations. The effects of anxiety and excitement were difficult to discern, but my therapist said if it was something you were looking forward to that would likely go well, then it was excitement. I vowed not to spin out about it. I needed to be inside him again, more than anyone I'd ever known, and I had plenty of advanced notice on this occasion.

I took a pill that evening, twenty-four hours before we were likely to be alone together.

.   .   .

AUSTIN CALLED EVEN LATER than usual. He'd spent all day with Jim and Ryan decorating the Cubby Hole for the dance party.

"It's circus themed. 'Under a Big Top.'" I pictured him making a sweeping *grand reveal* gesture. "You don't have a black leotard, do you?"

"Is there anything about me that makes you think I would own a leotard?"

"I have some running tights that'll work."

"For..."

"Your costume."

I groaned. "Can't I get away with, like... a rubber clown nose?"

"Gunner's already pulled something for you. He likes to style everybody. We all get together and raid his trunk, do shots, and try on looks. A bunkhouse pregame with the boys on a Friday night—that's my happy place." Of course Austin could define *happiness*.

"I'm looking forward to it," I said. "What time should I get there?"

"Any time after three. Just come up to the lodge. Jim knows where to put you. If Luke checks you in, and he doesn't already know, tell him to ask Jim. Oh! And if you have a fanny pack, bring it."

"I don't have a fanny pack."

"No worries. Somebody'll have an extra."

"Alrighty, then." I didn't ask any further questions. "Bear Run, here I come."

27

I ARRIVED AT THE ENTRANCE TO THE CAMPGROUND AT 3:03 p.m. with inflamed sinuses and a flushed face that broadcasted *Took a dick pill; came to fuck.* But it was worth it. I'd woken up with a hard-on so promising, even pressure from the seat belt during the drive had been a trigger.

I wouldn't be disappointing either of us.

After being buzzed through the gate, I headed toward the lodge, carefully navigating mud puddles left from the thunderstorms that had passed through the previous night.

I immediately spotted Austin stocking bags of ice behind the pool complex. I stopped in the middle of the road to watch him. I'd spent days scrolling through his social media pics, but none of them captured how handsome he was. As if he'd felt my presence, he looked my way.

When he recognized my truck, his face lit up. He yelled for me to wait, quickly padlocked the freezer, and came running across the wet grass. He was wearing my red sneakers.

"Hi there!" He leaned in through the open window to

give me a salty kiss. The part of me that had pined for him all week finally unclenched.

A car honked. Glancing in the rearview mirror I saw there were two vehicles waiting to get to the lodge.

"I'll ride up with you." Austin ran around the front of the truck and hopped into the passenger seat, throwing his radio into the cup holder.

His citrusy scent filled the cab. He laced his fingers through mine as if he'd done it a million times.

The car behind me honked again, impatiently this time.

Austin grinned. "Ride or die!"

I pressed the gas.

THREE MEN SAT in a row of camp chairs at the foot of the steps leading into the lodge. Considering there were benches and rocking chairs up on the deck, it seemed an odd place from which to take in the view.

Austin leapt out of the truck and started flexing and posing in front of them. A few observers scattered around the parking lot erupted into catcalls and whistles. Austin looked back and winked at me. "Gotta give the people what they want."

Having seen him the past few times on my home turf, it was an uncomfortable reminder of how much he belonged to this place. These men adored him. I couldn't fault them for it. He portrayed the Best Cub they wanted him to be—it was his job—and I'd try to be a good sport about it.

When the audience response died down, Austin curtsied.

Score paddles popped up from the laps of the three seated men. First a ten, then another ten, and finally, after a long pause and a playful glare, the last man finally turned his paddle around.

A nine.

Austin cried out, threw back his head, and clutched his chest. As he moved past them and started up the steps he muttered, "Bitch!" to the third judge, but they grinned at each other.

I followed, and the score paddles popped up in rapid succession.

Ten. Ten. Ten.

Austin cheered, and there was a smattering of applause. A steady stream of vehicles had been coming up the mountain, and there were more people in the parking lot than I'd realized.

I blushed a few shades closer to crimson, smiled tightly —*Thanks?*—and scurried up the steps.

"What the fuck?" I muttered when I caught up to him. "I didn't even *do* anything."

Austin scowled at me like I was insane. "Except be unbelievably hot."

"Enough to be heckled for it?"

Austin gestured dismissively. "They give everybody tens. It's a subversion of beauty norms for people who don't typically experience affirmation in the real world. I'm here for it."

A couple on their way out of the lodge slowed to hand Austin blue slips of paper. One of them leaned close to whisper something in his ear, and Austin grinned. He gave the man's arm an affectionate squeeze. "Thanks, bro. You guys have fun!"

They nodded to me and murmured hello as they passed. With a gleam in his eye, the one who'd spoken to Austin tucked a piece of paper into the V-neck of my T-shirt and dashed after his companion.

Once we were through the door and into the lobby, I plucked out the paper to examine it. It was red in color, some kind of game money like a Monopoly bill, with a cartoon bear in the center, and the words *Best Daddy* printed above it in a nineteenth-century typeface. As we waited in line to check in, three other men approached us, once again handing Austin blue bills that said *Best Cub*, then handing red ones to me. As I stood there, brain buffering, Austin thanked them.

"Well, look at you getting bear bucks right off the bat," he said. Seeing my confused expression, he explained, "It's for the contest."

"Are they giving me these because of... our age difference?"

Austin rolled his eyes. "They think you're a hot daddy, Prof. It's not that deep."

"But that's not"—I motioned between us—"what this is."

He shrugged. "Beauty's in the eye of the beholder. Remind me to give you mine later, though. When you check in, they'll give you a set, one for each category. The event fee covers the first set, but if you want more votes, you can purchase extras."

"Gee," I said dryly, "exactly like real politics."

Austin laughed. "It is kinda like a campaign. There's a lot of shaking hands and kissing strangers. Everybody gives out their bucks tonight, at dinner or at the dance. Wherever. Then, tomorrow at the pool party, the two individuals from each category with the most bucks will walk in the final competition."

"Walk?"

"From the cabana bar to the end of the pool and back. The final vote's in the form of applause."

"You guys sure fucking love to *clap* for people," I muttered.

"It's love!" Austin said.

JIM AND LUKE were both working reception, but Austin steered me into Jim's line. On the floor of the office behind him, a corgi mix wearing a pearl collar squatted on a velvet pillow next to a large water bowl with lettering on the side that read *Gin & Regret*. I'd seen her a few times with Jim over Memorial Day weekend. I smiled at her, but she turned away with a look of bored disinterest.

When Jim finished helping the man in front of me, he greeted me warmly. "Well, hey there, Paul." He leaned across the counter and lowered his voice. "I knew you looked familiar. But I didn't know who you were until Austin told me after you'd left. You're *the* Paul Carter. I loved your books!"

"Thanks for reading them." I always had to bite my tongue to keep from apologizing that there wasn't another one out yet. Readers didn't need to know I was struggling. "It's really kind of you to tell me."

"Don't get me wrong, I adored *The Boy Who Didn't Come Back*—we all love to see a mainstream bestseller with queer representation—but, honey, *Divining Virginia*... The mysticism's right up my alley. One of my favorite books."

"Really? I don't often hear that."

"He thinks everybody hated it," Austin said.

"What?" Jim's mouth dropped open. "No."

I shrugged uncomfortably. "It wasn't the most successful."

"Well, I guess that depends on how you define success. I, for one, thought it was phenomenal," Jim gushed. "I'm gonna hunt you down later and get you to autograph my copies."

"I'd be happy to."

Austin smiled, looking smug.

The dog gave a low, grumbly bark like someone muttering under their breath.

"Oh, hush, Karen Walker!" Jim shook his head. "Please forgive her rudeness. She can't stand to think somebody might be more famous than she is." Jim turned to Luke. "Honey, grab me the keys to the Summers's place." He slapped a clipboard in front of me and scribbled an *X* at the bottom of a form. "Jody would've been so thrilled to know you're staying there. We promised him we'd hold on to the place until we can find another writer who wants to take it over. I offered it to ol' what's his name, but he only comes once a year and always wants to stay in the same cabin."

I silently prayed Austin hadn't set me up for one of those timeshare scenarios where they'd hit me up with a sales pitch at the end of the weekend.

Sensing my hesitation, Jim made a dismissive gesture. "You're just signing in, honey. I promise it's not a lease or a mortgage." He laughed.

I scanned the safety and liability boilerplate and scrawled my signature.

Jim slid the key across the counter along with a laminated name badge and a rainbow spread of bear bucks. "Did Austin explain to you how all this works?"

Austin smiled. "He already picked up a handful right here in the lobby."

Jim inclined his head and stage-whispered, "Sounds like we've got a contender."

"Wait'll everybody sees his Big Top look." Austin waggled his eyebrows.

I started to move away so Jim could help the next guest, but he stopped me. "One more thing, honey. Which color lanyard did you want?" He pointed to three boxes containing variously colored lanyards similar to those given out at conferences.

"Um." I realized I'd seen other men wearing them. Knowing that hankie colors and leather armband placement communicated sexual roles and proclivities, I assumed the lanyards conveyed similar significance.

Before I could think of how to ask, Jim rattled off an explanation of the options he was clearly used to repeating. "Blue means you're single ready to mingle. With consent. Green, you're married or partnered but open. Terms negotiable. Red means you're not participating in sex, monogamous, or in an exclusive relationship."

Jim cut his eyes to Austin, who had braced his elbow on the counter, chin in his hand, nonchalantly watching me. Luke was watching too.

Austin and I hadn't discussed labels. It wasn't a conversation I'd expected to have this early, but considering there was likely some truth behind his joke about talking about his feelings, maybe it was easier to communicate my own this way.

I wasn't interested in anyone else. Austin was the only one. He was the reason I was here. The choice was simple.

I took a red lanyard from the box.

Austin shifted his hand to cover his mouth, but he couldn't entirely hide his smile or the blush on his cheeks.

Out of the corner of my eye, I noticed Jim quickly occupying himself with something on his computer.

Austin stood up straight. He drew in a breath like he was

about to say something, but then he shook his head, exhaling without a word.

"What?" I searched his dark eyes. Austin wasn't wearing a lanyard. None of the staff were. Maybe because they wore uniform shirts. My heart pounded, and my voice sounded faraway. "Is this okay?"

Nodding furiously, Austin slipped the red lanyard over my head. He clipped my name badge through the hook and kissed me on the cheek.

28

RETURNING DOWN THE NARROW ROAD AGAINST THE FLOW OF approaching vehicles required concentration and both hands on the wheel. I kept trying to hold Austin's hand and then dropping it to get through a few tricky spots. Every time I stole a glance his way, he was watching me.

"What?" I was dying to know what he was thinking about the choice I'd made.

He smiled. "You're so handsome."

Austin directed me to pull into a service space behind the pool complex at the bottom of the hill, grabbed my lanyard, and used it to pull me over the console for a kiss. He opened his mouth to mine, and our tongues had barely touched when his radio went off.

"Who was stocking the ice?" a grumpy voice demanded.

Austin jerked away from me and waved out the window at Sawyer, who was staring at us from the ice cooler. "Coming!" Austin called. He plucked his radio out of the cup holder. "Unfortunately, I'm on the clock. I gotta go get screamed at, then finish setting up both bars before dinner.

But I'll see you up there, okay?" He quickly kissed me one more time and jumped out of the truck.

"Wait. Where am I staying?"

"Oh, right! It's down near the boathouse at the far end of Trailer Park Avenue. There's a footbridge over the creek. It's the only one on the other side."

"There's a cabin down there?"

"No. It's a trailer. Don't gimme that look. It's really nice. It's a double-wide."

Trailer Park Avenue was a misnamed loop of gravel drive near the front gate nestled between the road through camp and the creek. Although the lots were tiny, every Airstream, RV, fifth-wheel, and trailer boasted elaborate multilevel decks and patios that rivaled the nicest neighborhoods in Edgewood. Awnings, drapes, and vine-covered trellises provided refuge from the sun, and there were more hanging baskets and beds of flowers than the set of a made-for-television rom-com.

I parked close to a prefab shed with racks of kayaks and canoes, grabbed my bags, and took the bridge to a shady path along the opposite bank of the creek.

The path ended at a clearing in the trees. In the middle of a starkly mown lot, a large gray box of a building sat on a scaffolding of metal bars three feet off the ground. Long horizontal stains along the exterior siding suggested there had once been a deck or screen porch, but now there was only a concrete block of steps leading up to the door, without even so much as a railing or an overhang.

As I unlocked the door with the key Jim had given me, I looked back at all the landscaping porn I'd driven past. The footbridge might as well have been a portal to another world.

I had to admit, the interior shocked me. It was sparsely

but tastefully furnished, with a gray linen sectional facing a stacked stone fireplace and a picture window overlooking the creek. A bar separated the main living room from a full-size, modern kitchen. Wide-plank floors, exposed ceiling beams, and skylights gave it the look and feel of a lake house.

Pretty fucking nice for a vacation rental—a palace compared to the cabin Eric and Ben had rented—but then it had belonged to a millionaire author.

The hallway leading to the bedrooms was a tunnel of empty bookshelves. The primary bedroom was minimal and spotless.

This was where Austin and I would finally be alone together. A serious upgrade from a tent.

I put away my things and spent some time setting the stage for tonight. I placed candles and a Bluetooth speaker I'd brought from home on the bedside tables. I tucked a few clean hand towels, a tin of breath mints, and a bottle of lube into one of the drawers.

I wanted everything to be perfect.

The anticipation made me anxious. I drank a beer and paced around the space until I finally decided to hike up to the lodge early. I didn't want to get Austin into trouble while he was working, but maybe I'd at least catch a glimpse of him.

I ARRIVED at the lodge with about an hour to spare until dinner, but there was a lot of activity in the kitchen, and the porches were packed with guys waiting, hanging out, and socializing. No one that I knew. When Ben and Eric and Eric's musician friends had been here, at least I'd felt like I belonged to a group.

I smiled and said hello whenever anyone made eye contact. Several guys gave me daddy bucks. I smiled and graciously thanked them, but the attention embarrassed me. I went to the lodge library and pretended to be engrossed in perusing the shelves.

I wondered if they had any Jody Summers books. I'd never read one, but staying at his place had made me curious, and they were considered the epitome of beach reads. Over the past four decades, the man had probably authored over a hundred bestsellers, the kind of juggernaut books sold in airports and grocery store checkout lines. By sheer odds alone, there should be a few. The branding had been consistent and familiar since I was a kid—glossy jewel-toned covers with the author's name in a gilded typeface taking up every bit of space it could, the title almost a secondary afterthought.

Here we go. A cracked paperback spine that had once been bright aquamarine. I slipped it out enough to peek at the cover.

Hollywood Pool Boy.

I smirked at the synchronicity. Although Austin was probably more of a *Dollywood* pool boy...

I was tempted, but I'd downloaded last year's Pulitzer Prize and Booker winning novels to my Kindle before leaving home.

"Finding anything good?"

The voice startled me, and I slammed the book back into its slot on the shelf. "Just, uh... browsing."

The guy smiled. He wore a T-shirt with an image of a leather man riding a bear. "I saw you earlier and wanted to give you this." He handed me a red bear buck.

I introduced myself, and we chatted until dinner was called and everyone started lining up.

"It was nice meeting you." He nodded at my lanyard. "He's a lucky man, by the way."

While I was in line for the buffet, more guys gave me their bucks, and so did almost everyone at the table where I sat to eat. I tried to employ the strategy I'd used when I did book signings. I asked them their names and got them to talk about themselves. Everyone was as friendly and welcoming as they'd been on my first trip. I did my best to engage in conversation while watching Austin work the room. He was so adept at being the center of attention, but whenever he passed and his hands were free, he squeezed my shoulder, letting me know he was aware of my presence too.

It made me feel proud.

When the others got up to leave, I lingered, facing my bucks in the same direction, hoping for a chance to speak to Austin when he came to wipe down the table.

He appeared with a rag in one hand and a fanny pack in the other. "I think you're gonna need this."

I made a show of putting my bucks in the pockets of my cargo shorts. "I can manage."

"Trust me. You've got a shit ton more cargo coming."

I narrowed my eyes. "It's not your doing, is it?"

Austin made a dismissive sound. "It's all you, Prof. These men have eyes." He leaned in for a quick kiss. "Listen, as soon as we finish up here, I've gotta head up to the Hole to help with some last-minute decorations."

"Do you want me to wait around for a bit?"

"Nah, I'll be a while. But I promise, tonight I'm all yours. Oh! Did you like the trailer?"

"Yeah. It's really nice. I'm impressed."

"Cool. Meet me at the bunkhouse around nine-ish. If I'm

not back yet, hang with the boys. Gunner's got your costume. You gonna be okay on your own?"

"Yeah. Don't worry about me."

"Go walk around a bit. Meet the neighbors."

I shrugged. "I might do some reading."

Austin rolled his eyes and chuckled. "Whatever makes you happy."

Before I left the lodge, I palmed *Hollywood Pool Boy* and slipped it into my new fanny pack.

BACK AT THE TRAILER, I showered, made myself a bourbon and Coke, and lay on the sofa staring out the picture window. It would've been the perfect spot for a sliding door onto a deck overlooking the creek. The lights of Trailer Park Avenue across the water made me feel lonely. Removed. Knowing Austin was somewhere nearby, I almost missed him more than I had at home in Edgewood. I picked up my phone to text Eric, but I didn't have any bars.

I propped *Hollywood Pool Boy* on a pillow on my lap and dove in. The opening chapter hooked me immediately. Jody Summers's writing was crisp, cheeky, and clever. Honestly, it was better than I expected and unlike anything I'd read before. The sex scenes were lyrical as well as shockingly graphic.

Damn. I've been missing out.

A few weeks ago, I might've beat off, but I was saving every bit of myself for later tonight with Austin.

29

I WAITED UNTIL NINE FIFTEEN TO WALK UP THE ROAD TO THE employee bunkhouse. A passing golf-cart driver slowed to offer me a ride, but I declined, claiming I wanted to stretch my legs. I was afraid if I arrived before Austin, I wouldn't know how to make small talk with his friends. The last time I'd been alone with a group of twentysomethings, I'd been teaching a class on *Mrs. Dalloway*, and I doubted that experience would serve me in this situation.

Hank answered the door wearing a bright-green leotard and waved me inside. As I'd feared, there was no sign of Austin. The bunkhouse reminded me of a messy army barracks with rows of bunkbeds strewn with clothes. Bailey, the slim boyish guy I'd seen working the buffet line in the dining hall, sat on an upper bunk with a hand mirror painting his face like a clown's. He smiled shyly.

"Come in, come in!" Gunner called out. He wore only a cheetah print thong and a wig fit for a madam in an old Western film. "Austin's still up at the Hole, but he'll be back in time to change into his costume."

I exchanged hellos with Albie and Kevin, who were

filling drink cups with ice and setting them on top of a mini fridge. They also wore leotards.

"We're going as trapeze artists," Hank explained. "We didn't want to wear a bunch of clothes and wigs and shit." He shrugged. "Probably not the most exciting costumes in the world, but..."

Given their lumberjack bodies, I doubted anyone would mind.

"Want a drink?" Kevin asked.

"Yeah. That'd be great." I doubted I could charm these guys the way Austin had my family, but I was determined to make an effort. A drink definitely wouldn't hurt.

Gunner gestured toward two long garments hanging from pegs on the wall. "Check these out. They're from my steampunk collection. The blue gown is for my bearded lady. And the red one is for you." He took it down and turned it so I could see the black satin lapels. "It's a tailcoat. Perfect for a ringmaster, right?"

"Yeah." Most of the enthusiasm in my voice came from relief that it wasn't a dress. "Very cool."

Gunner held it against my chest and shoulders, eyeballing the size. "We have a top hat in that box right there, and as for boots—Austin said you wear the same size shoe, right? I've got some riding boots that are a little big on me, so they should fit you perfectly. We just need to find you the right bottoms."

Kevin snorted. "Pretty sure he's found the right bottom."

Albie snickered behind his cup.

Gunner ignored them. "We talked about black tights or leggings, but it's gonna be hot in the bar. The coat and hat make the look, so you can't lose those. But I'm thinking, you've got great legs, why not ditch pants altogether and go with a black jock?" He tilted his head, appraised me, and made a circling gesture toward my crotch. "You're not, by any chance, wearing one right now, are you?"

I grimaced. "I don't suppose black boxer briefs would work?" It was probably a hopeless suggestion.

Gunner made a skeptical noise. "No worries. You can have one of mine." He must have seen me cringe because he hastened to add, "I have new ones still in their packaging. I tend to go through them."

"Cool," I murmured. I'd never worn a jockstrap *as* clothing. At least the tails would cover my ass.

"So beyond the costume, what about a bit of a makeover?"

"What did you have in mind?" I asked hesitantly.

"Your mustache has a great shape. With a little wax, we could curl the tips. It'd be epic. But it would have more impact without the full beard." Gunner turned to Hank. "Don't you think he could rock a 'stache?"

Hank nodded. "Yeah. Assuming he wants to do it."

I stroked my chin self-consciously. Austin had said he loved mustaches, and I could grow my beard again in ten days if I hated it. I shrugged. "Sure. Let's do it."

"Excellent! How would you feel about going bald?" Gunner shook his head. "Sorry. Bad word choice. I meant, shaving it off."

My cheeks flushed. Fuck. I was *that* dude, the one clinging to his thinning hair, trying to run out the clock with a crewcut.

Hank interjected. "You don't have to go along with him. Gunner does this to everybody. Trust me, we've already disappointed him with our trapeze artist looks."

Albie and Kevin raised their cups, acknowledging their part in it.

"*Trapeze artists,*" Gunner muttered, rolling his eyes. "Y'all look like a bunch of half-dressed superheroes." To me, he said, "But he's right. Don't let me pressure you."

"No, no. My barber's suggested it a few times. Less kindly than you. I've considered it."

"You could definitely pull it off. You have a great head shape. I've got some clippers in the bathhouse next door. We could run over there real quick before Austin gets here," Gunner said in a tempting tone. "Might be fun to surprise him."

I blew out a breath. I hadn't done much to surprise Austin, and he'd accused me of *coming from a place of no.* "Okay."

"Yeah?" Gunner grinned, excited.

"Yeah. Why not?"

KNOWING how Gunner felt about his shoes, I let him carry the boots and the hat box, and I followed with the tailcoat and jock. The staff bathhouse was smaller than the one down at the pool complex and only had basic amenities—sinks, toilet stalls, a small changing area, and a communal shower—but, as with all the public buildings on the property, the rustic materials were thoughtfully used.

We had the place to ourselves.

Gunner produced a cordless trimmer and a salon cape from a set of lockers. After removing my T-shirt and lanyard, I sat on the wooden bench in front of him and let him fasten the cape around my neck.

This was a trust exercise. I couldn't stop bouncing my knee.

Gunner put his hand on my shoulder. "If you're gonna do this, do it for you, okay?"

"I am."

He turned on the clippers and tipped my head forward. Bits of my hair skittered down the cape. It was over in minutes. He paused to brush the loose hair off my neck, then came around to face me. He cocked his head and narrowed his eyes at me through his false lashes. "How long has it been since you've seen yourself without a beard?"

"Um. Twenty years?"

"No shit. Wow." He grinned. "This is gonna be fun."

He spent a lot more time buzzing my cheeks and trimming my mustache. Finally, he whipped off the cape, and shook it out with a flourish.

I walked over to the sinks, resisting the urge to run to the nearest mirror because I didn't want Gunner to know how truly vain I was. I was mostly concerned with looking like I was trying to be someone I wasn't.

Damn. I did look younger. And hotter if I could say so myself.

Gunner joined me, setting a can of shaving cream and a razor at the edge of the sink. "So what do you think? Pretty good, huh?"

"This is"—I smiled at him in the mirror—"a damn good edit."

Gunner laughed. "Perfect analogy. It's all you, just... revealed."

I sighed. "I should have done this sooner."

Gunner shrugged. "Everything tends to happen in its own perfect time."

I ran my hand over my head. "It feels like a cat's tongue."

"Yeah, it's as close as the clippers can get, but it's quick, and it *looks* bald. You might just want to shave your cheeks and neck for now and do your scalp later. Or even when you get back home when you have plenty of time. It can take a while to get it perfectly smooth."

While I shaved and dressed, Gunner swept my hair off the floor, and then he gave me pointers on how to style the tips of my mustache with wax.

"You look fantastic."

"Thanks," I said, offering Gunner a handshake. "For the costume and the edit."

He took my hand and pulled me in for a hug. "My pleasure. Thanks for trusting me."

The screen door opened with a screech, and Austin called out, "Where's my big top?"

30

AUSTIN APPEARED SPORTING A GARGANTUAN, UNDENIABLY FAKE mustache. Pomade glistened in his hair, which was parted on the side and scraped flat against his scalp. His cheeks were clean-shaven and rounded with rouge. He wore a black singlet, which showed off his chest and highlighted his package, and lace-up wrestler's boots. The spitting image of a vintage strongman. *Of course.* He was also wearing a red lanyard.

His mouth fell open when he saw me.

"Nice 'stache," I said nervously. Standing there in the costume he'd chosen for me, awaiting his reaction, I'd never felt more naked. The tailcoat did offer some coverage, but wearing a jockstrap *instead of pants* still stretched the boundaries of my comfort zone. I self-consciously doffed my hat, revealing my bald head.

"Damn, Prof! I honestly didn't think you could get any hotter." He crossed the room and reached up to rub the stubble on my scalp. "Oh! Velvety." He dropped his gaze to my mouth. "Nice 'stache yourself, by the way. This is my backup. My real one's not quite thick enough. I looked like one of those fifteen-year-old boys who's trying too soon and not quite there yet. Yours, though. Yours is legit!"

"Can you kiss with that monstrous thing on your face?" I glanced at Gunner, who was politely ignoring us, intent on sweeping the floor again.

"One way to find out." Austin's kiss filled my nose with synthetic hair and the smell of adhesive, but apparently, my dick didn't mind too much. "Mm. Smashing 'stache," he said. "I'm into it." He stepped back to take me in again from head to toe, opening the front of my tailcoat and cupping my mesh-covered cock. "You look fucking amazing."

I wasn't *hating* my legs in a jockstrap and riding boots, so I chose to believe him.

We returned to the bunkhouse, where the guys cheered my transformation and announced we were just in time for shots.

Albie said Austin had told them about my house. It turned out that Kevin's family owned the cabinet company where Ben and I had sourced some of the materials for my kitchen remodel, and we ended up chatting about Craftsman architecture.

Austin slipped his hand into mine. He said little, but he listened and watched me with a soft warm smile. It was easier talking to them with him at my side. I invited them all to come over sometime when they were in town. After Charles and I had split up, I'd never hosted anything remotely resembling a party, but I could picture these guys in my home, maybe with Eric and Ben too, having a few drinks.

Bailey asked me what I taught, and when I said twentieth century British lit, he wanted to know if I ever taught the novel *Maurice*. To include the other guys in the conversation, I explained that it was E.M. Forster's posthumously published gay love story.

They surprised me with the thoughtfulness of their questions. They seemed genuinely interested. Bailey said he wished he could've studied more queer history when he was in college. I taught a course on Bloomsbury authors every spring, and I usually went with *Howards End* because it was more well-known, but I could easily swap it out next year.

This was the first time in months I'd thought about returning to teaching without a sense of dread or apathy.

Austin kissed me on the cheek and whispered, "You're sexy when you get all professory. They like you."

These guys were intelligent, kind, and their acceptance was almost as intoxicating as the alcohol. I truly understood why this was his happy place.

A RADIO SQUAWKED. "Gunner, Gunner. Jim. Where the hell are y'all?" Jim shouted over a din of music and noise. "It's almost eleven."

"We're doing last looks," Gunner lied. "About to head up now."

"Well, fix your wigs and come on."

Hank helped Gunner zip the back of his dress. Bailey pulled on a rainbow wig and started frantically digging through a pile of clothes asking if anyone had seen his clown nose. Austin went to the mirror with a handful of blue bills he'd seemingly produced out of nowhere. "Where're your bucks, Prof?" he called over his shoulder as he slid a few of his own into the neckline of his singlet.

"Um... in my trailer."

"You didn't bring the fanny pack?"

I shrugged. "I still have pockets." I pulled out the single red bill the golf-cart driver had given me on my way here.

"Give me that." Austin snatched it from me and opened my coat. "You need to tuck some into your jock. Like this. It's kinda like a tip jar. It needs to be seeded."

Albie snickered at the word and reached to hand me another bill. With a smirk, Kevin slipped me one too. "For your seeding."

One by one, the others presented me with their contributions. *God. These undeniably beautiful young men, voting for me of all people.* My face flooded with warmth, but I managed to murmur my thanks.

"See?" Austin smiled. "It works." He continued tucking and arranging the bills behind the elastic band of my jock, slipping his fingers into the pouch a little deeper than was necessary a few times and *accidentally* grazing my dick.

With the pill in my system and the promise of being alone with him later, my cock started to swell uncomfortably. "If you keep that up," I muttered, "we're gonna have to skip the party."

"We don't have to stay long." With a look of intense heat, Austin waggled his eyebrows. "There." He stepped away and turned me toward the mirror. "Check it out."

Good grief. "It looks like I'm wearing a fucking papier-mâché tutu."

"But it *matches*," Austin insisted as if that were enough to convince me to appear like this in public.

BAILEY SNAPPED a few group selfies on the porch of the bunkhouse, and Albie and Kevin peeled off in an ATV. After Gunner convinced Austin to leave behind his cartoonishly large Styrofoam dumbbell—"Props are a pain in the ass to keep up with!"—the five of us crowded into Hank's king-cab truck.

Austin did bring a backpack. "A change of clothes," he whispered, unzipping the flap enough for me to see my red Nikes. "For later."

Vehicles jammed the parking lot near the Cubby Hole. We had to park down the hill in the Village and hike the rest of the way. There had to have been twice the number of people as last time I was there. Hundreds of bodies crowded the outside deck watching stilt-walkers, jugglers, fire-eaters, and poi performers on the ground below.

Austin made a crack about the abundance of sword-swallowers.

When we finally reached the top of the stairs, a large figure in a long-sleeved Victorian dress stepped in front of Gunner, barring his way. "Oh, hell no!" Jim said, hands on his hips. His beard had been teased into a sort of chin bouffant and sprayed with glitter. "I've about had it with all you bitches trying to steal my look."

Heads turned to see if the confrontation was real or not —more than a few of them bearded ladies—but Jim and Gunner were laughing and exchanging air kisses.

"There's your competition, Prof," Austin whispered.

I followed his line of sight to the handsome man with the full head of dark hair perfectly graying at the temples. He was super butch and obviously didn't give a fuck about costume themes. He was shirtless with a carpet of perfect fur covering his defined pecs. He wore a single armband around his left biceps, black leather chaps over jeans, motorcycle boots, and aviator sunglasses.

He caught me staring, grinned around the stub of his cigar, and up-nodded.

"S'up, Smokey?" Austin said, playing it cool.

I snorted. "Smokey?" I said under my breath. "The Bear? For real?"

"Yeah. He's always doing the whole cigar-smoking-daddy schtick. Jim told me he goes to all the events around the country snatching up as many contest titles as he can."

The man's pockets were stuffed with red bills. "I doubt he'd find me much competition for anything," I muttered. "Other than maybe night vision."

"Well, you are," Austin said earnestly.

I rolled my eyes and kissed his fake mustache. "You're sweet. But I don't really care about this contest. I'm here for you." I opened the door for him, braced myself against the thumping assault of dance music, and followed him inside.

The domed ceiling had been draped with red-and-white striped fabric, and with the round shape of the room, it made a believable approximation of a circus tent. Aerial artists spun on ribbons above a crowd of clowns, more bearded ladies, a few Tiger Kings, and men in bear onesies.

We made our way to a small open space at the bar beside a guy in gray body makeup who was manspreading on a stool to accommodate the prosthetic elephant trunk between his legs.

We ordered bottled waters from Luke, who was dressed as a circus cowboy. He told us to check out Sawyer. He'd convinced him to wear a lion's head hoodie. Under a fringe of fake mane, Sawyer didn't look too thrilled about it, but when he caught Luke's fond expression, his scowl melted into a smile.

"I'll be right back," Austin said. "I gotta go talk to the DJ."

I watched him move through the crowd, constantly stopping to collect blue bills from literally everyone he passed. He treated them all the same with a smile and a quick chat that made them laugh. He was fucking *loved* because he loved everyone.

I didn't watch him with jealousy—maybe a little possessiveness—but mostly with wonder. I felt... *proud* of him. Humbled to have been chosen by him. Fortunate to know him in a way others didn't.

I'd intended to blend into the wall and observe the spectacle, but I too was continually approached by men leaning in to say hello, complimenting my costume, flirting, and gifting me with their red bucks. After a few of them tried to tuck their bills into my jock, I quickly became adept at intercepting with handshakes.

Austin returned and grabbed me by the hand, trying to pull me off the wall. "Come on. I requested a special song for you."

I resisted, shaking my head.

The song changed.

"This is it!"

I didn't recognize the music, but the female vocals sounded familiar, and the lyrics...

Oh.

It was a remixed version of the godforsaken "I Hope You Dance."

I rolled my eyes and groaned. "I feel very attacked!"

He leaned in to shout-speak into my ear, almost taking out my eye with his fake mustache. "I put you refusing to dance with me in the bonfire last weekend, so this is happening. It's magic. You're powerless." It was clear from his expression that I wasn't getting out of it this time.

It wasn't that I couldn't dance or that I had no sense of rhythm, but I knew I could never match Austin's level of performance.

I didn't want to disappoint him.

But what choice would've disappointed him more?

I heaved a sigh and allowed him to drag me onto the floor.

I needn't have worried about what I was expected to do. Once he had me under the disco ball, he wrapped his arms around me, and rocked me from side to side in half-time.

The music, the pace, the crowd didn't matter. The message did.

In a top hat, tails, a jockstrap tutu, and boots, with red lanyards tangled between our hearts, I slow-danced nose-to-nose with my strongman.

And nobody had ever looked at me this way.

Except he always looked at me this way.

We kissed, and he ground himself against me. He was hard.

We both were.

Over the loud music, Austin shouted, "Wanna go do butt stuff?"

31

WE ATTEMPTED TO SLIP AWAY WITHOUT ANYONE NOTICING, but Jim, who was hanging out with some of the staff on the side porch, spotted us halfway down the stairs. "Y'all are leaving already?"

"He needs to show me something," Austin said innocently.

"Uh-huh. I'll bet he does."

"Take care of my boys!" Gunner yelled.

Austin lifted his foot so Gunner could see his shoes. "These are mine, bro."

Gunner inclined his head toward me. "I was talking to the professor."

"I'll be careful with them," I promised. "I'll take everything off as soon as we get back to the trailer."

"We figured as much," Jim said.

"So his motorcycle-cop boots are *boys*," Austin murmured. "Interesting. I wonder what their names are."

"I'm pretty sure he called them riding boots."

Austin looked me up and down with a filthy smirk. "Not with that mustache."

· · ·

IT FELT like it took forever to get to my trailer. Austin had to run back to the bar to get the key to Hank's truck so he could retrieve his backpack. I almost panicked trying to find the key I'd hidden too well under the concrete steps.

Finally, we were alone in the air-conditioned hush.

This was the moment I'd been looking forward to all week.

I cupped Austin's face, and we kissed until his fake mustache came off in my mouth and my top hat tumbled to the floor with a bang. "Shit. Hold on." I wrestled out of the tailcoat and hung it along with the hat on wall hooks by the door. I plucked the bear bucks out of my jock, crumpled them into a wad, and tossed them onto the coffee table.

"Jock and boots," Austin growled.

"Help me get them off." I dropped onto the sofa, lay back on my elbows, and stuck out a foot.

"I was digging the look," he pouted.

"I'm trying to get us naked here, sir."

He yanked off my boots and socks and stripped out of his singlet, shedding blue bucks like falling leaves. "My costumes sure don't last long around you."

He swapped out his wrestling shoes for my Nikes. *Fuck, that was hot.* While he was still squatting tying the laces, I stood and stepped into his space. I towered over him, the swollen pouch of my jock at his eye level. He reached up and gently kneaded me through the mesh fabric. "Damn," he breathed, pulling the elastic band away from my body and releasing my cock. "You're so fucking hard."

I silently prayed I stayed that way.

He wrapped his hand around my shaft and stroked the sensitive underside with his thumb. He tasted the bead of precum at the tip, his tongue barely making contact. I pushed toward his lips, needing more, and thank God, he didn't tease me. He gripped my cock by the base and took it all in a single mouthful.

I nudged the back of his throat, gagging him a little, but he breathed through his nose and held me encased in loose, wet heat. He swallowed around my length and moaned.

Cursing from the vibration, I placed my hands on his head and tried to restrain myself from pushing as deep as I wanted to. His throat would never be deep enough. I needed to lie on top of him, to crush him under my weight as he squeezed me between his thighs.

I pulled out, awed by the sight of my wet cock sliding from his stretched lips.

He dragged air into his lungs and looked up at me through watering eyes.

I swiped the tears off his cheek with my thumbs. "Bedroom," I said. "Now."

Austin sprang up and hustled down the hallway, and I hurried after him, afraid of losing momentum. He launched himself onto the bed, spinning at the last minute like a pole vaulter.

I crawled on top of him, marveling at how the intensity of the first moment of full body contact never dimmed. Austin pulled me down into a kiss, and we writhed against one another, shifting and trying to renew the sensation.

I broke the kiss and pulled back so I could push his legs apart with my knees. I dragged my cock across his sac, and then it dropped, the head nudging his taint, but...

That wasn't where it should be.

Nothing should have *dropped*.

Fuck.

I braced his legs with my hands and investigated the situation, pretending to watch myself tease his hole.

Keeping the panic from my face, I continued moving my hips and trying to reestablish contact, but I was half-hard at best. Every time I pressed against him, I tucked my dick between us. The angle was all wrong for the stimulation I needed.

I moved back up to our original position. Nothing would bring me back more effectively than full body contact and kissing.

If I could get it back.

Shit.

I'd done everything right this time. I'd been popping boners *all day* with only the slightest stimulation. Mere minutes ago, in the living room, I'd been as hard as I'd ever been in my life.

Stop thinking about it. Stop talking to yourself about thinking about it. Be present. Look at him. He's smiling at you.

But there was also concern in his eyes. It was only a flicker, and he was trying not to let it show, but he knew what was happening.

"Lemme suck it some more," he said, his tone too casual.

God. He's trying to save the situation.

"Um... I might need to go pee first." It was a possibility. I'd drunk a full bottle of water at the bar.

"That's cool," he said like it was no big deal.

I smiled and retreated to the bathroom. It wasn't a surrender. I was regrouping. Taking a breath.

Unfortunately, the only sure-fire way to avoid panicking was not to panic in the first place.

It was an impossible head game.

When I returned, I found Austin propped up against the headboard.

I stood at the foot of the bed, flaccid now, and unsure of how to continue.

Austin patted his chest. "Come up here and feed it to me."

The thought of straddling his neck, flopping myself into his mouth, and going through the motions...

Trying.

"Um..." I stalled, rubbing my hand over the rough velvet of my scalp, considering my options. "Let me lie down next to you for a bit."

He rolled onto his side to make room for me, and I lay flat on my back with my shoulder against his chest. Taking matters into my own hands was probably my best bet, but I still wanted some contact.

I sighed, gave my dick a few tugs, and tried to embrace him watching me as a new level of intimacy. He'd choose to see it as a turn-on. It was all a performance anyway.

And it wasn't nothing.

Austin trailed his fingers through my chest hair. I focused on breathing, trying to relax and allow pure sensation to take over.

As I found a rhythm in my strokes, he tweaked my nipples, gently at first, then slowly increasing the pressure.

Okay. That's doing something.

I nodded for him to keep going, and jacked myself harder, more rushed and frantic than if I'd been alone but hopeful.

He released my nipple and leaned in to tease it with his mouth. He sucked and flicked it with his tongue, and...

It should've worked—it probably worked for most men, and it usually worked on me—but in that moment it tickled in a way that was irritating more than arousing, and I flinched.

He immediately stopped. "Sorry."

I shook my head, furious with myself for making him feel like he'd done something wrong.

"What can I do to help?" His voice was low, unsure, so unlike him. In any other situation, no matter how inappropriate, he would've teased me. I would've acted appalled, he would've laughed, and when I couldn't help but smile, we would have moved on. "Or not. I don't have to do anything if you don't want me to." It was excruciating how carefully he spoke.

If I gave up, I'd need to release him. Let him find a better prospect. He deserved more.

But I wasn't ready for him to give up on me.

"Maybe if you kiss me..." It always started with his kiss.

He brought his lips softly to mine. It was perfect, gentle and sensual to start, then blooming at the right speed with the right amount of low simmering heat.

I jacked myself frantically, every muscle in my body straining, gasping like a drowning man with his face just breaking the surface.

He granted me a breath, and even that was perfect, like a warm caramel pulled in two.

I stared into his eyes, my mouth open in a silent, desperate plea, yet still wanting to protect him from my fear.

He touched the tip of his nose to mine, looked at me with incredible tenderness and empathy, and whispered, "It's okay."

And I let go.

My body went limp, deflating on a sigh. A moment of sweet release before hope receded to guilty relief.

"Fuck. I'm sorry." I shrank away from him, avoiding eye contact. I took a deep breath. "I don't get it. I took the pill last night. Perfectly timed for the delayed effects. I woke up hard. I was hard on and off all day. You know." I gestured toward the living room, clenched my teeth. "It was working."

Austin hummed, trailing his fingers in soothing circles through the hair on my belly. "It's probably the alcohol. Technically, you're not supposed to drink on those meds. Everybody does, of course, but..."

I covered my face with my hands. "I'm so fucking embarrassed."

"Aww, come on." He pulled my hands away and forced me to look at him. "You don't have any reason to be."

"It's just so frustrating to not be able to *do* what I need to. And to feel like I'm disappointing you."

"Paul. Stop." Nothing stopped me like him using my given name. "I understand why you're frustrated, but I'm not disappointed. Not even close. You came. You hung out with my boys. You pulled off this whole Sandy-at-the-end-of-*Grease* move. And you danced with me, which was *major*." He settled beside me, laying his head on my shoulder and draping his arm over my belly. "Now we're here in this super nice trailer, enjoying all this amazing body contact." He squeezed me against him. "And it's only the first night."

Was it really enough for him? What if I couldn't resolve this and he came to resent it? "I'd understand if you wanted to go back to the party."

He stilled. "You wanna go back to the party?"

"I meant... you could go by yourself."

He propped himself up on his elbow and stared at me. "You think I want to hook up with other people?"

"I'm not accusing you of anything. You're twenty-six years old, and there're hundreds of guys up there who could make you happy and—"

"Are you asking me to leave?" Disbelief warped his voice.

"God no. No." Him thinking I wanted him to leave was a

thousand times worse than if he'd wanted to go. "I just don't want you to feel like you're missing out on anything because of me."

"I don't. I'm not." His eyes were wide, his expression earnest. "I'm happy being here with you."

"You could have anyone. Why me?" Somewhere down the road, he might wish he'd made a different choice, and it would hurt worse to hear it then.

"Well..." I saw him make the calculation that he should try to lighten the mood. "Because you're hot, and you're really smart, which is really, *really* hot. You're fun to aggravate, and you love my singing—"

I huffed out a laugh. "Come on. Be serious."

He waved his hand through the air, flailing, struggling to find the words. "It's... the *spark*. I don't know if I can explain it. I'm not a writer. It's a light in the dark, and I'm just following it. With other guys, it's like chasing lightning bugs in the woods. There's a thousand of them. They wink out, move around, disappear, but with you, the closer we get, the light keeps growing. Like you came out here to find me too." He laughed nervously and groaned in frustration. "You show up. You picked a fucking red lanyard for me. And you care about what happens to me when the party's over."

I swallowed. "Yes. I do. Which is why I don't want you taking on my shit. I want to protect you."

"I have a word for you," he said abruptly. "*Karezza*. Ever heard it?"

I frowned. "I don't think so. Is it Italian?"

"It could be. It means, like... affection and touching without being overly focused on completion. It's supposed to be good for all kinds of different... sexual disorders and stuff."

"Oh my God. See? You shouldn't feel like you have to *google* how to fix me."

"I didn't. I heard about it from Jim."

"You told Jim?"

"No. It came up while we were decorating earlier. One of his random, new age, *teachable moments*." He rolled his eyes and chuckled. "The man listens to too many self-improvement podcasts."

I stared at him.

He sighed. "Listen. All week long, what I've been looking forward to the most is spending the night with you, spooning, waking up with you..."

I sighed. I could've thought of more doubts—I could've *conjured* more reasons to worry—but my heart said I had no choice but to believe him. "Really?"

"Yes. Really." He toed off my shoes and let them drop to the floor. "Now let's get under the covers and fucking cuddle."

32

THE ALARM I'D SET FOR AUSTIN WENT OFF LIKE AN AIR-RAID siren. Ignoring the pounding in my head from dehydration, side effects, and regret, we made out. We kissed and frotted, hitting the snooze button three times too many until the need to pee was greater than his fear of being late for work.

We showered in the large glass enclosure. Having enough room to kiss under the spray while we lathered each other was heaven. I was seriously considering hiking out to the pole after breakfast, calling Ben, and telling him I wanted a do-over on my bathroom remodel at home. To hell with the charming original clawfoot tub. The tiny circular curtain wasn't going to cut it.

I lined up Austin's cock with mine and stroked us together. "You wanna get off real quick?"

"It doesn't have to be about getting off," he said with a coy smile, massaging my shoulders.

"It does if you're blue-balled."

He slid his hands up the tense muscles at the back of my neck and squeezed my skull, pressing his thumbs against my temples. "Karezza, remember?"

"You're killing me," I lied, not wanting him to stop.

"Karezza," he whispered sotto voce.

"Italian for torture-edging."

He laughed. "Hang in there. I'll have a couple hours free after the contest. We can come back here and take a special nap."

"Fine," I said petulantly, stepping away and giving him room to rinse off. While he leaned back into the spray with his eyes closed, I chanced an apology. I needed to reassure him that I'd had a moment of weakness, testing a fear that I'd lose him, but I wasn't going to give up. "Listen. About last night—"

"I had a fucking blast."

"Good. But I'm sorry I—"

"Shh." He clumsily swiped his fingers down my face like he was petting a horse. "Karezza," he said as if it were a calming incantation.

"Is this the new *butt stuff*? Are you going to keep repeating it until it loses all meaning?"

"I think *butt stuff* is a little obnoxious. This is the last time I'm gonna say *butt stuff*. And speaking of time. Here." He traded places with me under the showerhead. "I gotta run. Literally. I'm gonna have to jog up to the lodge."

I cut off the water and grabbed him a towel. "I'll drive you."

"I'd hate for you to lose your parking space."

"I'd hate for you to lose your job."

"Food won't be ready for another hour," he warned.

"That's fine. If you can hook me up with a coffee, I'll sit outside and read."

"Karezza!" he said, making jazz hands.

"You're relentless."

. . .

I SAT at a table near the cabana.

After breakfast, I'd gone back to the trailer to change into board shorts, then headed to the pool. I read while watching Austin and Luke set up the bar. Market tents crowded the far side of the pool area, one for the DJ, a few for T-shirt vendors, and another with a simple table and three chairs.

The Bloody Marys arrived and joined me. When Barry spotted *Hollywood Pool Boy*, he said he'd been friends with Jody Summers. "It's a shame he couldn't have written at least one book with a leading male couple. It was a different time." I accepted one drink and carefully nursed it for over an hour as we chatted, the party growing around us.

Austin had been right. It was like a holiday weekend, only more. Before today, I wouldn't have believed the pool complex could hold this many people. A beer pong tournament blocked the covered walkway adjoining the bathhouse; forty guys played some kind of unrecognizable keep away/volleyball/dodgeball game in the pool; and everywhere there wasn't a table or a lounge chair had become a dance floor.

"Speaking of pool boys," Barry said, looking up and shading his eyes.

"Y'all over here gossiping about me?" Austin said from behind me, placing his hands on my shoulders.

I tipped my head back and smiled up at him.

"Just talking about how cute you two look together," Barry said, batting his lashes. "Now that's a video I'd like to stream."

"I'll send you a link to our OnlyFans." Austin winked at me.

I blushed and shook my head while the Marys hooted and cackled.

Austin tapped my shoulder. "Grab your bucks. They're certifying finalists for the contest. I already turned mine in. Come on."

Barry pulled a red bill out of his cigarette case and slid it across the table to me. He scowled at his buddies. "Don't tell me. Y'all already gave yours to Smokey, didn't you?"

"Bitch, we didn't know Paul that well yet!"

I put Jody's book in my backpack—I'd resisted using the fanny pack on principle—and followed Austin to a tent where the score paddle guys were tallying bear bucks and making notes on a clipboard. They counted and recounted my bills, whispered among themselves, and then one of them looked up at me and smiled. "All right. Listen for Jim to call your name."

Austin dragged me back to the cabana where Gunner, Hank, and Kevin were talking to Luke. "He's in!" Austin announced.

"I don't know about all this," I said, spreading my hands in a helpless gesture.

"Wear the jock from last night," Gunner said, mistakenly thinking I was talking about my board shorts and flip-flops.

I scowled. "I'm not strutting around in broad daylight in nothing but a jockstrap."

Austin waggled his eyebrows. "You could."

"Trade shorts with Kevin," Gunner said.

Kevin was wearing coach's shorts with snaps like the kind my ninth grade PE teacher had worn, only Kevin's were about six inches shorter and his thigh muscles were the size of tree trunks.

Kevin shrugged and started to take them off, but I held up my hand to stop him. "No, it's cool. Thanks. Don't get me wrong, you look great in those, but... they're not exactly my style."

Hank shot Gunner a withering look. "Let the man wear whatever he wants. He doesn't have to try that hard."

"That's right," Austin said. "We were barely at the party last night for fifteen minutes. Prof picked up most of these bucks in the dining hall in his street clothes."

"All right." Gunner raised his hands in surrender. "Point taken. Authenticity is powerful."

Austin put his arm around me and whispered. "Just be yourself."

The volume of the music dropped, and Jim's voice boomed over the speakers. "Testing, testing. Can y'all hear me okay?"

"Shit. It's starting," Austin hissed. "Luke! We gotta get my shots ready!" He kissed me and dashed behind the bar.

Jim emerged from the DJ's tent carrying a microphone and a clipboard. "Look at all the beautiful people here today. Everybody having a good time so far?"

The crowd applauded, but thunder clapped and everyone's gaze snapped to the southwest. The sun still blazed in the blue sky, but a bank of dark clouds had crept over the mountains.

"Uh-oh. Mother Nature's telling us to get this show on the road. Y'all better get out of the pool. Safety first. Make room for everybody but keep the catwalk clear." It seemed impossible this many people could fit inside the pool complex. "Get close. This is your chance to rub up on a handsome stranger. If you haven't already."

The unmistakable intro to Missy Elliott's "I Can't Stand the Rain" thumped from the speakers, and Jim shot the DJ a glare. "All right, Danny. I know you think you're being cute with this song choice, but you're playing with some dangerous weather magic."

The DJ shouted something I couldn't hear, and Jim carried

on. "Okay. An illustrious panel of self-nominated busybodies"—the score paddle guys waved—"have counted the bear bucks and certified our finalists. Here's how it's gonna go down. I'll announce the category and call the names of the top two contestants. They're gonna step forward and stomp around this pool for you so you can get one last good look at 'em. The winner shall be determined by the volume of your deafening applause. Let me hear it." Jim held the microphone out for the crowd's response, but he made a disappointed face and shook his head. "I said, *deafening* applause."

This time, the crowd obliged him with a roar.

"Now that's what we're looking for. Danny, for the love of the Goddess, play us something else, please."

The DJ executed an abrupt song change and blasted the Weather Girls' ubiquitous gay anthem "It's Raining Men."

"Now you're asking for it," Jim said sourly. "It's on you." He consulted his clipboard. "First up, we've got our contenders for Best Otter, Adam and—y'all, I swear, I'm not making this up—Adam and *Steve*."

Two lanky, bearded, hairy-chested guys emerged from the crowd, one with a crewcut wearing a silver Speedo, and the other with his long hair piled up in a man-bun and long denim shorts hanging from his narrow hips. They worked their way down opposite sides of the pool, dancing and flirting with the spectators before returning to flank Jim. He called them by name in turns, and they stepped forward to receive their ovations. I felt personally vindicated when Steve won wearing skate punk shorts. He bowed, and after accepting a quick hug from Adam, they melted back into the crowd.

I was relieved by how quickly it had gone, but I still couldn't see myself doing it. Austin, who was arranging Jell-

O shots on a tray with Luke, caught my eye and winked. I glanced at the approaching storm front and prayed for an intervention.

The contest continued with a pair of smooth, musclebound bulls who posed and flexed their way down the catwalk and back. They could've been boyfriend twins. It took three separate rounds of applause to determine the winner.

Thunder rumbled, closer this time, and the wind kicked up. The silver undersides of the leaves flashed against the darkening sky.

"I tried to warn you, Danny," Jim said. "Bring me the cubs. I'm looking for Marcus and Austin."

A short, stocky guy stepped forward wearing booty shorts and a half-jersey with the number sixty-nine on it. Austin abandoned Luke to the shots pyramid they were building. He paused to kiss me, but instead of joining Jim and Marcus, he raced over to a guy with a colorful tie-dyed sarong knotted around his waist. After hurriedly conferring with him, the guy nodded, removed the sarong, and gave it to Austin.

"What the fuck is he gonna do with that?" I muttered to no one in particular.

"Austin, honey, we're waiting on you." With his hand on Marcus's shoulder, Jim watched with the rest of us as Austin wrapped the fabric around his neck like a long scarf with the ends trailing over his back. "He's getting into some flowy quick drag for us, y'all." Austin trotted back to the cabana and took the tray of Jell-O shots from Luke. "Oh, I see. He's gonna bribe everybody with some free liquor too. He's coming for you, Marcus."

Marcus said something the microphone didn't pick up.

"Didya hear that, Austin?" Jim bellowed. "Marcus said you better work."

Handing out shots, Austin tossed back over his shoulder, "I'm already working!" And the crowd roared.

This pageant was descending into WWE SmackDown territory.

The slower pace of Madonna's "Rain" suited Austin's performative cocktail service, but Marcus had already made it to the turning point and waited awkwardly for Austin to catch up.

After dragging the walk out to three times as long as any previous contestant had taken, Austin finally reached the end of the pool and someone helpfully took his empty tray. When he turned, his eyes sought mine, and I realized he was standing in the same spot where I'd first seen him. He smiled, and even though everyone could bask in it, it was for me.

He posed, letting the wind move the sarong to great effect like he'd personally invoked the weather for this moment, but when he started back, a gust tore it from his neck. He shrieked, briefly losing his game face, but he managed to snatch the fabric before it fell into the water and danced back with it fluttering over his head like a flag.

Talk about cock of the walk. In my red shoes...

The crowd ate it up.

The applause declaring Austin the winner wasn't even close. I almost felt sorry for Marcus, but Austin tied the corners of the sarong around Marcus's neck like a cape and they took a victory lap around the entire pool together.

"Moving along to our daddies," Jim announced pointedly. "Let's have Smokey and Professor Paul!"

Hearing my name called, my heart started to race. Gunner nudged my shoulder, urging me forward.

As I left the shade of the cabana, Austin met me, glowing with the high of his performance.

I hugged him, and whispered in his ear, "How the fuck is anyone supposed to follow that?"

He pulled back and murmured against my lips, "Nobody better than you." He kissed me hungrily as a wave of catcalls moved through the crowd.

"Are you trying to give me a visible boner?" I asked under my breath.

"You're welcome." Austin smiled mischievously.

"Austin, honey," Jim said. "We need to borrow your man for a minute."

His man. I liked the sound of that. Simple and more appropriate than *boyfriend*.

Smokey was waiting next to Jim in the same outfit he'd worn last night with a few notable exceptions—no jeans under his leather chaps and a painful-looking metal cock ring and ball stretcher highlighting his endowment.

All righty, then. Sure. Let's compete with that.

Austin released me. "Go walk."

"I'm not sure what to do with my arms," I whispered.

"Don't overthink it."

Sure. No problem.

I walked.

I had no idea what song was playing. I saw people clapping and yelling, but I couldn't hear anything but white noise. Maybe it was the wind in my ears, or negative ions from the approaching storm, or that one strong-ass Bloody Mary...

I might have left my body for a few moments.

I definitely couldn't feel my arms at all, and I hoped whatever my face was doing passed for smiling.

I made it to the end of the pool and stopped. I

recognized a lot of faces, even if I didn't remember their names. Sweet guys who'd come up to say hello, who'd welcomed me at meals, who'd given me the bucks that had brought me to this moment. What was the word for the complicated, conflicted form of gratitude I experienced? *Thanks?*

I had to have been the most awkward contestant in the history of this event—like amateur mall fashion show bad—yet they cheered for me.

Out of the corner of my eye, I saw Smokey making his way back to Jim, which meant it was half over, thank God.

How long had it been so far? The part of my brain that processed time had also gone offline.

You can do anything for sixty seconds.

When I turned, I saw Austin in front of the cabana waving pompoms, doing some kind of *routine*, and for a moment I thought maybe they were cheering for him.

We all wanted to believe we could meet someone out of our league who could see something in us we couldn't see in ourselves and love us for it. Or love us in spite of what we couldn't hide. Love us anyway.

We hoped.

Maybe it was my hope that everyone saw and cheered.

The final round of applause felt like "Happy Birthday" on steroids with my crew of Bloody Mary drinkers, lumberjacks, and pool boys chanting "Prof! Prof! Prof!" Being claimed by them—not just by Austin but by all of them—mattered more to me than the title ever would.

Best Daddy. What did it even *mean*? It was glamour, myth, projection. The reasons why people found you attractive were about them. The labels they gave you were out of your control. But sometimes their stories about you were wonderful, and your wins were theirs too.

Jim proclaimed me the winner, and Smokey crushed my fingers in a gesture I'd have been pressed to call a *handshake*. My head cheerleader, who was yelling like he'd lost his ever-loving mind, nearly tackled me in a hug and dragged me back to the cabana where I was greeted with backslaps and congratulations.

By the time my ears stopped ringing and my heart rate slowed, Jim was calling the winner of the final category, Best Bear. The man reminded me of what Austin might be like twenty years from now. As Jim presented him with a leather sash that read *Mr. Bear Mountain Lodge* the first drops of rain hit the metal roofs.

It was like a starting gun had gone off. The guests ran for cover, Jim hurriedly thanked everyone, and the guys on staff leapt into action. Sawyer yelled for Luke, who took off running, and moments later, they were speeding up the road in some kind of badass ATV.

"They like to fuck in the rain up at the waterfall," Austin said, grinning as he padlocked the beer cases.

"There's a waterfall?"

"I'm only half-kidding. There's also a dam up there Sawyer tinkers with. I'll take you up there tomorrow." He came out from behind the bar and kissed me on the cheek. "I'm gonna go grab some tarps."

"Do you need my help?"

"Hang tight for a minute. When I get back, we'll go rescue some tent campers. On the way down earlier I noticed some poor soul had set up in the cursed site. I'll be right back."

I looked around at the people waiting out the storm in the cabana. The Bloody Marys had gathered around an ashtray to smoke, Barry declaring he was too drunk to run through mud, and—

Christ.

Charles was pushing through the crowd toward me wearing board shorts, a blue lanyard, and a smirk. "I almost didn't recognize you," he said.

I drew myself up to my full height and squared my shoulders. "I thought it was time for a change."

"Well, you look great. And congratulations on your... latest achievement." He chuckled. "I voted for you, for what it's worth."

"Thanks," I said, managing to not roll my eyes.

"Speaking of titles, I meant to ask you last weekend. How's the new book coming along?"

"It's coming," I said, nodding. "It's a... departure from my previous work. I'm trying something different."

"Intriguing." Charles narrowed his eyes. "You seem happy."

Living well is the best revenge, I thought. I'd never put that in a book, though. It was too cliché. Besides, true happiness didn't need revenge. "I am," I confessed.

Austin returned with tarps under each arm, his soaking wet T-shirt clinging to his torso.

"I can definitely see why," Charles murmured. "He's very impressive."

"He is," I said. *In ways you can't even see.*

"Charles! Bro!" Austin calling the dean *bro* amused me even more than him ignoring his preference for *Charlie*. "You came!"

"It was a last-minute decision," Charles said, all smiles. "I wasn't sure about tent camping, but I found the most amazing site right on the creek. Someone must have had to leave early or something. I can't imagine why it would've gone unclaimed."

Austin and I shared a look.

"Didya have a chance to set up some weather protection?" Austin asked.

"The tent came with a rain fly." Charles waved dismissively. "Took less than a minute to pop it on."

Austin winced, sucking air between his teeth. He arched an eyebrow at me. "You wanna tell him?"

"Tell me what?" Charles asked.

Austin jerked his head in the direction of the trail. "I think we better talk on the way."

33

AUSTIN WAS A BETTER PERSON THAN ME. I MIGHT'VE applauded karma's late arrival and left Charles to deal with his own choices, but Austin inspired me to rise to his level. To my credit, I devised the tarp-and-log dam that diverted the stream of runoff away from Charles's site and a few others farther up the Soggy Bottom.

If Sawyer would dig out a series of trenches and install more permanent versions of these structures, they'd have a long-term solution.

"Sawyer's gonna be pissed somebody else thought of this first," Austin said. "But you definitely earned your dad title. And there's still time for a nap."

We walked back in the rain, holding hands. We were so soaked there was no reason to run at this point. We strolled down Trailer Park Avenue, basking in the rain like it was sunshine.

My red Nikes were trashed and muddy. I ordered Austin to leave them outside on the steps.

The air conditioning in the trailer felt like a meat locker.

By the time we grabbed clean towels from the linen closet, our teeth were chattering.

We dried off quickly and fled to the bed, pulling the covers over our heads to trap our warmth.

"Reminds me of our first night in the tent."

"Mm. Sweet." Austin turned so I could spoon him.

I wrapped my arms around his waist, my belly perfectly fitting the curve of his back, my thighs cradling his ass. My cock swelled, and I humped against him.

I brushed my mustache against his neck, and he turned his head so I could nuzzle his ear.

"Mm. You smell like petrichor."

"*Petrichor*?" he asked. "What the hell's that?"

"The delicious earthy scent that accompanies a rainstorm after a long period of dry weather. It's one of my favorite words."

"I think you made that one up."

"I did not! Google it!"

"Shh. We're napping." He nestled his cheek into the pillow and breathed slow and deep like he really intended to sleep. But he wriggled and arched back against me until my cock was trapped in the crease of his ass.

As much as I'd enjoyed the option, I hated to spend an erection this hard on another *intercrural* session. I was right there, and the temptation to angle and find his hole was too much.

I shifted my body lower and rutted up until the tip kissed his hole.

I was leaking like crazy, and when he bore down, the head slipped inside him.

I didn't want to hurt him, but I also couldn't risk stopping to get the lube out of the bedside table. I flexed my cock, purposefully pumping more precum into him, and pushed in an inch deeper.

He groaned, reached back, and lifted his butt cheek, spreading himself open for me.

I pinched saliva from my tongue and slicked the exposed part of my shaft, working as much moisture as I could along the seal between us. He relaxed the ring of muscle, and I pressed a fraction of an inch farther into him.

I slowly rocked back and forth, entering him by increments, grabbing his hips and pulling him onto my lap until I was fully encased in his crushing warmth.

Holy fuck. It felt like...

What was the word for this?

No, no, no. No words are required. Nobody needs your words right now. Stop thinking of words.

"Paul." Austin breathed my name like he was talking in his sleep. Dreaming. He clenched, purposefully gripping me, and the pressure at this stage made me harder.

It felt like I was growing inside him, reaching into him with each thrust.

He met every stroke, contracting and relaxing his interior muscles with perfect timing.

It was happening.

No shoes, no costumes, no expectations.

It was a miracle. A revelation.

How could such a moment be so profoundly *quiet*, accompanied only by stuttered breaths and soft grunts, the rustling of the duvet over our heads, and the faraway shushing of rain on the roof?

I never wanted it to be over.

I didn't even want to get off at this point, but I was too close.

I was coming.

I reached the edge of the cliff and fell, inevitably spilling over and into him.

And he caught me, contracting uncontrollably with the force of his own release, taking all that I had to give him.

I stayed inside him as long as I could, ears ringing, panting against his back.

When he felt me finally slip from him, he turned in my arms to face me, his grin crooked and smug. "See?" he said as if he had convinced me. "You can. Sometimes you will. Sometimes you won't. But you *can*."

I *could*.

I didn't *have* to—with Austin, it was safe for me to try—but I could.

We could.

He held up a hand. "Up top." His eyes twinkled with mischief, leaking the secret of the light inside him, that he was beautiful and sweet because he was empathetic and wise.

"I'm still not high-fiving you," I teased.

I kissed him instead.

"I talked to Jim yesterday," he said, his tone now serious. "They're not gonna keep me on past the summer. He said I need to *find a bigger platform for my talents*."

I sighed. "I know you're disappointed. But I agree with him. You're funny, gorgeous, and smart. You'll find something perfect for you."

He nodded. "I will. I texted Honey."

"Yeah?"

"She told me to call her on Monday, and we'll set up a time to meet and talk about the opening at YA."

"Austin. That's fantastic!"

"The position starts with the new school year, so if it

works out, I'll actually have to quit here before the season's over. Which is kind of a bummer, but..."

I hummed. "It'll be nice to have you in Edgewood, though, where we can, you know, see each other on a regular basis."

He laced his fingers through mine. "And see where this goes?"

"Yes. Absolutely."

EPILOGUE

Two Months Later

THE STAFF AT BEAR MOUNTAIN LODGE HAD CUT IT CLOSE, scheduling Austin's going away party for the weekend before public school started.

I was standing in the trailer's kitchen, contemplating whether I should start drinking now, when Austin emerged from the bathroom dressed in a white button-down shirt with the sleeves cut off, khaki shorts, red high-top sneakers, and a matching tie. "Ta-da!"

I smiled at the deconstructed version of the outfit he'd worn to his final interview. "Don't you look fancy."

"It's my lucky tie now," Austin said and kissed me on the cheek.

AUSTIN HAD MET with Honey a few days after the Bear Run. She'd shown him around the Youth Alliance facilities and shared their vision for the new after-school program for eight-to-twelve-year-olds. They wanted it to be fun and physical like a summer day camp that continued throughout the year, and they needed an activities director who could hit the ground running.

She'd invited him to come back and give a presentation to the board the following week.

The campground had been slow the weekend after the Run, so I'd rented a cabin and brought my laptop to update his résumé and make him a slide deck.

Austin had a ton of ideas for adapting adult training programs for young people. All the pieces of his purpose came together in the position—his education, his love of kids, his personal-training certifications. He was made for it. He admitted to being worried about references from his last teaching job, but I assured him no employer would be more understanding than Youth Alliance. I encouraged him to tell them his story, share what had happened to him in high school, and why he felt he had to leave North Crest Middle. It was important they knew where his passion originated.

Since his subletter was still living in his apartment, he'd grabbed some clothes and spent the night before the presentation at my house. I ironed his shirt and khakis for him and let him borrow a tie. He'd chosen a bright red one I rarely wore because it matched his new hi-tops. I'd gently questioned the choice, but he'd insisted red shoes were the only option for something this important. It was authentically *Austin*, and so far, his magic worked on everyone. The board at Youth Alliance had offered him the position a few days later.

When I'd wondered aloud if Honey had told my mom, Austin said, "She already messaged to congratulate me."

"Messaged you *how*?"

"On Facebook."

"You're friends with my mom on Facebook?"

He'd shrugged. "I'm friends with Veronica, John, Robert..."

"My *dad* has a Facebook account?"

I'D STILL HAD a little over two months left to produce a first draft before my own classes started. I wanted to embrace a new phase of my career with the same kind of courage and hope Austin had. Once I'd acknowledged the story in front of me, the words flowed. I did have a book—all the content I'd written about him—and it was a love story.

And love stories had a form I could learn. I'd asked Veronica if I could borrow a few gay romance novels, and she'd sent me home with two boxes of paperbacks and started texting me recommendations and links faster than I could've ever hoped to consume them all.

So many of these authors were damned good writers. Their books opened a portal for me to a world of happy endings and an audience that would accept a book about Austin and me.

I'd pitched it to my agent along with several sample chapters. She'd said we couldn't sell it as a Paul Carter novel, but she was excited about the potential for me to start a new brand under a pen name.

Austin had suggested I *take his name* and publish as Paul Fox. I'd pretended he was only joking, but after brainstorming dozens of possibilities, I kept coming back to it.

It was a leap of faith to tie my career to him, but the book had been his idea, and he was the inspiration.

We weren't going anywhere.

We'd agreed we wouldn't rush to move in together too soon. Austin would stay at his place on school nights—except for Wednesdays—weekends at my place, and special occasions at the campground.

I made some inquiries. I spoke with Jim, and Sawyer, and my mortgage broker. The monthly payment to purchase Jody's trailer and lease the lot was the same cost as renting a cabin for one weekend. Plus, none of the cabins or rooms at the lodge had the square footage or amenities the trailer did.

I'd immediately called Ben to tell him our epic deck project was a go, and then I ordered another print of *The Starry Night* to hang above the mantel in our new happy place.

Telling my mother I'd purchased a trailer had been almost as much fun as telling Austin. She'd mistakenly thought—or had chosen to believe—that Trailer Park Avenue was a tiny-home community near my parents' country club.

Having a permanent spot at the campground had softened the blow of Austin having to give his notice and inform the other guys he was leaving. He'd dragged his feet about it for almost a month. YA had offered him the position at the end of June, but he'd waited until after July Fourth to tell everyone.

Jim had told him, "Now we'll never really lose you, and we've gained Paul."

THEY WERE TREATING his going away like a holiday weekend, and of course, it wouldn't have been a party for Austin without karaoke.

Austin had been texting me every day with song options

for both of us. I doubted he believed I'd actually sing, but I'd already chosen a song, and I was going to surprise the fuck out of him.

It had been stuck in my head for a couple of months. I'd lost count of how many times I'd caught myself humming it.

When I'd told Eric about it, and that I wished there was a karaoke backing-track version with a nineties grunge vibe, he'd shifted into producer mode. He called Lance, Alex, and Noah and asked them to record something for me. I'd stopped him before he could book studio time. It would've been a crime not to involve my brother-in-law.

We'd all met up one Saturday in John's garage to rehearse, record, and mix the track. The guys had gigged at the campground a few times with Luke Cody as a band called Surfer Cowboy, and they offered to play live, but I couldn't front a fucking live band. It was one song, and it was crucial that it be karaoke.

At the end of the session, Eric had given John his card and told him he should consider doing engineering professionally. John was over the moon about the prospect, but as we were leaving, he sighed wistfully and said, "Damn, I wish I could come to the party."

"It's a men's campground," Lance said. "There's no reason why you can't be there."

Before I could protest, John had turned to me, his eyes shining with hope like a kid asking if he could sleep over at a friend's house. "I'm totally cool with being nude!"

I'd promised him that wouldn't be required.

I was pretty sure Veronica would shoot down the idea, not because she didn't want her husband hanging out with a couple hundred gay guys but because she'd be jealous she couldn't attend.

. . .

Whᴇɴ Aᴜsᴛɪɴ and I arrived at the Cubby Hole, John was on the side porch drinking one of the good beers from the secret cooler and chatting with Lance, Luke, and Jim.

Austin greeted John with a back-slapping hug and made a crack about Veronica giving him a hall pass, but he didn't question how John had come to be there.

Inside, the bar was decked out with balloons, a "Back to School" banner, and a blackboard with Austin's name rendered in chalk art.

The pair of microphone stands and the lyrics monitor set up in front of the DJ alcove sent my heart rate through the roof.

I tried to appear to be socializing instead of obsessing over being the first to perform. Luke caught me preparing to shotgun a can of liquid courage and whispered that I should avoid beer because the carbonation would make me burp while trying to sing. He suggested a single shot of bourbon as a wiser choice.

The lights flashed and the dance music that had been playing faded out. John was in the DJ booth armed with the thumb drive containing my custom track, grinning like a maniac, shooting me a thumbs-up, and waving me over.

I stepped up to the mic. My face grew hot even as a cold flash of panic moved through the rest of my body. I didn't have a clue what to do with my hands.

Don't fuck this up.

The crowd quieted except for Austin, who clapped loudly and yelled, "Prof!" He was probably expecting me to make a toast or give a speech, but on this occasion, I had more than words for him.

As the opening bars of "Can't Help Falling in Love" began to play, the crowd erupted into cheers, recognizing the familiar melody. Someone whistled.

"Oh my God!" Austin said, his voice carrying over the music. "What is *happening*?"

Surely everyone heard my shaky breath on the mic, but at least I'd remembered to inhale before I began. I focused on the monitor, even though I didn't need it. There weren't a lot of lyrics to remember, and the words were simple as the best poetry often was.

Austin had taught me it didn't matter how well you sang as long as you executed the song with feeling, but I feared I might not get through it without choking up.

Honestly, when I was in the right mood, the original Elvis Presley version always wrecked me a little.

I came in too soft on the opening line about fools rushing in, but when it had happened during rehearsal, Eric assured me this was one of those songs where it was an appropriate artistic choice to start out faltering and tentative and then grow stronger.

The refrain was a straightforward confession, right there on the second line, and there was no point in uttering those words if I didn't sing them directly to Austin.

When my eyes found his, they were welling up with tears and light. His mouth hung open in shock, and he clutched at Luke and Hank, who supported him as he swooned. I hadn't seen him cry before, but I wasn't surprised that when he did, it was from happiness.

Our friends couldn't have known this was the first time I'd declared my love for him, but they sang along, accompanying me to the special twist in my arrangement.

In the middle of the song, Lance's guitar effects crashed in like a wave, shredding the sweet lullaby and transforming it into a feedback-saturated, grunge power ballad.

At the back of the room, Lance raised his fists in

triumph. I'd asked for *Smashing Pumpkins covering Elvis,* and he'd fucking nailed it.

As the final notes reverberated through the room, Austin wrapped his arms around me, and we swayed together, safely grounded in the present. The crowd erupted into thunderous applause, their cheers and claps creating a joyful noise for both of us, for him and me together.

"Damn, Paul." Austin pulled back and swiped at his cheeks. "How the fuck is anybody supposed to follow *that*?"

I smiled, knowing I was only the opening act to an hours-long, full-blown Austin Fox concert. Maybe with a few choice duets. "I'm sure you'll find a way." I kissed him softly, dancing us in a slow circle.

"You *sang*," Austin said, shaking his head in disbelief.

"Well, I wrote an entire book about you, and trust me, words alone aren't enough to tell you I love you."

"Wow." He closed his eyes briefly, savoring the moment, and exhaled. "I waited for you to say it first so I wouldn't scare you."

"How soon would you have said it?"

He chuckled, and the laugh lines at the corners of his eyes deepened. "The morning after."

"The *first* morning after?"

"Mmmhmm. Told you that's how it would happen for me." His smile softened, his brow furrowed, and in a low, earnest voice he said, "I love you."

"Ahh." I'd underestimated the power of those simple words. "Now *that* definitely bears repeating."

"I love you," Austin said.

"I love you too."

ALSO BY SLADE JAMES

BEAR CAMP

The Uncut Wood

Grumpy Bear

The Cubby Hole

Muscle Cub

The Day Pass

Honey Bear

ACKNOWLEDGMENTS

Special thanks to:

M.K. Varrich and Amanda Johnson for beta reading. ("A Little Bit Veronica!")

Mia Monroe and Kelly Fox for supporting me behind the scenes and beyond the books.

Annabeth Albert for chatting about authors who are also professors.

Coach Lisa for the fitness certification details.

Patrick for sharing personal reflections on what it's like to be a gay male sixth-grade teacher.

Susie Selva for being my friend as well as my editor.

Lori Parks for spotting the tiniest yet most important things.

Steven, Darlin' and Clementine.

My mama.

And, most of all, thank you for reading!

If you have the extra time, please consider leaving a review or posting a recommendation online. It helps others find my books, and I appreciate every single one of them.

ABOUT THE AUTHOR

One summer, not so long ago, Slade James started writing gay romance, turned fifty, and met the love his life. (In that order, in a matter of weeks!)

Slade and his partner, Steven, live in a magical land in the American Southeast where three states converge. They call it "GeorBamaSee." They can be found playing disc golf in the parks, hiking in the mountains, kayaking in the creeks, and living in their own real life romance.

Get a free, exclusive Bear Camp story when you sign up for my newsletter at sladejames.com.